HANNAH KAYE

GOLDWATER RIDGE

A SADIE AND CLYDE ADVENTURE

Jellysquid Books
Broken Arrow, Oklahoma

ISBN: 978-0-578-68183-2

This is a work of fiction. All references to historical events, real people, or real places are used fictitiously. Names, characters, and places are products of the author's imagination. Any resemblance to actual persons, living or dead, is purely coincidental.

Cover illustration by Elise Yeomans

Interior illustrations by Sarah Phillips

Published by Jellysquid Books
Broken Arrow, Oklahoma

For my sisters
Sarah, Laura, and Claire
I love you, you bunch of beanheads.

CONTENTS

ACKNOWLEDGMENTS

I used to think writing books was a solitary activity. I was wrong. There are so many people who helped bring *Goldwater Ridge* into being, and without any one of them, this crazy story never would've been told. So thank you, thank you all.

To God, the greatest Author of all—*Soli Deo Gloria.*

To my parents, who taught me to love stories and who believed in me from the beginning. To my sisters, who are and always have been my chief source of inspiration. To my husband John, for being my biggest fan, loving and supporting me every step of this journey, and encouraging me through the best and worst of it all. To my son Sam, who I hope will one day come to love this little book that grew as he did.

To my fan club (Mom, Grammie, Nathan and Sarah, Drew and Laura, Claire, and John) who read the book as I was still writing it, demanding I give them another chapter every time I left them on a cliffhanger, and whose questions and comments may or may not have influenced the outcome of the story.

To James, my writing buddy and accountability partner, who is always up for brainstorming with me, checking in on my progress, or letting me rant frustration to him. To Erica, whose encouragement reminds me why I write in the first place, and whose input and advice is worth more than any gold nugget. To Emily and Casey, my critique partners— brave souls who delved into the mire of my first draft in order to give early feedback. To Samantha, for her editing expertise. To Elise, who never ceases to amaze me with her incredible talent.

And of course, to all the wonderful people who believed in this project enough to fund its publication: Julie Gumm, Brayden and Abby Lans, Claire Walters, Andrew and Kaitlyn Tindle, Jeff Voris, Drew and Laura Burkhart, Nathan and Sarah Phillips, Emily Martin, Josh and Katy Parker, Mark and Louise Walters, and Jerry and Linda Voris.

To you all, I am so very thankful.

-HK

1

A HAT, A HORSE, AND A DESERT

THE flat desert horizon stretched out in front of me, empty as a blank sheet of newsprint that didn't have a story on it yet.

FEARLESS YOUNG JOURNALIST LOST FOREVER IN ENDLESS DESERT. ARIZONA TERRITORY SWALLOWS UP WATER, LIFE, HOPES, AND DREAMS.

Extra, extra, read all about it.

I rolled my eyes, shaking my head to clear away the headlines penning themselves in my mind. I had to admit it—a story about me, plodding along through a desert, didn't sound all that captivating. Now, if the newspaper suffered an editing error and printed that a fearless young journalist had gotten lost forever in endless *desserts*, that would be a headline worth reading!

Desserts—what a thought! I closed my eyes, shutting out the shimmering heat, the relentless midday sun, the dusty, cracked ground, the sweaty old horse, and the countless cactuses. I imagined myself back in Aunt Helen's kitchen, laying into a heaping plate of her famed angel food cake. Smothered in sweet cream and topped with summer's last blackberries, fat and juicy and exploding with bursts of tartness in every bite—

"Stop it, stop it, stop it!" I shouted aloud, smacking my forehead as if I could knock the fantasy out of my head and leave it lying in the desert dust where it belonged. I'd thought back to the comforts of home many times since I set out on my journey, but these past few days the bouts of wishful thinking had gotten worse. It was no use to keep dreaming of food like that, not now, not in the desert. Aunt Helen and her cakes were…how far away was Philadelphia now? Over two thousand miles?

My empty stomach gave a forlorn rumble.

"Come on now, keep it together," I muttered to myself. I reached into my pocket, pulling out the crumpled note that started me on this journey three long months ago. I grabbed the pencil I kept tucked perpetually behind my ear—you never know when you might need to take notes— and absently tapped my lower lip with it as I glanced at the wrinkly paper. It was my habit, anytime I got homesick or doubtful, to remind myself what I was doing here in the first place. I paused before unfolding the note and smiled faintly at the name scrawled on its outside:

Billy Bob Clyde

The note was unsigned, but I'd instantly known who it was from. Ever since Pa headed west in search of gold five years ago, not a single soul had called me Billy Bob Clyde. He was the only one who ever used my full name. Most people called me William now that I was half-grown, which was a relief. Being skinny and slight at thirteen is hard enough. Being skinny and slight and dragging along a name like that is downright unbearable. Besides, William was a far more respectable name for a reporter. It was hard to imagine "Billy Bob Clyde" on a byline even in a small-town paper, let alone the *New York Post*.

"Maybe that's why all the big shots write under their initials," I said aloud. "I bet they've all got dumb names they'd rather not have published for thousands of people to see and laugh at."

My horse, Abraham, twitched her ears and snorted her agreement.

Speaking of dumb names, yes, Abraham was a she. And if horse children are even half as mean-spirited as human children can be, then

I'm sure poor Abraham was mocked ruthlessly when she was a filly. Abraham and I had that in common.

I was proud of her name though. The man I bought her from told me that the farmer *he* bought her from told *him* that she'd been named in honor of President Lincoln. As the story goes, at the exact moment Abraham was born, the farmer's wife rushed into the barn with the news that Lincoln had won the 1860 election. I thought it was a pretty special story, until I did the math and realized that if it was true, Abraham must be nearing thirty years old. Which meant I was trying to cross a desert riding what was probably the oldest horse in the West. Still though, I'd grown pretty fond of the old girl, name and all.

I wish I'd been named after President Lincoln. Being named for a great man was miles better than being named after three mediocre ones. I was named after all three of my Pa's older brothers, mostly because Pa was always owing them all money and favors. At some point in his past, he had sworn to each of them separately, in return for some favor or another, that he'd name his firstborn child after them. I can only thank my lucky stars he made no such promises to his sister. Growing up with three first names was bad enough. Imagine having four, and one of them being Helen.

Of course, Aunt Helen had done mountains more for me than any of Pa's brothers. She'd been the closest thing I had to a mother, since mine had died when I was a baby. And when Pa went west, she and her husband, Uncle Henry, had given me the best home I could ask for. I was comfortable, provided for, and loved. Which is why there had to be a good reason for me to pack up and leave that home in exchange for a lonesome trek across a desolate desert.

That reason was the note I held in my hand. Its message, written in Pa's handwriting, was simple and short:

"A present for my boy—look inside. A man's hat can be the difference between life and death. So you gotta be sure you've got a good one, one that won't lead you astray."

The note arrived pinned to a lumpy package, and inside was a black felt hat, the type that was commonplace in the West. It was sturdy and dusty and well-worn. My fingers tingled when I lifted it from its wrapping for the first time, as if all the wildness of the West was woven into its fibers.

Of course I was excited to get a package from Pa, whose letters had abruptly cut off some time ago. But the hat and the cryptic message gave me an unsettled feeling. If a good hat was, as Pa said, a matter of life and death, then why did he send his away? Didn't he need it anymore? Was he in trouble? The more I read the note, the more convinced I was that there was more to it. It was some sort of code. I pulled out the underlined words:

Look inside.

Hat.

Won't lead you astray.

It dawned on me then—*there was a message inside the hat!* But I figured it out too late. For some reason, Pa had written his secret message in chalk, and like any boy would've done, I tried the dusty hat straight on my head as soon as it was out of the package. By the time I figured out the hat itself was the real message, my hair had rubbed out half of it.

"What kind of pea brain writes an important message in chalk?" I'd moaned to Uncle Henry and Aunt Helen, rubbing chalk dust off my forehead in frustration. "And on the inside band of a hat, no less?"

Aunt Helen blamed the oversight on what she called Pa's "general foolishness," which is the sort of thing you'd expect a sensible older sister to say about her youngest brother. It's true, Pa was known for being impulsive and adventurous. But foolish? Never. The Pa I remembered was a clever man, if a little eccentric, so I knew there must be more to the message than met the eye. I just had to figure out what it was.

That was easier said than done. Soon all that was left of Pa's message were some white smudges where the chalk dust had ground itself into the hatband. But before it had all been lost, I'd copied out the letters I could still read, and this is what I got:

COME   GOLD   TER RI   CA   OK

It wasn't much to go on, but there was one very important word: gold. You don't just toss a word like that around, so I knew this was a message worth salvaging. I was sure of it—Pa had something he was trying to hide, something important, so he'd put it in the hat to make sure it was kept a secret. A secret he meant for me to discover. And if I was good at anything, it was digging up the facts and putting together clues. Finding out the truth is at the very heart of being a reporter, and I resolved I wouldn't rest till I'd figured out the facts. Pa was counting on me.

After some digging, I discovered there was a small mining town in southern California by the name of Terrieville. That's what I guessed the letters "TERRI CA" must mean. So the message, I figured, was that Pa had found gold in Terrieville, and he was trying to hide it from someone. You sure don't get a message that exciting every day!

But as attractive as the thought of piles of California gold was, it didn't mean half as much to me as the other two words I could make out:

Come, okay?

My heart caught in my throat the first time I read them. *Come, okay?* That meant—and I hardly dared to believe it—not only had Pa found gold, but he was asking me to help him. He trusted me with his secret, and he wanted me out West with him. Me! When Pa left home and sent me to go live with Uncle Henry and Aunt Helen, I was barely eight years old, a skinny little kid with missing front teeth and a lisp. Pa hadn't seen me since, but somehow, he'd decided I was the one he'd call for when he needed help. It made me feel bold, noble even, and I wanted desperately not to let him down.

So, in the spring of 1889, barely a week after receiving Pa's message, my adventures began. I left my aunt and uncle, my studies, my after-school job typesetting for the local paper, and set out for Terrieville, California. I was bound for an unknown journey of adventure, daring, risk, and—I hoped—gold. Aunt Helen dabbed her eyes and Uncle Henry shook his head, but they couldn't talk me out of it. My friends chased the train to the end of the platform, waving and cheering and raising such a ruckus you'd have thought I was Captain Cook leaving on a voyage.

"You'll read about me in the papers!" I hollered to them from the window of the train as the station slipped from my view. And what a story it would make—if I lived to tell the tale, that is. At this point, it was questionable.

I traveled west by rail as far as Kansas City. That's where I bought Abraham and joined up with a wagon train full of settlers moving to Texas. When they stopped, I kept going, my nose always pointed west. I rode with a posse of Mexican bounty hunters straight through the New

Mexico and Arizona territories, and right up to the edge of the Sonoran Desert. But at that point, the posse got word that the *banditos* they were tracking had turned south and were making a mad dash for Mexico, and they wanted to hurry and cut the outlaws off at the border.

"You ought to come south with us, *Jovencito*," Marco Casado, a posse member who'd taken me under his wing, urged me. The whole band had picked up on his nickname for me—which translated roughly to something like youngster or whippersnapper. I never was sure if it was a term of endearment or teasing.

But Marco hadn't been teasing when he told me to come with them.

"Do not to try to push on to California alone," he said with a concerned frown. "The journey is too long and harsh for one boy to make."

"I'm not trying to get to Mexico, Marco," I protested.

"Better to be in Mexico than dried up dead in the desert, *Jovencito*."

As true as that was, I wasn't willing to get knocked so far off course. If I went south, who knows when I'd have a chance to continue on to California. I was trying to get to Pa, and if that meant taking my chances in the desert, so be it. I told Marco no thanks, I'd keep on trekking westward. On my own.

That was ten days ago.

My empty stomach complained loudly, bringing my mind back to the present. Unrelenting sun beat down on my head, and I shoved my hat back on. I was amazed how quickly I felt cooler, just by having a good layer of protection on my head.

Pa sure wasn't kidding about that life and death thing, I thought as I pocketed his note and tucked my pencil back into its spot behind my right ear. I couldn't have made it this far without this hat, that's for certain.

A hat wouldn't keep me from starving, though.

"Hats are not good for eating," I told Abraham, just in case she was getting any ideas. She glanced back at me with hurt in her big shiny eyes, as if offended I would even think her capable of such a thing. But I wasn't fooled by the innocent act. She'd eaten my map three days ago, and while I couldn't blame her at the time—I knew she was as hungry as I was— I sure did miss that map. We'd been plodding along blind ever since, and though I kept the mountains to my right and the morning sun at my back to make sure I was headed west, I couldn't be sure where I was, what

natural landmarks to watch for, or even make a guess at how much longer
I'd be in the desert. I hoped it would end soon. It would have to, or I
wouldn't make it.

I thought I'd rationed my supplies well enough, but I guess I
underestimated how much a horse can drink. My water jug ran dry that
morning. The saddlebags Marco made sure had been stuffed with food
when I entered the desert were empty too—except for a few stray crumbs
lodged in the seams near the bottom. I'd tried to dig them out earlier, but
they'd gotten crammed under my fingernails and besides, eating them
wouldn't fill my stomach and would only make me thirstier.

Just as I started wondering if cactuses tasted any good, I came across
a wooden sign. It was leaning so much that I couldn't even read it until
Abraham nosed it over hopefully. She snorted in disappointment when it
didn't prove edible, but I was just happy that its painted words, while
faded, were still readable.

CACTUS POKE, ARIZONA
HOME OF THE FAMOUS GOLDWATER POTATO
4 MILES DUE NORTH
THE LAW IS RESPECTED HERE.
ABSOLUTELY NO OUTLAWS ALLOWED.

Even as hungry, thirsty, hot, tired, and lost as I was, I frowned
doubtfully. What kind of crazy folks would settle and build a town here
in the middle of the desert? I tried to conjure a memory of my lost map,
but I couldn't recall seeing a town marked anywhere near where I thought
I was. Maybe there wasn't a town at all. Maybe it was a trick, a trap set by
bandits to catch unsuspecting travelers. I discarded that theory a second
later though; if they were trying to make their town sound appealing and
attractive, they'd picked the wrong name.

Still, a town meant people, and people meant food and water. I looked
north, toward the mountains, and wrinkled my nose. I didn't want to go
north; I wanted to go west. Pa needed me to get to California. But
westward, the desert stretched out in front of me without any visible end.
Without a map, I might never find my way out of it. Just looking at the
shimmering heat of the flat, brown horizon made me thirstier.

I read the sign again. It was only four miles out of my way, after all. And what was that about the town being famous for its potatoes? Steaming heaps of them filled my imagination, mashed smooth and dyed golden with thick yellow butter. I swear I could almost taste them.

That decided it for me right there.

A quick stop in town couldn't hurt. I turned Abraham's head northward. I'd get something to eat, restock my supplies, and see if they had a map I could buy. Then I'd get back on track. I could spare an hour in Cactus Poke.

Two, at the most.

2

CACTUS POKE IS ABOUT AS FRIENDLY AS ITS NAME MAKES IT SOUND

"**WHOA** there," I called to Abraham. We'd come to the edge of Cactus Poke. I squinted through the dust we'd kicked up, trying to make sure this wasn't some elaborate mirage the desert had conjured up to taunt me. But no, it was real—and tiny. I could take in the whole town in one glance: one short road lined on either side with a single row of buildings. No wonder I couldn't remember seeing it marked on my map. At the end of the street, brown foothills rose toward the mountains, dotted sparsely with scrubby shrubs. Cactus Poke was nothing but a speck wedged between the desert and the mountains.

Abraham snorted and shook her head sharply, unhappy that I'd stopped us. She pushed forward, itching to gallop again, but I held her back.

"I get it, old gal, you're hungry too, but we can't go careening down Main Street at full tilt," I explained. "Got to be respectable, make a good first impression." Of course, a bad first impression would make an awfully interesting headline in the Cactus Poke Times:

GOOD-FOR-NOTHING STRANGER RAISES RUCKUS ON MAIN STREET, TERRIFIES CITIZENS.

Abraham whinnied, and I took that to mean she agreed, so I clicked to her gently, nudging her into an easy walk down the street. Small, faded buildings rose up on either side of us—a bank, a general store, a church, a town hall, all looking a little bit tired. I shouldn't have worried about making the news; Cactus Poke didn't appear to have a print shop.

I'd gotten so used to the emptiness of the desert that it didn't strike me as odd at first how quiet the town was. I was halfway down the street before it occurred to me that it didn't matter if I was making a good first impression. There wasn't anybody around to impress—not another soul in sight. I looked up and down the road and peered into the little alleys between the buildings. Nothing. Not a circle of kids playing marbles or a man taking aim at a spittoon. Not a single horse flicking its tail at flies or stray dog nosing around in search of scraps. Not even a lonesome little tumbleweed.

A prickle of unease crept up my back. I reined my horse in the middle of the road. When her hoofbeats stopped, the silence was tangible.

"Hello?" I called. Nothing. Not even the sound of my own echo. The town, as far as I could tell, was deserted.

The terrible thing was, I was definitely being watched. I could feel it. Someone—or something—had me in its sights and was keeping well out of mine. I shuddered.

"This place gives me the creeps, Abraham," I murmured, keeping my voice low. "Something's not right." Her ears flicked backward, and I knew she could sense it too. We both would've been perfectly happy to ride straight on through, leaving Cactus Poke behind us. My stomach took that moment of hesitation to growl loudly, reminding me why I was here in the first place.

I was hungry. And thirsty. And lost. And Cactus Poke might well be the only town for hundreds of miles in any direction. I slumped in the saddle with a groan. I rubbed furiously at my stinging eyes with the heels of my hands, and my traitorous imagination once again conjured up tantalizing images of Aunt Helen's angel food cake, all light and fluffy, but this time it added the extra insult of serving it with gleaming goblets of fresh-squeezed lemonade, tasting like pure sunshine and happiness and—

I was jolted from the cruel fantasy by the unexpected sound of a splash. I looked up, astonished to see that while I was despairing about what I didn't have, Abraham had found something to be thankful for right here: a trough, miraculously full of water. She plunged her head right in and was busy drinking to her heart's content, washing away the desert dust and grime.

The trough Abraham found was right in front of the saloon. I laughed. This was the same Wild West I had read about, after all. Maybe the saloon was where the town's population went to escape the blistering afternoon heat. Maybe everyone was inside right now! I dismounted and looped Abraham's lead around the hitching post. I bounded up onto the boardwalk, which creaked loudly under my wobbly legs, and tried the door.

Locked.

Unwilling to give up so easily, I tugged, shoved, and rattled that door. I knocked, I hollered, I begged. Nothing. Not one doggone response. Abraham observed my worthless efforts with a passive stare, water splashing off her nose in fat drops that plunked back into the trough.

"Hey, don't backwash," I chided her. "I'm probably gonna have to drink after you. Betcha that's the only water in this whole place. It's lucky you found a full trough at all, since it sure hasn't rained…" I trailed off.

It *wasn't* lucky the trough was full. That water had to be put there on purpose. I knew it couldn't have rained enough to fill it, not that much, and certainly not recently. That meant somebody had to have filled it up, probably this morning by the looks of it. Somebody who was probably still in Cactus Poke. Probably the same somebody who ran the Cactus Poke Saloon and was, for some reason, refusing to help me.

"Let me in!" I aimed a furious kick at the door. Pain shot through my foot and ankle at the impact, but the door didn't budge. "Come on, please! I need help!"

Something hard fell on me, bouncing off my shoulder. I yelped and jumped back, and it clattered down onto the boardwalk. I bent to pick it up. It was a small sign, with a hole near the top. A long rusty nail lay beside it. I glanced up at the door to see a little rectangular shape where the wood was less faded. I felt a little sheepish for not noticing the door had a sign nailed to it, and even more embarrassed because it hung at eye-level...if you were about a head-and-a-half taller than I was. I stood up a little straighter and said a secret prayer of thanks that nobody had seen me make such a fool of myself.

The sign, painted in the same neat handwriting of the sign outside of town, cleared up the locked door mystery. It read:

CACTUS POKE SALOON CLOSED BY ORDER OF BROTHER PARSON. LIQUOR IS THE DEVIL'S DRINK AND THE DEVIL AIN'T WELCOME IN CACTUS POKE.

"Is *anyone* welcome in Cactus Poke?" I demanded of the sign, giving it a little shake. But, remembering the water trough, filled up in an act of consideration for thirsty travelers, I rubbed the frustration out from between my eyebrows and sighed. I was about to toss the sign aside when I caught sight of some writing on the back. It was a little smeared, but I could still make it out, and when I did my heart soared:

STRANGERS AND VISITORS CAN FIND WHOLESOME HOME COOKIN' AT THE OLDE TOWNE CAFÉ ON THE NORTH END OF TOWN. OPEN FOR BREAKFAST, DINNER, AND SUPPER.
CLOSED SUNDAYS.

A flicker of doubt crossed my mind. Was it Sunday today? I wasn't sure. I'd been wandering in the desert too long to keep track. But I figured I had a six out of seven chance of the café being open. Those seemed like good enough odds to me.

"Hold down the fort here, Abraham. I'm gonna go check out the café." She gave me a bored glance and went back to drinking. I set out down the street headed north—toward the mountains and away from the desert—with a new hopeful spring in my step as I kept an eye out for the café.

It was the northernmost building in town, the last sign of humanity before the town gave way to wilderness. It was impossible to miss, nestled against the backdrop of the craggy mountains like a lighthouse at the edge of a stormy sea. But instead of a beam of light, the café radiated the unmistakable smell of bacon, and that was the only beacon of hope my soul needed.

In my excitement to find the café, I'd forgotten the feeling of being watched that had dogged me since coming to Cactus Poke. But as I bounded up the steps and reached for the door, I caught something out of the corner of my eye, like a shadow flickering across the ground. It made me jump and I whirled to face it, but the street was just as deserted as before. I could see all the way down it, and the desert stretching endlessly beyond. Nothing in my line of vision moved, except Abraham's tail as she swatted at flies back at the saloon. I hesitated a second longer, waiting for the spooky feeling to leave me.

"Probably just a shadow from a vulture flying overhead or something," I muttered to reassure myself. But circling vultures weren't the most comforting thought either. I turned my back on the street and whatever might be haunting it. Spooks or no, I had to get something to drink.

I yanked open the door and stepped inside, but as I closed it behind me, my knees went weak. A wave of the most wonderful, comforting, mouthwatering smell washed over me. It was better than Aunt Helen's kitchen on Christmas Day. My shriveled stomach did a series of quick backflips. My vision swam and my head went all airy. I swayed on my feet, half collapsing back against the door with a moan. This was it for me, then. I could see the tragic headline now:

FAMISHED TRAVELER PERISHES WITHIN INCHES OF FOOD AND WATER.

It would be a good story, too, front page material, doubtless. Maybe it would even get picked up by a big paper back East, maybe I'd die famous and schoolgirls in pretty ribbons would pen sentimental poems about my untimely death in the margins of their copybooks and—

The sound of breaking ceramic shattered my tragic fantasy.

I opened my eyes to see two people, a gray-haired man and a gray-haired woman, frozen mid-action like they were in a tintype photograph—he with a spoon midway to his mouth, she still holding a coffee pot poised to pour, not noticing the mug she'd been filling was now smashed to bits on the floor in a puddle of coffee. They both stared straight at me. I jumped back to my feet, steadying myself against the door.

"Begging your pardon," I croaked, my throat feeling even drier than it had in the desert. "But would this happen to be the Olde Towne Café?"

"Café's closed," the old man grunted. "Don't you know nothin' boy? Today's Sunday."

If I looked as bad as I felt, I must've been the most pitiful sight west of the Mississippi. My lip trembled, and I didn't even try to stop it. If there had been any spare moisture in my body, even just a single drop, I'm sure I'd have cried it out.

"But you've arrived just in time for Sunday dinner," said the old woman kindly, giving the man's shoulder a little nudge.

"Kay Fay," the man said, a warning in his voice. His mouth turned downward beneath his bushy gray mustache.

"My kitchen, my rules, Lawrence," Kay Fay retorted. He narrowed his eyes, but didn't say anything else as she brushed past him toward the squat stove that sat in the far corner.

I didn't wait for her to change her mind. I scrambled to the table and hurriedly sat down—on the far opposite side from the old man, I might add, who eyed me warily from underneath wiry white eyebrows. I made myself busy looking elsewhere.

The Olde Towne Café was a simple place, but little touches of hominess—like the faded gingham curtains trimmed with old lace decorating the window, and a cracked vase filled with dried wildflowers sitting at the center of the table—made it feel friendly. Hooks and dusty shelves on the back wall housed tin plates, ceramic mugs, and a neatly folded stack of threadbare dishtowels. Aside from the short black stove in the corner, the only furniture was one long wooden table that ran the whole length of the room. Sturdy backless benches sat on either side, matching the table's length.

The old man sat at the corner of the table nearest the stove. I was a full ten feet away, on the corner diagonally opposite him. He didn't seem to take the hint that he was making me uncomfortable; every time I sneaked a peek his direction out of the corner of my eye, he was still studying me. I noticed he had even leaned forward a bit, like he was trying to inspect me more closely.

"Gracious, child, you aren't traveling alone, are you?" said Kay Fay as she turned back toward the table. Her tone surprised me; it might just as well have been sweet, round, rosy-cheeked Aunt Helen who asked a question like that. But Kay Fay was as different from Aunt Helen as Cactus Poke was from Philadelphia. They both had gray hair, but that was where the similarities ended. Kay Fay was too skinny and sharp to be grandmotherly, all elbows and angles. Her face, marked by deep crow's feet at all its corners, was tanned and leathery. She looked like a cactus—battered for years by relentless sun and wind, but still standing sturdy and proud, if a little prickly.

"I, uh," I floundered, not sure how I wanted to answer her question. Part of me—the hungry and lost part—wanted to be fussed over and comforted and taken care of. But the other part—the fearless rugged adventurer who had braved a desert alone for weeks—balked at being called a child.

"I have a horse," I said with a short nod, as if that explained everything.

Kay Fay paused for a second, looking at me quizzically, then laughed. It was a rough, cackling kind of sound, but not entirely unpleasant.

"I bet you do, stranger!" she said. "Drink." She plunked a tin cup in front of me. I swear, I wouldn't have been able to tell the difference between that lukewarm, gritty water and the Fountain of Youth, that's how thirsty I was. I downed it in seconds. Kay Fay refilled it and I guzzled that one too. Five cups later I finally came up for air, feeling like a man reborn.

Kay Fay gave a satisfied nod when I at last leaned back and sighed in contentment, swiping my sleeve across the droplets on my chin.

"Now let's get some food in you, young'un," she said, stepping over to the back wall to rummage for dishes among her shelves.

"Thank you, ma'am," I said, remembering I had been brought up right and needed to show it. The old man was still glaring at me from across the room, but his eyes weren't meeting mine. He was looking at my hat. I hadn't thought to remove it when I sat down, since my mind had been a little occupied with *not dying of thirst*. Was that all that was bothering him? I guess it was Sunday dinner, after all. I whipped the dusty hat off and set it on the bench beside me, then, in an attempt to look a little more respectable, rubbed at the grime and sweat on my forehead. I cast an apologetic smile in the old man's direction.

Without breaking eye contact, he slid all the way down his bench to my end of the table in one long, continuous scoot, not stopping until he sat directly across from me. I wondered how many splinters got stuck in the backside of his trousers as he did that. But his pants seemed to be the last thing on his mind. He placed both hands, palms down, in front of him and leaned as far forward as the table between us allowed.

I instinctively shrank away from him as far as I could without falling backwards off the bench. Undeterred, he jutted his chin out and stared right into my face, with an eyebrow raised in suspicion. One of his strikingly blue eyes glared at me, wide and round, and the other squinted menacingly.

"Where'd you say you come from again?" He demanded in a tone that left no room for funny business.

"I, uh," I stammered. "That actually hasn't come up yet." My eyes caught on a polished gold star pinned to his vest, embossed with the word *SHERIFF,* and I quickly added, "Sir."

"Well I'm bringin' it up now!" The sheriff smacked the table with one of his open palms. "Where were you afore you got to Cactus Poke?"

My doggone pride gets the better of me at the worst possible times.

I squared up my shoulders and decided right then and there I wouldn't let myself get pushed around by this old geezer, sheriff or no. I hadn't trekked two thousand miles, crossed a whole continent, and braved a desert by myself, just to get bullied by an old man.

"Uh, the desert?" I shrugged, daring him with my eyes to challenge me.

"You mockin' me, smart mouth?" The sheriff stood, pushing the bench behind him back with a rough *screech* on the floor. He leaned in even closer, though I don't know how he managed that without falling over on top of me. When I got a good look at him, towering over me like that, I regretted crossing him. The sheriff had a chiseled face that looked like it was carved from stone, like a statue of a war hero. His age was evident in the shiny bald patch on top of his head and the wrinkles that creased his sunbaked skin, but nothing in the world could convince me to describe him as past his prime. His back was ramrod straight, his shoulders broad and muscled. He seemed vibrantly alive, like a raw force of nature. His wild, ice-blue eyes glinted with something that almost wasn't quite human, like they were emitting a cold light all their own.

"No, sir," I said quickly. "I'm not mocking anybody, least of all you."

The sheriff frowned at me, but he drew back a few inches, to my immense relief.

"See that you don't," he grunted. "You mock me, you mock the *Law*. Don't they teach you respect for the Law where you come from?"

I ventured a smile to lighten the mood. "Back home, I hear the West is a lawless place."

"NOT IN CACTUS POKE, IT AIN'T!" the sheriff roared. The tips of his ears turned bright red and he looked like he was itching to grab me by the collar and give me a good shake. He would've too, I'm sure of it, if Kay Fay hadn't reappeared just then and rescued me.

"Pintos and johnnycake," she announced, setting a steaming bowl down directly between me and the sheriff. "Eat up, stranger. Lawrence, I don't wanna hear your voice raised like that again. It's Sunday, ain't it?"

The sheriff sat back, folding his arms across his chest, and I could breathe again. He didn't stop staring at me though, his mouth set in a grim line and that unnerving intensity never leaving his eyes.

Tension hung thick in the air between the sheriff and me, but my stomach was mighty distracting. I grabbed the spoon and was about to start shoveling, but caught myself at the last second and bowed my head to say grace. That brief silent prayer was less a note of thanks for the food than it was a plea for safety from the sheriff, but the Lord must've heard it anyway, because when I looked up again, the sheriff's expression was a half-shade softer.

If I forgot to say thanks during my prayer, I made up for it in that first bite. My eyes rolled back in my head and my heart sang. A savory gift straight from the very gates of heaven, that's what those beans were. A generous helping of thick-cut bacon topped the hearty bowl, satisfying my stomach and my soul. The johnnycake was yellow as a sunflower and thick as a deck of cards, crisp on the outsides and melt-in-your-mouth soft on the insides.

"Ma'am, this is the best food I ever tasted in my whole life," I said between spoonfuls.

Kay Fay laughed at me. "That's the desert talking, boy, and nothing else." But her smile said she was pleased as she grabbed a rag to start cleaning up the coffee spill from earlier.

"Desert's nothing to fool around with," said the sheriff with a nod. It was the most pleasant sentence he'd spoken to me yet. "What brings a young whippersnapper like you to Goldwater County anyway?"

I should've been straight with him, I know that now. I should've told him about splitting from the Mexicans, and about Abraham eating my map. I should've told him about California, about Pa, about the message in my hat. I should've told him the truth, the whole truth, and nothing but the truth. But my mouth was full of beans, my mind was on my stomach, and the fact that he'd said "Goldwater" made me remember the sign I'd seen that had pointed me to Cactus Poke in the first place.

So when the sheriff asked, "What brings you to Goldwater County?" I said:

"Potatoes! I heard you were famous for them." I looked hopefully to Kay Fay. "You wouldn't happen to have any on hand, would you?"

The shards of the broken mug Kay Fay had just finished collecting fell from her hands, crashing back to the floor and splitting into even smaller pieces. She stared at me, wide-eyed and open mouthed.

The sheriff jumped up, jostling the table so hard a few of my precious beans sloshed out onto the table.

"I knew it!" he shouted, leveling a finger in my face. "I knew it the moment you walked in this door. You got an awful lotta nerve, you know that? Steppin' foot in this town and takin' advantage of our hospitality after what you did! I ain't never seen such boldfaced arrogance in all my life!"

I leapt to my feet too.

"Whoa now, hold on," I said, raising my hands in front of me. "I don't have a clue what you're talking about!"

"Don't think for a minute playin' dumb'll get you off the hook." He shook his head. "You outlaw types are all alike."

Outlaw?

"Nothing else for it," continued the sheriff with a grim expression. He reached out a big hand as if he meant to grab me by the shirtfront. "I'm puttin' you under arrest as a suspect in the Town Hall robbery. It'll go best for you if you surrender quiet-like."

"What, no! You're crazy!" I shouted, jerking back from him. I fell off the bench, landing hard on my rear, but scrambled to my feet a second later. My heart was pounding and my palms were sweaty. It was time to get out of Cactus Poke. I rushed for the door.

"Stop, in the name of the Law!" the sheriff shouted as he struggled to get out from around the table.

I hesitated for a second, my hand already on the door. Then, I made the decision to break the sacred Cactus Poke Law for the first time.

I bolted.

3

I'M AN OUTLAW NOW, APPARENTLY

"**ABRAHAM!** We gotta go!" I shouted as I flew down the café steps. Abraham was still halfway down the street from me, and she gave a snort of surprise to see me coming for her at a full sprint. She stomped her hoof in agitation and tossed her head.

"I'll explain later, just get ready to run!"

But I didn't have to do much explaining. Abraham reared with a frightened whinny as the door to the café burst open behind me.

"You git back here, you low-down no-good yella-bellied outlaw pup!" The sheriff roared. The whole town echoed with his voice.

"You've got the wrong man!" I yelled back, my voice cracking into a squeak on the word *man*. I didn't slow down, but I did risk a glance over my shoulder. I guess I didn't get as big a head start as I thought; that, or the sheriff was gaining on me. He was just a few yards behind me. I willed myself to run faster.

I noticed two very important things about the sheriff in that one quick glance. First: he only had one leg. His right one cut off a few inches above where the knee should've been. He stumped along on a heavy wooden peg, strapped to his thigh outside of his trousers. The second thing I noticed was that this didn't seem to be slowing him down in any way whatsoever. He doggedly kept pace with me. In fact, he ran like he was confident he could easily outpace *and* outlast me. He looked like he could run like that for miles.

If I wasn't scared of the sheriff before, I was now.

I had barely a second to get in the saddle when I reached Abraham, and I was thankful for the practice I'd had making quick getaways with the bounty hunters. I leapt onto her back and yanked the looped lead off the post in the same motion, and Abraham broke into a run a split-second before my back end hit the saddle. Even at that, we only escaped the sheriff by a hair. He was so close that Abraham's tail smacked his face on our way out.

"You won't get off that easy!" The sheriff yelled after us. I looked back to see he'd pulled a pistol out of his holster and was taking aim.

"Run, girl, run!" I urged Abraham breathlessly, holding my hat tight on my head and bracing myself to hear a shot ring out. But when we reached the end of the street without any bullet holes to show for it, I allowed myself a little breath of relief. Never mind that I was headed straight back for the desert that had seemed so brutal an hour ago. At that moment, it looked downright friendly by comparison.

"Yeah!" I cheered as Abraham and I galloped toward the wide-open freedom of the desert horizon. "Good riddance, Cactus Po—!"

Before I could get the town's name out of my mouth, something snagged me from behind and jerked me backwards—*hard*. Abraham, still running full tilt, shot out from underneath me. I didn't even realize I was hanging in midair before the ground flew up and smacked me in the face.

"Ohhhhh," I groaned, trying to get my arms to cradle my spinning head, but they wouldn't move. They were pinned to my sides by a sharp pain that wrapped all the way across my ribs and back. I coughed, trying to remember how to breathe.

Through the ringing in my ears I could hear the clip-clop of a horse's hooves right next to my head. I blinked dust out of my eyes and squinted up to see a freckle-faced waif sitting on a red and white horse.

"Goin' somewhere, stranger?" she asked, flashing me a sweet smile.

She didn't look a day older than twelve, and was kinda pretty in a girlish sort of way, with round ruddy cheeks that glowed with a just-scrubbed-clean sort of shine. The two dishwater blonde pigtails poking out from beneath her hat looked like they'd been braided without first being brushed. She wore a man's shirt and trousers that hung loose on her skinny frame, and in one hand she held the end of a rope. The other end of that rope, I realized with a start, was wrapped tight around my chest.

The girl jumped down from the horse, her boots smacking the dry ground inches from my nose. I inhaled a good lungful of dust, and then my chest and head throbbed at the effort of getting a sneeze out. The girl didn't seem to notice or care; she walked a few feet away and stooped to pick something off the ground.

My hat.

"Hey," I coughed, my voice refusing to come out. "Don't...don't touch that. It's...special."

She ignored me, turning the hat over in her hands and running her finger along the brim with an expression of what I took to be awe...and maybe a little bit of fear.

"You're with him, ain't you?" she said in a whisper, staring at the hat, then me, then the hat again. Her sweet and sassy smile was gone. She crouched beside me and leaned in close, her eyes wide as saucers. "You know where he is."

"What are you talking about?" I yelled, the air finally returning to my lungs. "Nobody in this town makes a lick of sense! Let me go, ya bunch of crazies!" I writhed against the rope, trying to break free, but I'd barely managed to sit up before a heavy wooden beam shoved me in the chest and plunked me back down into the dirt. Or to be more specific, it was a heavy wooden leg.

"Good work, Sadie," said the sheriff, glowering down at me. At the sound of his praise, Sadie snapped out of whatever it was that made her look at me with such fear in her eyes. She beamed and gave a ridiculous sweeping curtsey, flourishing my hat like she was a circus master. She tossed her end of the rope to the sheriff, and he yanked me to my feet.

"Now don't you try any funny business," he warned, patting his holster with his free hand. "Ol' Trusty don't miss twice."

23

"But you haven't even shot at me once yet," I said, then bit my tongue. Listen to my big mouth, trying to give him an excuse to pull his gun on me again.

"Yes I did," he said. "Gave ya a warning shot, while you was riding away, cause I'm merciful like that. Grazed right past your head. Mighta even hit your hat."

"No way!" I protested. I was in no position to argue with him, but I couldn't help myself. I can't stand it when people don't have their facts straight. "I know I would've heard it if had been that close!"

"You callin' me a liar?" The sheriff demanded. His ears turned red again and he yanked Ol' Trusty from its holster. He stuck the gun in my face.

I would've laughed, except it was instantly plain the sheriff wasn't joking. Ol' Trusty wasn't a gun at all; it was nothing but a thick chunk of wood, like a short club, crooked at an angle that made its shape vaguely resemble a handheld revolver. It even had a knothole where the trigger would've been on a real gun, and the sheriff's finger curled through it menacingly. My eyes got wide as I searched his face for any sort of giveaway, anything at all that would convince me the sheriff knew he was being absurd, that he was holding nothing but a gun-shaped stick. But he was serious as a statue. He really believed he had shot at me, just like he really believed he was threatening me now.

That's when it hit me—the sheriff was insane. That unnerving light in his eyes made sense now. So did his reaction back in the café when I mentioned those potatoes. He wasn't just over-zealous or easily excitable, but actually crazy. Loony. Full on, certifiably, honest-to-goodness out of his mind.

I looked past the sheriff and up the street, fully expecting Kay Fay to appear, take him firmly by the elbow, and say, "Come on now Lawrence, back to bed with you. Time for your medicine." But when she didn't show up, I looked to Sadie for help. I caught her eye and raised my eyebrows, nodding my head toward Ol' Trusty with a significant glance.

But there was no sympathetic look of understanding from Sadie. She flicked her eyes to the gun and back, then gave me a blank look for half a second before turning her attention back to the sheriff.

"Want me to fetch Deputy Duke, Sheriff?" she piped up.

"Naw," he said. "Trusty and I got this varmint well in hand. You run along and tell Duke we've got need of him at the jail."

"Okie doke," said Sadie, swinging back up into her saddle. "Giddyap, Pinto," she said, nudging the horse into a walk, and catching hold of Abraham's lead as well. "How 'bout we show this sweet old gal to the stable?"

So Abraham got called sweet and got taken to a stable by a pretty girl, while I got called a varmint and got taken to jail by a crazy old man. That didn't seem right to me.

But then again, I thought in exasperation as the sheriff marched me back up the deserted street, nothing in Cactus Poke seemed right.

DEPUTY Duke Hastings was exactly the kind of person you'd expect to find hanging around a spooky old town like Cactus Poke. He was skinny and hardened, and shorter than average, with dark shaggy hair and a cynical smile he kept permanently pasted to his mouth. He was pale, and had dull gray circles hanging under his tired eyes. A long, jagged scar cut from his eyebrow down across his cheek and onto his chin, though it was impossible to guess what kind of injury it had come from. I had the horrible feeling there was something wrong about him, something a little bit *off*, but I couldn't give it a name, even though it made my skin crawl a little when I looked at him. He reminded me of the ragged stray dogs I sometimes saw slinking through the back alleys of Philadelphia's crowded streets—the dogs I often took long detours to avoid.

But I couldn't avoid Duke. He sat on the other side of the bars a few feet away from me, tilting on the back two legs of a rickety wooden chair with his feet propped on the desk in front of him. His boots nudged aside a small wooden desk plaque that read *SHERIFF L. HODGES*. Behind him, the wall was plastered floor to ceiling with faded wanted posters with crumbling edges, depicting the faces of countless outlaws. Even though it looked like I was the first prisoner he'd had the privilege of guarding for a long time—maybe even the first ever—Duke looked at me like I was more of an annoyance than anything.

"Save me a whole lotta trouble if you'd jist confess," he said, absently picking at something in his teeth. "I ain't got time to go rummagin' through all this junk lookin' for clues."

Duke was referring to the crate he held on his lap, labeled EVIDENCE. It held everything I owned—excepting Abraham and her saddle. Duke pawed through it lazily, not taking much interest in anything. And why would he? Was there something incriminating about my handkerchief, or my box of matches, or my bedroll? They'd even confiscated the pencil stub from behind my ear.

Duke stopped when he came to my note from Pa, which, despite my protests, he'd taken along with the rest of my stuff. His eyes skimmed its message with a tiny bit of suspicion (the first emotion I'd seen on his face yet) but after a second, he folded it up and his expression went blank again.

"Billy Bob Clyde," Duke said, waving the note at me. "So your last name's Clyde, and first name is…" He gave an all-too-familiar snicker, "Billy Bob?"

My pride prickled. I may have been sitting in a jail cell in the middle of a desert after being chased down by an old man and lassoed by a girl, but I had to retain at least some smidge of dignity. I wasn't going to stand for being laughed at on account of my name as if Duke was some sort of overgrown schoolyard bully.

"Actually, I usually just go by—" I hesitated, unsure if William was any less laughable a name than Billy Bob Clyde. William seemed far too formal a name for a place like Cactus Poke. It would be like wearing Sunday clothes to a cattle drive. I had the strangest feeling that if I said the name out loud, I might get it dusty. The West was no place for a William.

When I didn't answer for a few seconds, Duke rolled his eyes.

"He don't even know his own name," he drawled.

"You know what? Just Clyde. Clyde is fine." It felt right as soon as I said it. I was Clyde now. Clyde, the rugged adventurer. Clyde, the desert-crosser. Clyde, the fearless hero.

Clyde, who'd gone and gotten himself arrested.

"Whatever you say," Duke chuckled.

It was a small victory, and to be honest, I didn't feel much better for winning it. I sat down on the sagging cot and sighed. I was sore and

26

bruised from my fall off Abraham. My stomach grumbled, reminding me of the unfinished bowl of beans I'd abandoned when I ran from the café. Most importantly, I was stuck in jail, accused of who knows what, and couldn't leave Cactus Poke, which by this time I'd decided was the worst town in the West.

"What's with this place anyway?" I asked Duke. "It wasn't on my map. Is it some sort of ghost town?"

"Why, did ya see a ghost?"

His answer took me off guard. A shudder ran through my shoulders as I remembered the flickering shadow I'd seen outside the café, and the spooky feeling of being watched that had followed me down the street. It wasn't until I noticed Duke's sly smile that I realized he was joking.

"Well no…not exactly," I answered, trying to shake off the cold, eerie dread that trickled down my back. "I just…I mean, where's all the people?"

"Colorado, or California, mostly," Duke shrugged. "Some went back East. People came here lookin' for gold, so when years passed and they didn't find any, most didn't see much reason to stay."

Duke gave a dismissive sniff and picked at a hangnail. He obviously wasn't interested in recounting the town's history to me. And frankly, I wasn't interested in hearing it. No, the only thing I was interested in was a way out of the Cactus Poke Jail, and the biggest thing standing in my way was a certain one-legged madman.

"So, about the sheriff," I began again. "He's…you know," I twirled my finger around my temple and crossed my eyes. "Isn't he?"

Duke shrugged by way of answer.

"Seems to me that's a bit…dangerous, don't you think?" I pushed.

"Dangerous?" Duke frowned. "No, Sheriff ain't dangerous. He's got some oddities, sure, but nothin' that makes him any less than qualified to uphold the law in this here town."

"Are you serious?" I buried my hands in my hair and yanked in frustration. "*Of course* he's less than qualified! He's completely out of his mind!"

Duke narrowed his eyes. "It don't seem to me that's any business of yours. Keep your nose out of it, why dontcha?"

"Because somebody's got to get to the bottom of this!" I shouted, my patience evaporating. "Look here, nothing in this town is right, and

I'm the one taking heat because of it. Look, if Sheriff Hodges is crazy, people ought to know it. That's a good reporter's job—to find out the truth of a matter and then tell it!"

Duke flinched. For the briefest moment, his passive expression flickered. The look he wore underneath was the same one I'd seen on Sadie's face when she picked up my hat in the road—fear. I don't know what I'd said to scare Duke, but it was clear I'd touched a nerve.

"Look kid," he said, not meeting my eyes. "Maybe some stories are better left unreported, all right?"

"What, like the story of a raving lunatic having total control of a town?" I snapped. "Wielding his power to oppress people? You want me to leave that story untold?"

"You ain't bein' fair." Duke said, his bored expression firmly back in place. "And Sheriff Hodges ain't mad. You're too young to know what it was like back then, so you can't understand. The sheriff, he was in the army." He gave me a significant glance. "During the *War*."

I frowned doubtfully. Lots of people fought in the War Between the States, and I knew a good number of perfectly sane army veterans. Even Uncle Henry fought, and you didn't see *him* losing his mind over an innocent request for mashed potatoes.

"So what?" I said. "It's been thirty years."

"Listen kid, war ain't kind," Duke said in a low voice. "Sheriff was an artillery captain in Grant's army. Won a medal or somethin' for his part at Shiloh. That's where he lost his leg. Shell fragment took it clean off. He laid a night and a day on the battlefield tryin' to stay alive afore any help came to him. You jist can't blame a man who's lived through somethin' like that if every now and then his mind wanders a little."

"I guess so," I admitted, feeling sympathetic against my will. No wonder he was tough as jerky; you'd have to be to survive that. But though I felt sorry for him, it didn't change the fact that he was crazy as a horny toad, and it certainly didn't mean I was ready to let him win.

"Look, I'm sorry he had a hard time, and I'm obliged to him for helping win the war and all, but that doesn't make up for him locking me up for no reason!"

"No reason?" Duke cocked an eyebrow. "Ha! If Sheriff hadn't nabbed ya, I would've. In case you forgot, you pretty much already admitted to being an accomplice of Outlaw Jack and assistin' in the robbery of the Golden Tater."

"I don't know how many times I've gotta say it!" I threw up my hands. "I am *not* an outlaw! I didn't even know Cactus Poke existed before this afternoon, so how could I have robbed—wait, the Golden *what?*"

"Tater," repeated Duke. "More properly, the Goldwater Potato, the most famous gold nugget ever discovered in Arizona Territory. Stolen by Outlaw Jack, otherwise known as the Black Hat Bandit." Duke jabbed a finger at one of the wanted posters, a centrally-placed one depicting a shadowy, faceless silhouette in a black hat. "So how 'bout you tell me how it's jist happenstance the tater got stolen only three days afore you came a-ridin' into town wearin' *that* hat, bein' all evasive-like when Sheriff asked you where you came from, and braggin' with your big mouth about how you was here to get some of Cactus Poke's famous *Potatoes*."

Well, when you put it *that* way, it did indeed look like a mighty unlikely coincidence. A mighty unfortunate one, too.

4

CRIMES AGAINST THE LAW

A TELLTALE *step-thump-step-thump* announced the arrival of the sheriff. He removed his hat when he came in the door—a white hat, I noted bitterly—and hung it on a peg beside Outlaw Jack's wanted poster. I tried to let my newfound knowledge of his past heroics soften my opinion of him, but when I looked at his intense blue eyes, I knew it was useless. You could tell me that the sheriff had single-handedly slain dragons and saved kingdoms, and I still wouldn't be able to see him as anything more than a crazy old geezer waving a stick in my face, convinced it was a gun.

"Report's finished. Learn anything useful, Duke?" Sheriff Hodges asked, sitting down in the chair Duke vacated for him.

"He wants to be called Clyde," Duke said, scratching at his chin.

"That it?" the sheriff looked doubtfully at Duke. "We gotta work on your interrogation skills."

Duke shrugged and stifled a yawn.

"Why don't you run along and fetch Sadie," said the sheriff, "seein' how she's a witness and all."

Something in my chest tightened at the thought of Sadie seeing me humiliated like this, so I was glad when Duke said,

"Sadie's tending the horses just now. Might be awhile afore she's able to git away."

"That's fine, tell her to take all the time she needs," the sheriff replied, his face softening a few shades. "Ain't no one takes care of a horse as good as my Sadie-girl."

Duke slinked out the door, kicking it shut behind him as he headed to the stable. It did my soul a little bit of good to know Abraham at least was in good hands. It did not do so much good to hear that possessive *my* come out of the sheriff's mouth. I got the message loud and clear— Sadie was none of my business.

I shook my head and blinked hard. *Snap out of it, Clyde!* My freedom was on the line here, and here I was daydreaming about a girl I'd barely met? I was disappointed in myself. *Focus, back on track now!*

"Um," I said, willing my voice not to crack. "Duke and I were talking, Sheriff, sir, and I've gotta say, I think there's been a big misunderstanding here."

"Good, you've prepared your defense, then?" Sheriff Hodges said with a curt nod. He turned toward the desk and rummaged around. He pulled out something that looked like Aunt Helen's old rag rug, faded and fuzzy and a bit reminiscent of a dead cat. It wasn't till the sheriff put it on his head that I realized it was supposed a judge's wig—and even then, I wasn't convinced it wasn't originally intended to be a mop. Then he pulled a hammer from the drawer (not a gavel, just a regular old hammer) and solemnly turned the plaque on his desk around. On the back face it read: *JUDGE L. HODGES.*

"You may begin," he said, and smacked his hammer on the desk. "How do you plead?"

I almost choked trying not to laugh. It would've been a horrible idea, and not just because the sheriff didn't know he looked ridiculous. The thought that my fate was in the hands of a man with a hammer in his fist and a rug on his head—and who had the power to act as judge, jury, and executioner—was enough to sober me right up.

"Uh, not guilty," I gulped. I decided to keep my story plain and simple, no flairs or embellishments he could twist and use against me. I told the straight and simple truth: I was on my way from Philadelphia to

California to meet my pa, who worked on a mining operation in Terrieville. I had to split from my traveling companions and cross the desert alone, and came across the sign pointing to Cactus Poke by chance. I came to town because I was hungry. No outlaws, no potatoes.

Sheriff Hodges stared at me for a long, tense moment when I finished.

"Seems like you got a mighty tight alibi," he said finally. But he didn't look too friendly when he said it. "In fact," the sheriff continued. "It's a little too tight for my likin'. And it ain't possible to prove. Accordin' to your story, before you rode into town this afternoon, you hadn't been seen by another soul—'cept your horse— for ten days. You coulda been anywhere between then and now. It seems like just the kind of story an outlaw would cook up."

"I'm *not* an outlaw."

The sheriff narrowed his eyes. "That's what an outlaw would say," he muttered.

"Look here, Sheriff," I said. "I'm just your average gold-hunter headed to California. No more, no less. I stopped in your town cause I was hungry and lost, looking for some Christian hospitality, which I have to say, your town is kinda lacking in." I paused for a second, then amended, "Except for Kay Fay."

"Normal gold-hunters don't carry coded messages," said the sheriff, holding up Pa's note. "Codes are only useful if you've got something to hide."

"It's not a code, it's just some of the letters got lost…it's hard to explain, but they were written in chalk. Pa's a little…quirky sometimes I guess. Look, I'm sorry your tater got stolen, but I had nothing to do with it. You searched my things. Didn't find any gold, did you?" I was talking too much, and I knew it. But I couldn't stop myself. "And I didn't even know such a person as Outlaw Jack existed till Duke showed me his wanted poster ten minutes ago! You gotta believe me, Sheriff— I wouldn't know Outlaw Jack from Adam, even if he were to walk in that door this minute!"

Sheriff Hodges snatched my hat up out of the evidence crate and shook it at me. "You're trying to tell me *this* don't seem like a mighty suspicious connection to the Black Hat Bandit?"

"Oh, for crying out loud!" I yelled, exasperated. "You got no proof of anything, and you can't convict me on a hunch! The only thing you've got against me is that I happen to wear a hat of the same color Outlaw Jack does. You can't really believe he wears the only black hat in the West!"

"Well, outlaw or not, you got one thing right," said the sheriff. "Neither of us can't prove nothin', one way or t'other. Ain't got enough evidence to git you on the charges of conspirin' with outlaws and stealin' the tater, though personally I still think it's likely to be true," said the sheriff. I sagged in relief, but he wasn't done yet. "So now on to the other charges against you."

"*What* other charges?" I shouted.

Sheriff Hodges ticked them off on his fingers as he named them.

"Disturbin' of the peace, disrespect for an officer of the law, resistin' arrest, obstruction of justice, and destruction of town property."

"Destruction of town property?"

He leveled his piercing glare at me from beneath his bushy eyebrows. "Did you or did you not knock down Brother Parson's sign from the saloon?"

"I…I mean…" I stammered. I suppose he had a point there.

And it wasn't exactly an accident either, I remembered, considering how I kicked and pounded on the door before it fell down.

"I can fix it," I mumbled.

"Is that a confession?"

"No," I said stubbornly, crossing my arms over my chest.

"Now I got to add lyin' under oath to your charges—that ain't helpin' your case any, boy."

"I'm not lying!" I protested. "And you didn't even put me under oath!"

"CONTEMPT OF COURT!" Sheriff Hodges bellowed. "Well, Mr. Clyde, I think I've seen all I need to."

"Wait, what?" I sputtered, leaping to my feet. "You can't have made up your mind yet!"

"Yep," he stood, taking off his wig-thing. "This court finds you guilty of crimes against the Law, foremost of those being a menace to society and an all-around suspicious character."

"That's not even a crime!"

He kept on like he hadn't even heard me. "And I still count you as a top suspect until the Town Hall robbery case is solved. I ought to banish you from Goldwater County straightaway, never to return."

That didn't sound so bad. I guess I could live with being an outlaw after all.

"But since I'm a merciful man," he continued. "I've decided to give you a chance to better yourself and change your outlawin' ways."

My heart dropped.

"You're hereby assigned ninety days of servin' the community of Cactus Poke, doin' good deeds, and repayin' your debt to society, startin' at sunup tomorrow." He pounded his hammer on the table so hard a little chip of wood went flying. "Court adjourned!"

"THREE MONTHS?" I yelled, grabbing the iron bars. By that time, Pa's message would be almost a whole year old! "I don't have three months! Wait! No! I wanna be banished instead! Can I appeal?"

"Sorry," the sheriff shrugged. He put the wig and the hammer back in their drawer and turned the plaque on his desk back to the *SHERIFF* side. "For that, you'd need to talk to a judge."

WHEN I left home, I never imagined I'd end up staging a jailbreak of any kind, let alone my own. But you know what they say about desperate times. Pa needed me to get to California, and I couldn't do that from behind bars.

My chance came easier than I expected. I'd imagined I'd have to wait till everyone was asleep, then sneak around carefully, trying not to wake Duke as I searched for tools to aid my escape. I'd have a few close calls where he'd stir fitfully in his sleep and I'd have to freeze like a statue until he settled back down and I could continue inching silently toward freedom. That's how it usually happened in books, at least.

But I wasn't destined to have a heart-pounding, high-stakes, book-worthy jailbreak. A few lazy hours passed where I sulked in the corner of my cell, writing furious editorials in my head to every major paper I could think of, complaining that officers of the law everywhere, including remote corners of Arizona Territory, should be held to a higher standard of sanity, whether they were decorated war veterans or not. Duke mostly entertained himself by throwing a wadded scrap of paper at the wall of wanted posters, bouncing it off Outlaw Jack's face over and over again. But about an hour before dinnertime, he abruptly stood up and opened the door.

"Hey, where are you going?"

"Shift change," he said. "I'm off duty."

"Whose shift is it now?" I asked, hoping it wouldn't be the sheriff.

Duke shrugged. "Not mine," he said.

"There's not another deputy?"

"Nope," he said, spitting out the open door. "Guess you could call us understaffed. But I ain't gittin' paid to stay late. Besides," he laughed. "You ain't goin' nowhere."

He let the door slam behind him.

I didn't waste any time at all. As soon as Duke's footsteps faded, I got to work. I didn't know how much time I would have before someone came back, and I couldn't miss the one opportunity I might get, so I had to take my chances.

Running my hands over the walls and floors in search of loose boards was unsuccessful. The next thing I tried was squeezing my arm as far is it could go through the bars, hoping I could reach something useful. The sheriff's desk was too far away to be of any use, but I found I could—if I stretched—reach the coat peg on the wall. After a few tries, I managed to get hold of the sleeve of a heavy leather duster hanging there—probably Duke's, though it looked like it would've hung big on his slouchy frame. I yanked hard on the coat and it sprung free of its peg. I pulled it into the cell with me and started turning all the pockets out.

"Come on," I muttered. "You've got to have something in here I can use."

I didn't need much. Just a pen, or a knife—something small and sturdy I could use to force the lock. But Duke's pockets were as useless as the deputy himself. All he had squirreled away in there were bits of lint, a crumpled copy of Outlaw Jack's wanted poster, a tattered bandana that looked like it had been his handkerchief for far too long, a dented harmonica, and—oddly enough—a small tin of cold cream. Ladies' cold cream, like what Aunt Helen put on before she went to bed.

"Not helpful, Duke," I said, tossing the cream aside. It rolled through the bars and out of my reach.

That was the end of my ideas. There wasn't anything else in the jail I could reach from inside the cell. The coat had been my best bet. Frustrated, I raked my hands through my hair.

I'd just about given up and decided the best thing I could do was teach myself to play mournful ballads on the old harmonica. The instrument had bounced under the bed while I was searching the coat, so I crouched to pick it up. That's when I came across something that very nearly made me weep with relief.

There was a worn leather case nailed to the bottom of my cot, hidden from view unless you were under the bed yourself. I pried the nail out with my bare hands and scooted back out from under the bed with my prize.

I unwrapped the leather to find a complete set of lockpicking tools. I couldn't believe my good luck! The tools had probably been stashed there by some nefarious outlaw, but I didn't care. It also didn't matter that I hadn't the slightest idea how to use them—just a second ago I'd believed I could teach myself how to play the harmonica—how hard could figuring out how to pick a lock be?

Turns out, it's hard.

I probably spent a good fifteen to twenty minutes digging around blindly in the lock's mechanism with one of the tools, a thin, pointy little thing that looked like something a dentist might use. I had to stick my arm through the bars and crook my wrist at an awkward angle just to reach the lock, let alone get anything like decent leverage. I was sure it was about to give way, so I gave my tool an extra powerful twist…and it sprung out of my hand, went flying across the room, and smacked Outlaw Jack on the forehead before rolling under the sheriff's desk.

"GAAHHH!" I yelled in frustration, banging my head on the bars.

"It's okay, took me awhile to figure them out too."

I nearly jumped out of my skin. I dropped the case of lockpicking tools and hurriedly kicked it under my cot.

But Sadie, leaning casually against the doorframe, just laughed at me.

"Don't worry, I won't tell Duke you were snooping," she giggled. "I'm actually a little surprised he didn't leave the spare keys stashed in there somewhere."

I was too stunned to answer, and not just by the fact that she'd managed to creep up on me and watch my miserable failure at lockpicking. She'd walked in on me mid-jailbreak and didn't seem to be a bit worried about it. I frowned at her suspiciously.

"Sorry about ropin' you earlier," she said. "I hope you ain't too sore."

My face flushed at the memory. "I'm not sore," I lied. "Actually, I'd forgotten about it."

Sadie raised a doubtful eyebrow and I squirmed. I didn't want her to know I'd spent the past few hours checking for bruises where her rope had caught me. It's a highly undignified thing, being yanked off your horse like that, especially by someone like Sadie—all capable and sure of herself. Even if she was skinny and freckled and a little disheveled, Sadie was the type of girl a fella wants to look his best in front of. Now that she was up close, I could tell she had a few inches on me, which in my present circumstances seemed like adding insult to injury. I straightened my posture a bit.

"So," I said, anxious to change the subject. I picked up the leather case containing my remaining tools. "You knew this was here? And you just left it, for anyone to find?"

"Other people's things ain't my business," Sadie replied. She reached through the bars and plucked the lockpicking kit out of my hand. "Or yours neither, for that matter. Duke put 'em in there, so that's his business."

"Why would a deputy be hiding jailbreak tools *inside* of a cell? That's the worst idea ever!"

"Duke's past is a little…questionable. Legally, ya know. I think he just hid those in there to prepare for the day when Sheriff found out about it and locked him up." Sadie shrugged, as if this were a perfectly normal thing to say—the sheriff's deputy was secretly a former outlaw. Every moment I spent in this town made me like it less.

"I brought you dinner," Sadie said, producing a basket that smelled mouth-wateringly of salt pork and biscuits. She smiled sweetly.

Okay, so maybe not *everything* about Cactus Poke was terrible.

"Thanks," I said. "I'd tip my hat to you, but it's evidence now."

Sadie laughed at that, which made me smile, too.

"We can shake instead," she said, sticking her hand out to me. "Sadie Wooten."

"Wil—" I stopped myself. "I'm Clyde." I reached through the bars and shook her hand. "Wooten? Not Hodges?"

"We get that a lot," Sadie said. "But Sheriff ain't my pa."

"Oh, that's a relief," I said without thinking.

"Why'd you say that?"

"Uh, well," I fumbled for words under her sudden glare. "It's just...he's a little, ya know..."

"A little what?" Sadie demanded, planting her hands on her hips and leaning menacingly toward me—and looking a whole lot like the sheriff when she did it.

"Scary?" I shrugged guiltily. I didn't dare say crazy. Not when I remembered how Sadie hadn't been at all unnerved by Ol' Trusty earlier, or how Duke had defended the sheriff's behavior. Maybe this whole town had agreed sanity wasn't a necessary quality. Maybe they were *all* a little crazy—living in the middle of nowhere for so long might've gone to their heads.

It must've been the right thing to say, because Sadie's frown melted.

"Yeah, you and Sheriff didn't get off on the right foot today," she giggled. "You know, I think that's the fastest I've ever seen him run."

Much as I liked seeing Sadie's freckled face smile at me, her attitude about this whole thing was getting under my skin. I was sitting in jail—unjustly, I might add—and here she was acting like it was some sort of joke.

"Why'd you get me arrested?" I demanded. "If it weren't for you, I would've gotten away. How come you're so keen on being friends now, when this mess is all your fault? I was just about gone, and then *you* showed up and ruined everything! Why didn't you let me skip town?"

"What, and let you go die in the desert?" Sadie rolled her eyes at me. She sat down in the sheriff's chair and propped her feet up on the desk, like Duke had earlier. "You oughta be thankin' me for stoppin' your fool escape and savin' your life."

"I made it in the desert on my own before," I said, jutting my chin out defiantly.

"Yep, and you stumbled into town half-dead, and a few bites of supper ain't enough to bring you back from that. If you'd got away, you and that ancient mare would be a nice dinner for the vultures by now," Sadie said. "You think you're some kind of storybook hero-type or somethin'? Don't be such a beanhead. Here's a fact: It's a hundred and fifty miles yet to California from here, and the desert don't jist up and end at the border neither. You'd never've made it, 'specially not carryin' no water."

I had to admit when she put it that way, my odds of survival didn't look great.

"I'm still not about to thank you for getting me thrown in jail," I muttered.

"Besides," Sadie said, ignoring my comment. "I hadn't made my mind up whether you was with Outlaw Jack or not."

"Have you made up your mind now?" I asked, rolling my eyes. "I am a convicted criminal, after all."

Sadie studied me, long and hard. "That's what I'm here to find out," she said. "So tell me, Mr. Clyde, are you in league with Outlaw Jack or are you not?"

"No. I'm not," I said, even though I was sure denying it wouldn't do any better with Sadie than it had with the sheriff. I figured I could repeat that over again for the rest of my life and still nobody in Cactus Poke would believe me. "I just happened to be in the wrong place at the wrong time wearing the wrong hat."

"All righty then," said Sadie. Then she smiled at me.

"Wait, that's it?" I sputtered. "You're just gonna take my word for it? No interrogation, no demand for proof?"

"Got all the proof I need," Sadie said. "I can tell when people are lyin' to me. And you ain't. Simple as that. You're an honest sort, Clyde. I believe you."

"You do?" I squeaked. A wave of relief flooded me at those three words, the words I'd been waiting to hear all day: *I believe you.* "You know, you've got more sense than the entire government of this town, Sadie Wooten! You wouldn't consider running for mayor, would you?" I asked, only half joking.

"Don't be too hard on Sheriff," Sadie said. "I'm sure he'll come around. Ever since the robbery, he's been real on edge. That tater meant everything to him—it was all that was left of what this town used to be. And Cactus Poke, it's the dearest thing to his heart."

"This old dump?" I scoffed.

"Cactus Poke ain't a dump," Sadie frowned. "It's our home and his

40

legacy. Sheriff founded this town, back in the old days after the war. When the tater was first discovered, you couldn't keep settlers outta this place. That's why the townspeople voted to change its name from Goldwater to Cactus Poke—they couldn't handle so many settlers at once, so they thought they'd try to make it a little less inviting."

"I'd have thought unjustly arresting folks would do the trick just fine," I muttered. Out of habit I reached for the pencil tucked behind my ear, looking for something for my hands to do, but I came up empty. I pursed my lips in annoyance, remembering it had been confiscated.

"You can say the Sheriff is mean and scary all you like," Sadie said. "But the honest truth is he loves this town, and his heart's broke over what's happened to it. And Outlaw Jack…" Sadie's face screwed up, and I panicked, thinking she was going to cry. I never knew what to do when girls cried. Was I supposed to offer a hanky? Or say something sweet? I always just seemed to make it worse.

But Sadie held it together, even though the corners of her eyes glistened. Instead, she clenched up her fists and spat viciously in the direction of Outlaw Jack's wanted poster. I jumped. Girls who cried made me make a fool of myself. Girls who spit, on the other hand, were an entirely foreign type to me. I'd never crossed paths with a girl like Sadie before. I wished she'd cried instead.

"What about Outlaw Jack?" I asked. "Who is he, anyway?"

"That bandit's the real reason people left this town," Sadie said. "He's been draining the life outta Goldwater County for years. It's him who scared off most of the settlers in these parts, and snatched up all the gold before anyone else could find it."

I glanced up at the wanted poster. I once again felt like I was being watched, like Outlaw Jack was eavesdropping on us from the wall. The shadowy, faceless form looming over me made me shudder.

"So why doesn't the sheriff do something?" I asked, forcing myself to look away. "You know, round up a posse and go get him?"

"And jist who would he take with him, Duke?" Sadie scoffed. "He can't hardly get Duke to sit in a chair to guard the jail for more than an afternoon."

"Well, the sheriff's got you, doesn't he?" I said. "I saw how you handled a horse and a lasso. It's not a stretch of the imagination to think you're pretty handy with a gun too. Seems to me you almost make a whole posse on your own."

Sadie turned pink all the way to her hairline and her eyes sparkled with pleasure at the compliment.

"That's nice to say," she said with a modest half-smile. "But I couldn't stand up to Outlaw Jack. He ain't like nothin' you've come across before." She lowered her voice and glanced over her shoulder, like she feared Outlaw Jack would creep up behind her any second.

"The Black Hat Bandit moves like a shadow," Sadie said. Her tone reminded me of how my friends and I used to tell ghost stories to each other by candlelight late at night, trying to scare ourselves. "Nobody's ever seen him, leastaways not up close. That's why his poster is all dark—we don't even know what he looks like, just that he always wears black. Nobody can find his hideout, and not for lack of tryin' neither. They say he knows the land around here better than any man alive. The land is on his side too. I've seen him from a distance, two or three times, standin' up at the crest of Goldwater Ridge, lookin' down on the town. But anytime anyone tries to go after him, he up and disappears, like smoke. But folks say you can *feel* it when he's close by."

I swallowed hard. Had I been imagining the creepy feeling that followed me through town? Or was it something more? Duke's question—*"Did you see a ghost?"*—echoed in my mind, this time with a sinister edge to it. I decided I liked scary stories much better when they were told within my school's sturdy brick walls. Out here in the untamed West, with only the flimsy town of Cactus Poke standing between me and the vast wilderness—and anything haunting it—they were a whole lot less appealing. I shuddered.

"I gotta go now," Sadie said, standing up. She dusted her hands off on her pants and smiled, sweet as a peach, but a spark of mischief glittered in the corner of her eye. "Sweet dreams, Clyde!"

Sadie bounced lightly into the blackness of the night. The door didn't close all the way behind her, creaking ominously on weary hinges. Eerie sounds floated into the jail: a loose shutter clapping against a building, the haunting wails of jackals out in the desert, and the lonely moan of the wind as it wandered Cactus Poke's deserted street.

"That's not funny, Sadie," I hissed, but Sadie didn't come back.

Outlaw Jack watched me in unsympathetic silence. If he'd had a face, it would've been smirking.

5

MORE OF MY HOPES AND DREAMS GET CRUSHED

"I don't see the point in repaying my debt to society when there isn't any society to pay it to!"

Duke and I stood in the deserted town street, facing each other showdown-style. By my guess, it was hardly eight in the morning (my pocket watch was still "evidence" so I couldn't be sure) but heat already rippled through the air in shimmering waves. I was lucky I'd been able to convince the sheriff to let me have my hat back, otherwise my brains would've fried. He charged me thirty cents for it though—imagine having to bail a hat out of jail!

I didn't get much sleep; Outlaw Jack kept staring at me from the wall all night, and anytime I shut my eyes, his shadowy form stepped off the poster and into my imagination, keeping me awake with his ghostly gaze. That didn't do much for my mood, and Duke was the only one around for me to take it out on. He seemed to be taking it pretty well. He looked a little bored, standing there with his signature smirk plastered on his pale face. He held a bucket in one hand, filled to overflowing with bubbly white paint, and in the other he had a ragged paintbrush.

"Sheriff's orders," he drawled, giving me a lazy shrug. "Whatcha gonna do about it?"

He held out the bucket to me and nodded toward the ladder that leaned up against the building's faded face. Above us, the sign that was supposed to read GENERAL STORE had surrendered most of its letters to the desert long ago.

"Look here," I said, not moving to take it. "The general store is closed. Been closed a while, by the looks of it. It's as abandoned as the rest of this spooky old town. This is a complete waste of my time, no matter what Sheriff Hodges says!"

"Lemme spell it out for you, kid," Duke said. "I. Don't. Care. You got a problem, you talk to Sheriff. He's the one that wants you to do good deeds around his town. So you either git up that ladder and start paintin' or you take it up with him. I ain't your man."

Duke set the bucket down between us, then backed up, crossing his arms over his chest. The bucket sat there like a challenge, a gauntlet thrown. I didn't pick it up; instead I kicked at it, sloshing a bit of goopy paint over the rim and onto the dirt.

Duke eyed me with a curious expression. "Ya know what?" He said after a second. "I think Sadie was wrong about you. She told me last night she thought you was a decent sort, kinda adventuresome and hero-like, ya know? But looks to me like you're jist a baby throwin' a fit when he don't git his way."

"Sadie said I was adventuresome?" I repeated, forgetting the paint bucket as my head filled instantly with a giddy sort of lightness. "She said that? Wow. I mean," I caught sight of Duke's smirk and stopped myself. "I mean, yeah, I guess I am a bit hero-like," I gave my shoulders a modest shrug, like I was used to hearing compliments like that. "But you know, I guess it just comes with the territory."

"What territory? The 'my daddy struck gold and now I think I'm entitled to special treatment' territory?"

"Uh," I said. "I was kind of thinking the fearless desert adventurer territory."

"Whatever you say," Duke chuckled. "But you ain't got me fooled. Her neither, I'd reckon. Besides," he said, nodding down at the bucket. "Sadie cares about this town as much as anyone, except for maybe Sheriff. And she cares about *him* more than he cares about the town. So *she'd* side with him on this."

"Oh." I heaved a defeated little sigh. "I guess that kinda ruins my chances with her, doesn't it?"

"Chances?" Duke raised an eyebrow at me. "You thought you had *chances*? With *Sadie*? Kid, lemme spare you a whole lotta hurt. You ain't never gonna be good enough for a gal like Sadie."

"Wh—what do you mean?" I sputtered, his words hitting me like a punch in the stomach.

"Sadie's somethin' special, kid. She can rope and ride and shoot and spit better'n most full-grown men," Duke said. "And she's got *standards*, ya know. She ain't just gonna swoon for the first boy to come a-ridin' into town who thinks he's all that. And let's be honest, man-to-man here: you don't got much goin' for you. You stumble into town half dead on a horse older than the hills and the first thing you do is run your big mouth so much you git yourself arrested. Then you run like a coward and git hauled off to jail after landing on your rear in the dirt. And then ever since, you've done nothin' but whine and complain to anyone in earshot. Jist what about *that* do you think would impress a gal like Sadie?"

Duke's words stung me like a hornet, and not just because he'd insulted me and smashed my daydreams about Sadie. I opened my mouth to snap out an angry reply but closed it just as quick, afraid I'd only prove him right. That was the worst part, I realized all at once. Duke *was* right! Sure, it hadn't been fair the way I'd been treated since coming to Cactus Poke, but there was nothing noble about the way I'd reacted, nothing at all. I did run like a coward, and I did whine and complain.

As if it wasn't bad enough to be told I wasn't worth the time of day to a fine and pretty girl like Sadie, another horrible thought hit me quick on its heels: what would Pa think of the way I'd behaved myself in Cactus Poke? All this time, I'd been trying not to let him down, but what would he say if he could see me now, pouting over a bucket of paint? Sure, my memories of him were a little nonspecific, but I knew Pa was a good man, a noble man who did the right thing and would want his son to do the same. I still needed to clear my name and get out of this worthless old town, but until I figured out a way to do that, Pa would want me to hold my head high and conduct myself honorably.

Without another word to Duke, I bent down and picked up the bucket and hauled it up with me as I started to climb the ladder.

Duke watched me for a second with a satisfied smirk, then turned before I'd even gotten to the top and began to walk away down the street.

"Hey, where are you going?" I called after him in surprise.

"Kid, you got another thing comin' if you think the most interestin' thing I got to do all day is watch you paint a sign."

"I thought you were guarding me. Ain't you worried I'll run away?" I said, then bit my tongue. There was no question about it: I had to figure out a way to get out of this town and quick. My grammar was already starting to deteriorate.

"Run? That's rich!" Duke chuckled. Based on Duke's range of emotions, getting a real laugh from him, no matter how small, would've taken the joke of the century. I guess I was that joke.

I narrowly resisted the urge to flick a spattering of paint across his nose.

"And just where d'you think you'll run to?" He asked. "Look around you, kid, and tell me what you see. Nothin', that's what. A thousand square miles of nothin'. The desert almost gotcha once; you think it'll let you escape a second time?"

"Maybe I'll go north instead and brave the mountains," I said, jutting my chin out defiantly. My newfound nobility wasn't holding up too well.

Duke's grin melted.

"To be honest, kid," he said quietly, "if you're a bettin' sort, my money'd be on the desert."

"Oh, really? Why?"

"Those are the Bitterroot Mountains," he said. "*Outlaw Jack's* territory. See that there?" He pointed to the rise overlooking the town, the first rocky slice of mountain looming up over the foothills. "That's Goldwater Ridge. People used to go up there sometimes, lookin' for him. They didn't never come back."

I remembered Sadie saying she'd seen Outlaw Jack spooking around on the crest of the ridge and my eyes scanned it expectantly for a glimpse of his ghostly shadow. But the ridge sat there, serene and empty. No shudders ran up my spine. No dread clenched my stomach. Outlaw Jack was nowhere in sight.

Ghost stories, as it turns out, don't keep well in sunlight.

I eyed Duke doubtfully. "I still think if I'm penned in by a desert on three sides and an outlaw on the fourth, I'd risk it with the outlaw," I said.

"Suit yourself," Duke shrugged, kicking at the dust as he turned to go. "But if he kills ya, don't come cryin' about it to me."

"But if I'm dead, how would I...you know what, never mind," I said to Duke's retreating back. He wasn't listening anyway.

I looked back up at the ridge. Maybe I could get away through the mountains; it probably wasn't as dangerous as Duke and Sadie thought. The real problem was, it wouldn't get me any closer to Pa. By the time I had hiked on foot through the mountains and survived off the land long enough to reach civilization, months might have passed. I didn't have that kind of time to spare any more than I had the time to be a handyman around Cactus Poke. No, I had to go straight and true, through the desert, and I had to go as soon as possible. But the only way I'd survive was if I had plenty of supplies, and if I could get Abraham back, and if I didn't have crazy old Sheriff Hodges galloping behind me in hot pursuit, brandishing Ol' Trusty.

I could make it if I had help from somebody in Cactus Poke, somebody who could load me up with food and water and then make sure the sheriff was distracted long enough to give me a decent head start. I weighed my options. Duke was out, that's for sure. He probably wouldn't care too much if I got away (I wasn't convinced Duke cared about *anything*) but he sure wasn't about to help me. Kay Fay had been kind to me once, but giving a stranger food and assisting a fleeing fugitive were two different things. I had a hunch her loyalties were with the sheriff. But Sadie...surely she'd help me out if I asked her.

Duke's words came back like a slap in the face. *"You ain't never gonna be good enough for a gal like Sadie. She's got standards, ya know, and you don't got much goin' for you."*

A glob of white paint splatted on my boot like a great white tear falling from my paintbrush.

"Get it together, Clyde," I muttered through gritted teeth, gripping the paintbrush with white knuckles and attacking the sign with far more aggression than artistry. Forget Sadie. Just focus on figuring out how to get out of town. "You'll think of something."

But seven painted letters later I still hadn't had any brilliant ideas. The heat was suffocating. Sweat rolled in big drops down to the end of my nose, like I was a candle melting from the top down. I took off my hat to mop my forehead and squinted at the desert as if it were possible to catch a glimpse of California glittering unreachably beyond it.

I didn't see California, but what I did see was almost as good. It was a cloud of dust, rolling across the desert like an overgrown tumbleweed. It was moving fast, and headed straight for Cactus Poke. As the cloud got a little closer, I was able to make out its source. Inside the dust were—hallelujah!—three horses, ridden by three men.

I was so shocked I didn't realize the brush slipped from my hand and streaked a white line across the sign as it fell, making the *N* in *GENERAL* look more like a lopsided *W*. There were people—real, honest-to-goodness people—headed my way. They could help me get out of here! I was saved!

As the riders reached the border of town, I scrambled down the ladder in a hurry, waving my arms.

"Hey!" I yelled. "Over here!"

The riders didn't slow as they thundered down Main Street, galloping past the general store and leaving me choking on their massive cloud of dust.

"Come back!" I coughed, staggering after them. "I need to talk to you!"

They kept on, but I sprinted after them, determined not to lose what was maybe my one chance to get rescued from Cactus Poke.

Just when I'd resigned myself to the fact that they were planning to ride straight on through town without so much as slowing down, the three men reined their horses right in front of the jail. I caught up to them a few seconds later, panting and still coughing on dust.

Sheriff Hodges stepped out of his office. He stood at attention on the boardwalk in front of the jail, looking like one of the tin soldiers I used to play with when I was younger. I could see the sun glinting off his badge, which gleamed like he'd just polished it. I hung back, not wanting to draw his attention. He watched the riders with a calm expression that said he'd been expecting them. He snapped off a smart salute, practiced to perfection from his military days. Two of the riders returned it, but the one in the middle merely gave a short nod.

"Sheriff Hodges," he said by way of greeting, looking down at the sheriff from atop his horse. "How go matters in Goldwater County?"

"Marshal," the sheriff replied, nodding back cordially. "We've had some problems in recent days, sir."

Marshal? *Sir?* Hope bubbled up inside of me. A federal marshal, and one that the sheriff treated like a superior officer—I could hardly believe my good luck!

"If you'll kindly come on inside," Sheriff Hodges continued, "I'd be happy to give you a full report."

He disappeared back inside the jail, his wooden leg *clomp-clomp-clomping* as he went.

The three riders dismounted and started hitching up their horses in front of the jail. This was my chance. I took a deep breath, wished myself luck, and stepped up to the marshal.

"Excuse me, sir," I said, and for once my voice didn't crack at an inopportune time. The marshal turned around and fixed me with an annoyed glare. He was huge, towering over me like an oak tree, and built like a bull. I did my best to look a little taller.

"Scram, shorty," said the first of the marshal's deputies, stepping between me and the marshal. He was a ferret-like man with a pinched face and patchy blond beard. He was tall too, but more like a corn stalk and less like an oak. "The marshal ain't got time for bothersome questions."

Ferret put his hands on my shoulders and gave me a hard shove. I stumbled back a few steps, but I didn't fall.

"Ooh, a tough one, ain't he?"

"Don't pick fights with children," said the other deputy in a longsuffering voice. He was suave-faced and handsome, with a bit of a swashbuckling look to him, like a painting I'd seen once of Captain Kidd.

"I'm not a child," I said, realizing as I said it that it was a very childish thing to say. I cleared my throat and started over. "I need to speak with the marshal, please, on a matter of legal urgency."

"The marshal has important business with the sheriff," said Captain Kidd. "He doesn't have time—"

"Let him talk," interrupted the marshal in a booming bass voice that made me jump after Kidd's soft-spoken tones. Kidd shot the marshal a look of unmasked annoyance, one I wouldn't have expected a deputy to give his senior officer, and the marshal added, "But make it quick."

"Yes, sir," I said, not letting my mind linger too long on the odd exchange. "I'll get right down to it sir. I'm being kept here against my will by the sheriff, held prisoner in Cactus Poke as a suspect for crimes I didn't commit. I haven't been given a fair trial, there isn't any evidence or witnesses against me, and I have urgent business elsewhere that I'm being kept from."

I should've left it at that, but the words were tumbling out faster than my brain could keep up, and I found myself saying, "And furthermore, I don't believe Sheriff Hodges is fit for service as a lawman. I don't know how well you know him, but I think his mental state is unstable at best, and at worst, he's completely out of his mind."

The marshal studied me for a second. I bit my lip, my heart pounding.

"Sheriff Hodges," he boomed, his voice so loud and rumbling that I know the sheriff heard it from inside the jail. I'd be willing to bet Duke heard it from wherever it was he'd slunk off to, and Kay Fay down in the café, and heck, probably even Outlaw Jack up on Goldwater Ridge. "Sheriff Hodges is a war hero, a dedicated public servant, and proven to be the best lawman west of the Mississippi. And you dare accuse him of incompetence?"

"It's not his fault," I amended. "I just think maybe in his…uh, declining years…that he's just not as sharp as he used to be. That's no sort of mark against his character, mind you," I added quickly. "Marshal, sir, all I ask is that you hear me out. Give me a fair trial where I can prove there's no real case against me and I can be on my way."

"This sounds like a *local* matter, sir," Kidd said to the marshal, giving him a significant look. "Best leave it to *local* law enforcement. We've got more pressing matters to deal with."

"Yes, yes, of course," said the marshal, nodding compliantly at Kidd. My heart sank. "I fully trust Sheriff Hodges's discretion, and I've no interest in meddling in a matter that falls under his jurisdiction. The sheriff's ruling stands."

"But, sir!" I pleaded, grabbing at the marshal's arm as he turned away. He shrugged me off without any effort. "You don't understand, I'm no outlaw! I'm innocent, and I gotta get to—"

"Get the hint, kid. Nobody cares," sneered Ferret, pushing me again, and this time I did fall down. By the time I'd scrambled back to my feet, the three men were disappearing through the door to the jail. I wasn't beaten yet, I decided, screwing up my courage to burst in after them. They *had* to help me. They were the only chance I had.

I charged at the door, ready to fight for my chance at freedom, but I didn't make it. Something snagged me from behind, yanking me by the back of my collar and pulling me to the side.

"What—HEY!" I half yelled, half choked.

"*Shh!*" Sadie hissed in my ear, then dragged me away from the door and down the boardwalk a few yards. I was too surprised to fight back. She didn't release her grip on me till she'd ducked off the boardwalk and slipped into the narrow alley between the jail and the town hall. She crouched in the dirt, pulling me down with her.

"What in the world—" I started, but she cut me off.

"Pipe down, would you?" she whispered. She pointed upward to a little window high up on the wall. It was tiny and barred, and too high for a full-grown man to reach. Muffled voices floated out from it, but I couldn't make out what they were saying.

"Why are we hiding?" I demanded in a stage whisper.

"I need to know what they're talkin' about," Sadie whispered back. Frantic intensity burned in her eyes. "Boost me up to that window, okay?"

"What? No," I said, pulling away from her. "Here's a better idea: I go in there and talk to the marshal and when I'm done I'll tell you anything I overhear."

"They won't talk about it if you're in there!" Sadie pleaded. "C'mon, help me out!"

"Talk about *what*? And why are you spying on them anyway?"

Sadie bit her lip and hesitated for a second, but then shook her head firmly.

"Ain't your business," she said.

"Well it sounds to me like it ain't yours either," I replied, pulling away from her. "Look, I'm sorry, but I'm going in there. I gotta talk to the marshal and get out of this crazy town."

I stood up, brushing dirt from my pants. I squared up my shoulders and stepped back out of the alley.

"The marshal won't help you," Sadie said softly. "He don't care what goes on in this town. Never has. Something ain't right about him."

I turned back to her. "What do you mean?"

"I can't quite put my finger on it," Sadie said. "But I don't trust him. Don't tell me he didn't give you a fishy sort of feeling. I mean, you saw how he let his deputy push him around like that a second ago. It's like he ain't the one actually in charge, he jist wants you to think he is."

I had to give her that.

"They're lyin' about something, I know it. I can spot a liar a mile off," Sadie's eyes flashed. "And Sheriff, he thinks the world of 'em. He'd tell 'em anything or do anything they asked, jist cause they flash those fancy badges around. They're bullies, Clyde, and I ain't even convinced they're real lawmen. Look," Sadie said, "I know you wanna go on to California. I'm sorry you're stuck here, and I get it, you wanna find a way out. But *please*, don't go trustin' those rattlers. The less they have to do with matters in Cactus Poke, the better."

"The better for you?"

"For everyone!" Sadie insisted. "Lemme say it plain: I think they're outlaws, impersonatin' marshals to gain Sheriff's trust so they can use him to get whatever they want."

"And what's that?"

"I don't know yet!" Sadie threw up her hands in exasperation. "Why do you think I wanna eavesdrop? I'm lookin' for proof! This could be my chance to expose those snakes for who they really are. Help me out, Clyde," she begged, grabbing my hand. "Please."

It would be nice to say my decision was based on logic and reason and genuine distrust of the marshals, and not entirely on the fact that Sadie was squeezing my hand tight. But I can't be sure, because when she held my hand like that and looked pleadingly at me, those big round eyes of hers trembling with unshed tears, every knight-in-shining armor instinct inside me woke up. Not good enough for Sadie, huh, Duke? I'd show him. More importantly, I'd show *her*.

"Sure, okay," I said, letting my hope of help from the marshal get snatched away on the desert wind and blown down the street like a tumbleweed.

"Thank you!" Sadie said, throwing her arms around my neck in a quick hug. "Okay, gimme a boost."

I braced against the wall and Sadie scrambled up to stand on my shoulders. She kept her head ducked beneath the window, so she'd be out of sight even if someone chanced to glance out of it.

"Can you hear okay?" I whispered up to her, and she nodded silently.

With Sadie's boots balancing on my shoulders and my back already beginning to strain a little bit, it was definitely the wrong time to have second thoughts. But I had one anyway: I was now a willing accomplice in whatever Sadie was up to. If her hunch about the marshal and his deputies being imposters was right, then exposing their fraud could be an act of heroism that would make papers from here to the Pacific. If Sadie was wrong, though, then we were deliberately spying on a confidential conversation between the sheriff and a man who carried the authority of the United States federal government. And that, I was certain, was something an outlaw would do.

Sadie listened at the window a good five minutes or so. I didn't hear a word of the conversation; I was concentrating too hard on not collapsing and sending us both crashing to the ground. Sadie wasn't that heavy, but then again, neither was I, and I'd like to see you try to hold a person the same size as you on your shoulders for five minutes straight. Just when my legs were starting to shake and every muscle in my back was screaming at me, Sadie hissed, "Git down!"

We both did, tumbling down into the dust in a heap of arms and legs. Sadie instantly popped back up, and dragged me with her.

"Get up, Clyde, they're coming!"

We raced around the corner, disappearing around the back of the building without a second to spare as the sheriff led the three visitors back into the main street.

"Duke!" Sheriff Hodges hollered. "Git out here, I need ya! DUUUKE!"

Nobody answered.

"Where do you think Duke's gone off to?" I whispered to Sadie. She shrugged.

"He makes himself scarce when the marshals are in town," she said. "I think he's afraid they'll recognize him."

"Confound that boy," we heard the sheriff mutter after a few seconds. "Never around when you need him."

The rumbling voice of the marshal answered him, but we couldn't make out his words.

"Sadie!" Sheriff Hodges called next.

"Yes, Sheriff?" she answered instantly, making me nearly jump out of my skin, yelling like that after all the whispering we'd been doing.

"Come on over here and help the marshal's horses freshen up before they head on, will ya?"

"Sure thing, sir!" Sadie yelled back, moving to go.

"Wait," I caught her arm. "Aren't you gonna tell me what's going on? What were they talking about in there? Did you hear anything important?"

"I was right, they're up to no good," Sadie whispered. "But I don't have time to tell you now. Go back and paint your sign. I'll come find you later."

"Promise?"

"I *promise*," Sadie said with an eye roll. "And Clyde," she added, her face breaking into a genuine smile. "Thank you."

6

BILLY BOB CLYDE, OUTLAW HUNTER

I never did go back and finish painting that sign; it could read *GEWERAL* till the end of time, for all I cared.

After my stint as an accomplice to espionage, Sheriff Hodges went off somewhere—I didn't see where—flanked by the marshal and his men. As soon as I was sure they were gone, I followed Sadie to the stables in hopes of wheedling some information out of her while she took care of the marshal's horses. It was good to see Abraham again, though she didn't look all that thrilled to see me. Apparently she'd been enjoying our imprisonment much more than I had, all snug and cozy in a well-stocked stable. She looked fatter and happier than I'd ever seen her.

Sadie's news wasn't good. Turns out the marshal had come to see if the sheriff had managed to capture Outlaw Jack yet, and when he'd told them that not only was Outlaw Jack still on the loose, but he'd managed to steal the Golden Tater, the marshal was furious. The sheriff had failed to protect his town, the marshal declared, and Cactus Poke was no longer inhabitable. Its townsfolk needed to prepare to pack up and leave for good.

"United States citizens," Sadie related, mimicking the marshal's booming bellow surprisingly well, "should not live in fear of phantom outlaws in the hills!"

"They can shut down a whole town?" I asked Sadie. Her jaw was clenched tight as she brushed the marshal's horse.

"They can do whatever they want," she growled, "as long as Sheriff believes they've got the federal government on their side. They've told him he'll be transferred to the law enforcement office in Tombstone."

"Tombstone?" I remembered seeing that name on my long-lost map. The name stuck in my mind (for obvious and morbid reasons) but it wasn't anywhere on my route. "Wait, isn't that down by the border? That's nowhere near here!"

"Four hundred miles southeast, to be exact," Sadie shook her head.

"And Sheriff Hodges is gonna do that? Leave his town?"

"It'd kill him to leave. He asked them for more time," Sadie blinked hard, and I realized she was trying her hardest not to cry. "Begged them, actually. I've never heard Sheriff sound that desperate. They said they'd give him seven days," she shook her head. "One week, Clyde, that's all, to not only *find* Outlaw Jack, but to defeat and arrest him too! One measly little week, after people have been searching for his hideout for years! It jist ain't possible!"

"Hang on a minute," I said, a knot of dread forming in my gut. "If the sheriff goes to Tombstone, what happens to me? You know, being arrested and all."

"I reckon Sheriff will probably have you come with us," Sadie said. "I don't think he'd just turn you loose. After all, you're bound by the laws of Cactus Poke, even if there ain't no more Cactus Poke."

"Well, I don't know about the rest of you, but *I* can't go to Tombstone, that's sure and certain!" I took my hat off and smacked it on my knee in determination. "I'm going to California!"

With that, I left Sadie and marched right back across town. The dust the marshal and his deputies kicked up as they galloped out of town hadn't even cleared the street yet. But I couldn't wait another second. I had to talk to the sheriff, and I had to do it now. I stood outside the jail, gathering my courage to go busting in with a plan for a wild grab at my freedom—for the second time today.

"You've got this Clyde," I said. Then I took a deep breath, straightened my black hat, and shoved open the door.

I caught the briefest glimpse of Sheriff Hodges slumped over at his desk, his face buried in his hands. He sat up straight and alert and pasted on his fearsome expression the instant I opened the door. But he wasn't quick enough, and I saw him—saw him as he truly was: a sad, tired, defeated old man. Seeing a man that proud look that broken was more disconcerting than anything Sadie had said about the marshals. Sheriff Hodges was no friend of mine, but he was important to Sadie, and Sadie was becoming important to me. My plan, awful as it was, could save the town and the sheriff. That was the only way to win my freedom—and her approval. I had to do it.

"I'm going after Outlaw Jack," I said without preamble.

The sheriff blinked at me blankly, his sharp blue eyes lacking their usual intensity. He gave me that empty stare for a solid five seconds before he shook himself and spoke.

"And jist what in tarnation put that fool idea in your head?" he asked.

"Look, Sheriff," I said, my rehearsed words spilling out fast. "You want me to do good deeds for the citizens of Cactus Poke, I get that. And that's the best good deed I can think of. I'm not going to poke around town painting signs and mucking out stables while there's real work that needs doing around here. And if I find him, if I find your stolen gold nugget, that clears my name of any suspicion in the robbery, right?"

The sheriff leaned forward a little bit, still not giving any thoughts away on his face, but I could tell he was listening to me now. And as he listened, the spark in his eyes rekindled.

"This is my deal," I said firmly. "You let me go after the Golden Tater. If I can find it, and bring the person who actually took it to justice, then I've proved my innocence, and you have to let me go."

I stuck out my hand to him, and for a moment, I thought he'd shake it without hesitation. But he seemed to catch himself from being too eager. He straightened and squinted at me, and though it was still the same unnerving expression he'd worn during our first encounter in the café, it seemed to me now that he was eyeing me with a little bit of a newfound respect.

"Boy," he said finally. "What in the world makes you think you're fit to go out and chase down Outlaw Jack? He's ruled the Bitterroot Mountains for years, knows 'em like the back of his hand. And you're nothin' but a wide-eyed whippersnapper who ain't even got any whiskers yet."

My hand flew to my chin self-consciously. I was tempted to jump into a defense about my baby-soft skin (the men on my mother's side of the family never had the ability to grow a full beard.) But I forced myself not to get derailed.

"I'm young, but that's what makes me strong. I've traveled over two thousand miles, the hardest bits of it on my own, so you know I can fend for myself just fine. Sheriff, I know it might seem like a long shot, but you owe me the chance to clear my name. It's a matter of honor, sir. Besides," I added, "If I fail, you're just back where you were before. If I succeed, though, you get your tater back, and Outlaw Jack, to boot. You've got nothing to lose here."

Of course, I knew exactly how much he had to lose, but he didn't need to know that Sadie and I had been eavesdropping. His town, his position, and his life were bargaining chips, and that's what I was counting on to get him to agree to this wild Outlaw Jack gamble. No sheriff in his right mind would send a thirteen-year-old alone after a seasoned outlaw. But Sheriff Hodges wasn't in his right mind, and I was staking my hopes on that.

A long moment passed while the sheriff studied me. He stared at me so long that I started to waver. Go hunt down Outlaw Jack? What was I thinking? I was going to get myself killed! Sure, finding Outlaw Jack, recovering the Golden Tater, saving the town, clearing my name, and earning my freedom would seal me forever in Sadie's mind as a hero, but I couldn't enjoy that if I was dead.

I felt the leathery grasp of the sheriff's hand in mine.

"You have seven days," he said, giving my hand a firm shake. I couldn't help but wonder if that handshake sealed my doom. "Find the tater, clear your name."

"I won't let you down, sir," I said in a voice that carried loads more confidence than I felt. He released my hand, and I turned to go. I hadn't made it out the door yet when he stopped me.

"Clyde," he said, and I flinched in surprise. It was the first time I'd heard Sheriff Hodges address me by name. I turned back to look at him. He'd stood to his feet (or, foot and peg I guess) and was giving me a soldier's salute. "Good luck, son," he said.

I swallowed hard, tried to return the salute as well as I could, and stepped back out into the sunlight.

"**AND** jist what do you think you're gonna do, ya beanhead," Sadie demanded, standing in the stable doorway with her hands on her hips. "Walk up into the mountains and bump into Outlaw Jack taking a stroll?"

I thought Sadie would've been impressed by my bold and daring plan, but she seemed far from it. Her reaction made me pause for the first time since declaring my outlaw-hunting intentions. As soon as the sheriff shook on my deal, I'd rifled through the box of evidence for my knapsack—grabbing my watch and pencil while I was at it— stuffed a few provisions and some basic gear inside, and set off to the stables to say goodbye to Abraham before heading out to the hills. After all, I only had seven days to catch an outlaw, and the first one was half gone already. I didn't have any time to waste.

But Sadie found me in the stables. She must've heard my plan from the sheriff, and she wasn't thrilled about it. In fact, she looked like she meant to stop me.

"No, of course not," I huffed. "I've got a plan, well, most of a plan, but it's still in the developing stages. I'm on a tight schedule with this. I figured I'd work out the details on the way. But yeah, it starts with going up in the mountains and scoping out the territory."

That was pretty much the extent of my plan, but Sadie didn't need to know that.

"This is something I've got to do, Sadie," I said. "I'm not going to Tombstone, and you aren't either, not if I can help it. This might well be the only chance I've got."

"It ain't a chance at all," Sadie insisted. Her freckles stood out starkly against the exaggerated whiteness of her face. She looked more agitated than I'd ever seen her. "This ain't bravery, Clyde, it's suicide!"

Even though she was probably right, and this might be the most foolish thing I'd ever done, a part of me was downright pleased she was so worried about me.

"Don't concern yourself about me," I said bravely, shouldering my knapsack with the determined air of a tragic hero headed to an unknown fate. "After all, it's not just about me anymore. I'm doing this for the good of everyone. Restoring the Golden Tater and confronting Outlaw Jack will save this town and everyone in it."

"Clyde…" Sadie said, wringing her hands and not meeting my eyes. She looked like she wanted to tell me something. My heart did a backflip. I'd read enough books to know this was the part of the story where the hero usually got a confession of undying love from the fair lady, and if it was a good book, he'd get a kiss too—the mere memory of which would be enough to sustain and bolster him through the most dire of straits that lay ahead. I'd never in my life been kissed before, and if my first one was destined to come from a gal like Sadie, well, who was I to argue with luck like that?

But Sadie didn't kiss me. She didn't confess her love either. What she did was pull out a gun.

"I guess you'll need this," she sighed, holding it out to me. "If you're so determined you're gonna go."

"I am," I said, quickly hiding my disappointment. "Um," I said, taking the gun and holster belt she offered me. "Isn't this Duke's gun?"

Sadie shrugged. "He ain't usin' it, and I ain't lettin' you go after Outlaw Jack empty-handed. You're already easy pickins to him as it is."

"Won't Duke miss it? I mean, taking a man's gun is—"

"Take it Clyde, jist take it!" Sadie snapped. "I—I already asked him if you could and he said it was okay, so there, that's all good."

I raised an eyebrow at her obvious lie, but she looked so desperate and fearful that I didn't protest. I strapped Duke's belt around my waist and felt the weight of his gun tugging conspicuously at my side. Now, I decided, was not the best time to tell Sadie I'd never fired a gun at a man before. I didn't think I could actually do it if it came to that. Not even if that man was Outlaw Jack.

"Okay," I said once the gun was secure. "Are you happy now?"

"No," said Sadie. "But it's the least I can do." That look came over

Sadie's face again, like she had something she was itching to say to me, but she held back again, biting her lip.

"Jist please, *please* Clyde, be careful," she finally whispered. "If you don't come back, I'll never forgive myself." And with that, Sadie turned and ran from the stables, her braided pigtails flying behind her. It wasn't exactly a confession of love, but it was something.

But rather than encourage and empower me, Sadie's worry tugged heavily at my heart like an anchor as I left town. Goldwater Ridge frowned down at me from above, and beyond it loomed the Bitterroot Mountains and my unknown fate.

I was barely out of town, just starting to get into the foothills, when I knew beyond a shadow of a doubt I was being followed. It wasn't just the rustling of movement behind me that gave it away; I could *feel* somebody's presence nearby. When I froze, the sounds stopped too. I spun to scan the area behind me. Nothing. There wasn't much place to hide in these hills. Maybe the rise and fall of the land had a few dips a person could disappear into, and the scrubby bushes dotted here and there could possibly obscure a person—if he were smaller than average and lucky.

"Duke? That you?" I called softly, cautiously. "Sadie said it was all right if I borrowed your gun."

No one answered. Whoever it was stayed hidden.

I hesitated a moment longer, then shook myself. Maybe it was just nerves. I turned and started uphill again. As soon as I moved, the rustling sound started back up.

"Show yourself!" I commanded, whirling to face the threat and drawing Duke's pistol, hoping I looked intimidating even though I felt very small.

From behind one of the bushes, my pursuer stepped out.

Or I guess I should say, he hopped out. He was nothing more than a large desert jackrabbit. He stood up on his back legs—he was over two feet tall—and sniffed the air in my direction curiously. One of his massive ears twitched as we regarded each other.

I breathed a sigh of relief and sheepishly put my gun away.

"You ought to know better than to sneak up on people like that," I scolded the hare. "If you'd done that to a meaner fella than me, you'd be dinner by now."

Maybe the desert sun had done some damage to my head after all—it seemed to me that the hare's eyes lit up when I said the word *dinner*. He hopped a few feet closer, his nose twitching expectantly.

"No, you don't get any food from me. Go on now," I said. "Shoo. I'm busy hunting outlaws."

I turned away from the hare and set my face toward the mountains again. Something about having a scare (even if it turned out to be nothing but a rabbit) made me all the more anxious to get up into Outlaw Jack's territory and get on with it. I had a job to do. When I glanced back over my shoulder, the hare had disappeared. Apparently I was of no more interest to him than he was to me.

As I hiked further in, the ground steadily grew steeper and rockier. I found myself stopping for breath more frequently, and studying my path carefully to ensure I chose the surest footing. Everything was quiet here, including the land as it subtly transformed from desert to mountains. If I looked behind me, I could see Cactus Poke standing like a last outpost on the shimmering shores of the endless desert. It looked so lonely.

"So long," I said, turning my back on the town.

Once I got past the ridge, I tried to head due north, straight into the mountains. But traveling in the mountains was nothing at all like traveling in the desert. They're two entirely different breeds of wilderness. In the desert, you pick a direction and go with it; you can go one way for miles and the ground doesn't get in your way. In the mountains, any direction you pick will almost always have some kind of boulder, or cliff, or gorge standing right in your path. There isn't much you can do except zigzag your way around it. By the time an hour had passed and the sun was at its hottest, I had changed directions so many times to get around various obstacles that I'd completely lost my bearings.

I could see why nobody had found Outlaw Jack yet. The Bitterroot Mountains were dotted with hundreds, if not thousands, of little dips, caves, and hollows an outlaw could disappear into. He could stay in a different hideout every day of the year and still have limitless options open to him. The massive improbability of me finding him in seven days began to weigh heavily on my mood. What was I thinking? A one-man search party with a looming deadline would be no challenge at all for Outlaw Jack to evade, especially since I'd never set foot on this terrain before. He might even find it insulting.

The hopelessness of ever seeing the smallest sign of Outlaw Jack was so overwhelming in my mind that I didn't even notice I'd walked into his hideout until I tripped over the remains of last night's campfire.

"What in the——?" I muttered, kicking at the circle of rocks with charred sticks piled in the middle before it dawned on me. "Oh!"

I whirled around, certain Outlaw Jack was standing behind me, ghostly eyes all aglow, waiting for me to realize I'd walked into a trap. But the place was deserted. Actually, the longer I looked around the campsite, the more I began to wonder if maybe I'd overestimated Outlaw Jack.

He hadn't even tried to hide his camp. Not only was it out in the open, on a relatively flat bit of ground without even the cover of a few boulders to obscure it from view, but he hadn't taken any great pains to cover his tracks either.

It was obviously a campsite, and a recently occupied one. Even the most inexperienced tracker could've told you that. Aside from the remains of the fire, footprints—human and horse— littered the dusty ground. Empty bottles lay scattered near a flattened-out spot where a bedroll might have sat. I picked one up, but the words on its paper label weren't part of my limited Spanish vocabulary. I tossed it aside. The rest of the camp wasn't much better. Some scraps of food and trash were tossed around the area, and a puddle of half-dried tobacco spit sat a few feet away from the fire. Aside from being messy, Outlaw Jack must also have been lazy—I mean, how long would it take to kick a little dirt over your chew spit? A second? Maybe Outlaw Jack wasn't as cunning and elusive as everyone thought he was.

That, or he'd wanted me to find him. This could be a trap, and if it was, he would still be close by. The thought of him lurking just out of sight like a mountain lion waiting to pounce made me uneasy. I shuddered, my hand twitching toward the gun at my belt. But even though I waited a few minutes, no outlaw appeared. I couldn't find anything worth picking up as evidence, so I left the camp. I'll admit I walked quicker than normal—not running, but close—and I glanced over my shoulder every few steps.

That must explain how I missed the ground's drop off until I was already falling into it.

Loose shale and dust slid out from under me and I lost my footing, landing hard on my right shoulder and instantly tucking into an ungainly somersault that smacked my backside hard against the rocks. I tumbled down the slope, the centerpiece of an impromptu rockslide, before finally skidding to a stop, lying flat on my back in a cloud of dust.

I'd fallen probably three quarters of the way down the slope of a narrow ravine, about twenty feet deep with a bone-dry creek bed at the bottom. Its walls were steep, but with a little concentration and well-placed footing, I decided it was possible to get back up to the rim. Of course, if I factored in my aching tailbone, skinned palms, and the three bloody cuts I found, (two on my shins and one on my forearm) then "possible" might take a little longer.

I brushed the dust off my pants as best I could and bent to pick up my hat, which my fall had hurled a few yards away, but as I reached for it, a shadow fell across me. I froze, crouched low like a rabbit sensing a hawk, moving only my eyes as I whisked them up to the ravine's rim. Something big and dark ducked out of sight just as I did. My breath caught. That was the side of the rim I had come down—the side with the camp.

Outlaw Jack was here.

It was terrible timing for him to show up. I was aching and shaken, not to mention stuck in the bottom of a ravine like a fish in a barrel. I hadn't been convinced I could fight Outlaw Jack before, let alone now. But, as Uncle Henry used to tell me when I asked him for war stories: "You don't have to have the high ground; it's enough if your enemy thinks you do." It was clear who had the high ground here—and I'll give you a hint, it wasn't the kid standing at the bottom of a gorge. But maybe, just *maybe*, I could convince Outlaw Jack I did.

"We got him now, boys!" I hollered, making myself jump at how sharply my voice split the silence around me. It bounced off the walls of the ravine like I had shouted down a well, and even though I instantly regretted my intimidation strategy, I had jumped in with both feet and there was no undoing it now.

The shadow did not reappear, but a few loose shards of flinty rock tumbled down the slope where it had been. He was still up there, probably peering down at me, but remaining unseen. I gulped, sensing the need to fill the conspicuous silence with confidence. Remembering the bottle I'd found at the camp, I decided to try out my Spanish.

"*Te tenemos rodeado,*" I yelled, trying my best to sound like I knew what I was talking about. "*Sal lentamente con las manos a la vista!* We have you surrounded. Come out slowly with your hands in sight!" Good words to know when riding with a band of Mexican bounty hunters. Not so great if you were alone and vulnerable, but I hoped Outlaw Jack wouldn't call my bluff.

The only answer was the wind's ghostly whistle as it whipped through the gorge. I snatched my gun, pointing it vaguely in the direction of the shadow with shaking hands.

"Surrender!" I yelled, then tried to follow the command with its Spanish equivalent, just to be safe. But I couldn't for the life of me remember what the Spanish word for *surrender* was. The only thing I could think of was "*Deditionem,*" which wasn't even Spanish; it was Latin, leftover in a dusty corner of my brain from some long-forgotten vocabulary lesson. As impressed as my Latin tutor would have been, I didn't think it was much help in the current situation. I shook my head vigorously. *Focus, Clyde!*

"Hand over the Golden Potato, Outlaw Jack! *Entregar la dorada…*" But my feigned confidence wasn't enough to carry me. I smacked my forehead in frustration. Now was *not* the time to realize I'd never learned the Spanish word for potato! "*La dorada…baguette?*" said my fool brain.

A moment of deadly silence. Then suddenly, I could feel him right behind me.

I nearly jumped out of my skin. "Don't hurt me!" I screamed, making a sound that was probably about three octaves higher than any self-respecting outlaw hunter had any right to make. As if begging for mercy in a pitch a concert soprano would envy wasn't bad enough, when I recovered my senses, I made the humiliating discovery that it was completely unnecessary. I wasn't in any danger at all. The rabbit, that same ridiculous jackrabbit from before, had appeared right behind me, and the touch I'd felt was him aggressively poking his nose into the backside of my knee. He now sat a few paces away, fixing me with the most offended gaze you could imagine on a rabbit's face; I might've accidentally kicked him when I scrambled away.

"What are you *doing?*" I yelled at him when I could breathe again. His ears flinched at the sound. "Are you trying to get me killed?"

The rabbit stood up on his hind legs and twitched his nose at me expectantly.

My pounding heart was still in the process of coming down from my scare, and I was in no mood to be friendly. "Get out of here and quit following me! This isn't a game!"

I whipped back around to face the rim of the ravine where Outlaw Jack had been. But the black shadow—and the chilling feeling along with it—had vanished. A shiver ran up my spine.

"What are you, some kind of guardian angel or something?" I asked in a hushed voice, turning back to the hare. But he was nowhere in sight. I looked again. Nothing. I turned a full circle, scanning the area around me for any sign of anything. No shadows, no bunnies, no outlaws, no angels. Just me, alone on a rocky slope, talking to myself.

"It's all in your head, Clyde," I said, taking a calming breath. I wiped my sleeve across my damp forehead before smacking my hat firmly onto my head. Phantom jackrabbits? I was losing it. I'd end up as mad as old Sheriff Hodges if I kept this up, sure and certain. Maybe that was Outlaw Jack's strategy: hide out so well that his enemies went plumb crazy trying to find him.

It wasn't a very reassuring thought.

"You'll be okay," I said, hoping I could convince myself. "It's just the pressure getting to you, that's all. First things first, get yourself out of this ravine."

That was easier said than done. It took me about fifteen minutes to recover the ground I'd lost in a matter of seconds. By the time I'd scrambled back up and crested the rim, I was panting hard and had several fresh cuts on my already battered hands.

I sat down on the lip of the ravine, took a few deep breaths, and shook my head to clear it. I pulled a corn muffin out of my pack and munched on it, feeling much better even after the first bite. I glanced around, half expecting that persistent jackrabbit to sneak up on me again, but he didn't. I felt a twinge of guilt at the thought of the rabbit though, and I broke off a crumble of muffin.

"Sorry," I said, even though I couldn't see the hare. With ears like his, maybe he heard me anyway. I scattered a small handful of crumbs on the ground. "I shouldn't have yelled at you."

I stood up, then hesitated. Should I go back to Cactus Poke and report on the camp I'd found? Maybe I could get Duke and Sadie to come out here with me and check it out. I doubted the sheriff could make it up here on one leg—I'd barely made it on two—but after a minute I dismissed that plan. I'd found a camp, but that wasn't enough. It wasn't Outlaw Jack, and it wasn't the Golden Tater. Going back now would give Outlaw Jack, if he was nearby, more time to get away. I decided to keep moving.

I wandered the Bitterroots for hours and found no other signs of the Black Hat Bandit. The sun hung low over the western peaks, and I started thinking maybe I should turn back. But I hated the thought of returning to Cactus Poke with nothing to show for my efforts but a few new bruises. It felt like giving up, and I couldn't afford to do that—if I didn't want to get carted off to Tombstone and have Sadie see me as a failure the rest of my life, that is.

So as the day crept toward dusk, I pressed on. I stumbled upon a small lake just in time to see the pink and gold sunset reflecting off its glassy waters. After weeks traveling in plains and deserts, the sight of a lake was a welcome relief. It was a beautiful and lonesome place, rimmed by mountains whose rocky slopes dipped into the water. On the near shore, where I stood, a copse of evergreen trees lined the muddy beach, thick enough to be termed woods. On the far shore, there was a break in the outcropping where a mountain stream fed into the lake. I don't know how long I stood there, drinking in the sight—the lake, the mountains, the sunset, the stillness. For a moment I forgot my sore muscles and bruised bones, I forgot Outlaw Jack, I forgot Cactus Poke, and I even forgot California. For a moment, everything was at peace.

I climbed down to the water's edge, a low, smooth spot where there was a stretch of muddy beach. My eye caught on something near the edge of the woods: an upright stone column, about shoulder height on me. It was engraved with a few words: a name, a date, a phrase in Latin. At a glance, it looked like any common gravestone. I would've passed by quietly at a respectful distance—except I could read the name from here, and what I saw sent panic knifing through my chest.

The name on the stone was Lawrence Hodges.

7

ASHES AND HOPE

A MILLION and a half possible explanations shot through my head all at once, none of them favorable: Maybe Outlaw Jack killed Lawrence Hodges, and the sheriff down in Cactus Poke was an imposter; maybe the sheriff I knew *was* Outlaw Jack! The craziness was all an act and I'd played right into his hands!

Then, if it was possible for it to get worse, it did. I thought of Sadie, and my heart sank.

"I can spot a liar a mile away," she'd said, and I believed her. So if the sheriff wasn't who he said he was, if he was lying to me—and the whole town—Sadie would know about it, and that meant *she must be in on it too!* If I didn't trust Sheriff Hodges, I couldn't trust Sadie either. And if I couldn't trust Sadie, where did that leave me?

Just as I was about to give in to full-on panic, I had the bright idea to go read the stone. I staggered forward, holding my breath as I prepared to come face to face with the truth carved on its weathered surface.

It read:

On this spot, February 20, 1869
LAWRENCE HODGES
Discovered the Goldwater Potato
Ex Cinere Belli, Novam Spem Luceat.

Never in my life had I been so happy to be proven wrong. I laughed out loud with relief, a sound that went bouncing off across the lake. The stone was a monument, but it didn't mark a grave.

"Drat these Cactus Poke folks and their obsession with that potato!" I laughed, shaking my head. "It's caused me more trouble than its weight in...well, gold, I guess."

But something about the stone still bothered me. Why build a monument to a gold nugget? What was so special about this discovery that it merited commemorating for all time? I reread the inscription a few times, paying special attention to the Latin phrase at the bottom. Lucky for me, Latin was fresh on my mind, thanks to my impromptu linguistics exercise in the ravine. I studied the monument, digging in my brain for vocabulary words to string together in a translation. After a minute or two, I got it.

"From the ashes of war, new hope shines."

It was an odd thing, I thought, to mark the discovery of gold with an epitaph like that. It seemed so momentous and weighty. If it had been me who discovered a giant gold nugget, I imagined the inscription would read something more like, *"So long peasants, I'm buying an island!"*

But Sheriff Hodges hadn't cashed in on his find, and he certainly hadn't run off and kept it all to himself. Instead, he founded a town where he could point others toward the hope of gold. As much as I wanted to find reasons to dislike the sheriff, it did seem like a noble thing to do.

For a moment, I pictured myself as a younger Lawrence Hodges, fresh from a war that left him forever broken and scarred. He was tough and he'd survived, but I couldn't blame him for wanting to leave it all behind him, to start over somewhere new, somewhere he didn't have to be surrounded every day by the reminders of all he'd lost, breathing in the ashes of a life that was gone forever. I imagined what it would have felt like to be in his shoes as he limped up to this hidden paradise after weeks in the endless desert. And then, as he stooped to take a drink, to catch sight of the glint of sunlight off of gold, shining up at him from beneath the muddy waters, bright as a promise.

From the ashes of war, new hope shines.

It made sense now, the sheriff's dogged refusal to give up. To Lawrence Hodges, Cactus Poke wasn't just a dot on a map. Nor was it just a town that needed his leadership. To him, it was a life reborn. It was a chance at healing.

It was hope.

But now, all these years later, the sheriff had lost even that, despite his grit and determination. The dream of a booming town supported by an influx of Goldwater gold hadn't become a reality. And even the Golden Tater, the one remaining shred of that dream, was gone too. No one who spent so much as an hour in Cactus Poke would argue that it was a place full of hope. Its people had abandoned it, Outlaw Jack drained the life out of it, and the marshal and his men (whoever they were) were about to extinguish it for good. The stone up here on the shores of this lonely lake might just as well have been a grave after all— Cactus Poke, and all it stood for, was as good as dead.

And try as I might, I hadn't done anything to save it.

Who was I kidding? Find Outlaw Jack and recover the Golden Tater? Save the town? Win Sadie's lifelong admiration? The very idea seemed laughable. Billy Bob Clyde the great outlaw hunter stood in the gloomy dusk, his confidence gone, his heart heavy, and his body tired. With a sigh, I made the decision to turn back.

"You win this round, Jack," I said aloud to the gathering darkness and any outlaw-shaped shadows lurking out there.

For a moment, I thought I did see something, away on the opposite shore. It stood in the gap between the rocks where the stream fed into the lake. In the dim twilight it was hard to be sure my eyes weren't playing tricks on me. But if I had to guess, I'd say it was a person. A tall, black-clad person, watching me.

At this point, I shouldn't have been surprised (but of course I was) when once again the rabbit jumped out at me, his oversized ears twitching in expectation. If he could've talked, I'd bet good money he'd have said "You called?"

"I wasn't talking to you!" I snapped. I looked back across the lake, and just as I expected, the shadow had vanished. "Dumb bunny."

The jackrabbit's ears drooped and he snuffled his nose on the ground, looking a little dejected. His sadness pricked my conscience and I bit my tongue, ashamed of how mean I'd sounded.

"Fine," I sighed. "Here, have at it. I'm going back now so I don't need it." I dumped my knapsack upside down, shaking the rest of the provisions out onto the ground in front of him. The rabbit looked at me with an expression I can only describe as total adoration, and he wasted no time in enjoying the feast I'd given him. I walked away, leaving the happy rabbit behind me.

Well, I thought drearily. *At least there's one living creature in Goldwater County I didn't fail today.*

It didn't take me long to get out of the mountains. Apparently I was much closer to Cactus Poke than I'd thought; I'd gotten so turned around that I'd traveled pretty much halfway back to town before I found the lake. But despite the unexpectedly shorter hike, my heart was heavy as I trudged back down into the foothills. A whole day gone, one of a very precious few, and all I had to show for it was a heart full of discouragement and a whole bunch of bruises.

Some hero I'd turned out to be.

Even though I hardly expected a hero's welcome on returning, I don't think I was prepared for how dark and quiet the town was. Between the rabbit and the shadowy figure, there had been more activity up in the wilderness than there was on the main street of Cactus Poke. Nobody came out to meet me, and no dinner-like smells came from the café. I didn't see a light in any windows. Even Abraham begrudged me a whinny of welcome when I ducked into the stables to tell her I'd made it back all right. There was no sign of Sadie anywhere. I trudged back to the jail and let myself in. Duke was off duty, so I had to get the keys down off the wall and unlock my own cell to be able to get to my bed. If that isn't the most lonely, pathetic thing you ever heard, I don't know what is.

I flopped face-first onto the lumpy mattress and fell into a dreamless sleep.

WHEN I woke up, the midmorning sun was already pouring through the jail's tiny window. I struggled to shake myself out of a thick daze as I sat up. I'd slept in my clothes—boots, hat, and all. Every bone in my body hurt, and I groaned as I tried to stand.

The jail was quiet. Nobody sat at the desk. I vaguely wondered where Duke had gone off to as I let myself out of my cell and left the building, squinting like a mouse against the glaring sunlight. I looked up and down the street, not the least bit surprised to find it empty, then followed my nose to the Olde Towne Café, where the smell of coffee beckoned me.

I pushed open the café door, convinced I'd lived this moment before. Kay Fay and Sheriff Hodges were there, drinking coffee, like they had been two days ago when I'd first come to town.

Two days? It felt like a lifetime.

"Oh my lands!" exclaimed Kay Fay as she took in the sight of me. "You're back! And in one piece!"

She rushed at me, arms extended like she wanted to catch me tight in a hug. But she stopped herself just short of grabbing me and instead gave my cheek an awkward pat.

"You had me so worried, child, going out into those wicked mountains all on your own," she fussed. "And then you were out there all night...you poor thing."

"Um," I said, stepping back. I felt even less like a child now than I had two days ago when she'd first called me one. "I'm all right, ma'am. I got back in last night actually; I just slept pretty hard."

Sheriff Hodges sat at the table, sipping silently at his mug, but he eyed me thoughtfully.

"May I join you, sir?" I asked. "I'd like to tell you what I found yesterday."

"Take a seat, son," the sheriff said with a nod. Kay Fay gave me another pat, this one on the top of my head (I narrowly resisted the urge to duck out of her reach) and then she brought me my own mug of scalding black coffee.

I sat down across from the sheriff. The cold blue light in his eyes that had scared me so bad when I first met him two days ago now just made me sad. I wondered how much of the old Lawrence Hodges, the one I'd discovered up at the lake, was left in his muddled mind.

"Well?" he asked, breaking into my thoughts. "Did ya find him? Did ya find Outlaw Jack?"

"Not exactly," I said. I told the sheriff everything—well, mostly everything. I didn't think the parts of the story where I made a fool of myself by falling into a ravine or getting scared by a rabbit were terribly relevant, so I left them out. But I did tell him every detail I could remember about the campsite, and the shadow that had persistently followed me throughout the day. He listened intently, only stopping me to ask a few clarifying questions—"Did the footprints in the camp look fresh?" "This shadow, did it give ya an eerie sort of feelin' right before ya saw it?"—but when I finished talking and he realized there was no conclusion to my story, no happy ending, not even so much as a next step to my plan, he gave a heavy sigh.

"It's always the same," Sheriff Hodges said, his voice laced with discouragement. "People who go lookin' for Jack always think they're so close to findin' him. But then he up and vanishes, not leavin' so much as a trail to sniff at."

"So I'm right back where I started," I groaned. "Except now he knows I'm looking for him."

"That looks to be about right," Sheriff Hodges nodded, giving me a resigned sort of smile. "But the week ain't up yet, boy. Maybe that head of yours'll think of somethin'."

"Maybe," I said, then had a thought that brightened my outlook a bit. "Hey, Sheriff, where's Sadie this morning?"

"Think she said she got some chores to do back at the house. Sadie'n me live in Ol' Widder Nell's boardinghouse across from the Town Hall. You'd probably find her there." He gave me a suspicious glance. "But what business do you have with *my* Sadie?"

"Just want to tell her how my hunt went yesterday and see if she's got any ideas about what I should do next," I said. He didn't let up on the staring. "Sadie and I have gotten to be friends," I said. "Uh, *just* friends."

"See that it stays that way," he grunted, then turned his attention back to his coffee. I took that to be a dismissal, so I got up, thanked Kay Fay, and headed out the door.

Widow Nell's boardinghouse wasn't hard to find once I was looking for it, though I'd passed it without noticing every time I'd walked the main street of Cactus Poke. To be fair, it looked like all of the other abandoned buildings. I guessed Nell herself had either passed on or left town long ago, despite her house still having tenants. I wouldn't be surprised if the sheriff still dutifully paid her his rent every month.

I got about halfway to the boardinghouse when I froze in my tracks. I was being followed again, I knew it. It's not the sort of feeling a man likes getting used to, but I had to admit it was becoming one of my more commonplace sensations. I looked up and down the street for any sign of a shadowy bandit and—there! I caught sight of a figure running along behind the row of structures. I only got a glimpse as it slipped past the alley between two buildings, but I could tell it was staying low and moving fast.

"You don't get to haunt me anymore, Jack!" I yelled, taking off after it. I sprinted down the closest alley and popped out on the other side of the buildings. You probably already guessed it—by the time I got there, the shadow was nowhere in sight. There wasn't anywhere Outlaw Jack could've gone, not unless he had an elaborate network of secret trap doors and hiding spots stuck all over town. He couldn't have outrun me, not that quick, and none of the buildings had back doors he could've ducked into. Even the windows were too high, and most of them had shutters, so he would've lost too much time if he'd tried to scramble up through them.

"I *know* I saw you!" I stomped my foot, frustrated and befuddled. "I'm too young to go crazy!"

But if I wasn't crazy, that left me with the most illogical—and unpleasant—explanation for his vanishing.

"I don't believe in ghosts," I said to the emptiness. More than that, I *refused* to believe in ghosts. "Ghosts can't steal gold nuggets. And—" I looked down and saw something that reassured me I was neither crazy nor haunted. "And ghosts don't leave footprints! Ha! You *were* here!"

There were footprints, all right. Not enough of them and not clear enough to follow, but enough to prove that someone, a person with a physical body, *not* a ghost, had been here just a few moments ago. I crouched down and studied the clearest of the prints for a second. Something wasn't quite right about it. I was no great tracker, but even I could tell that this boot-print was noticeably smaller than the ones I'd seen in Outlaw Jack's camp yesterday.

"So that means…" I said aloud, hoping a plausible explanation would come to me by the time I reached the end of my sentence. It didn't, and I trailed off. "Sadie. I gotta find Sadie," I concluded. Two brains would be better than one when it came to this, especially if one of those brains belonged to Sadie. With one last glance up and down the row of buildings, (and no shadows in sight) I left the footprints and resumed my walk to the boardinghouse.

It was quiet inside. The first door on my left as I entered had a little bronze number 1 hung on it, and beneath that, an engraved plate that said L. Hodges. The rest of the doors were blank underneath their numbers. The only other thing of note on the first floor was a little wooden box with a slot in its lid. It was labeled RENT, and, true to my suspicions, it was stuffed to bursting with coins and bills, even though the cobwebs clinging to it made it clear it hadn't been moved in years.

"Sadie?" I called as I started up the stairs. "It's me, Clyde."

She didn't answer, so maybe she hadn't heard me. The second floor was barren and deserted, so I climbed up one last flight to a gable attic and was met by a door with S. Wooten written on its plate. I knocked, and the door swung open without resistance.

"Uh, hello?" I called. "Sadie, are you in—?"

My words caught in my throat. Sadie's doorway looked like a portal to a different world. I blinked hard, twice, but the magical sight didn't disappear.

Lush green velvet draped all around, hanging from the walls and ceilings and puddling in glistening heaps on the floor, cloaking the attic with luxurious softness. Garlands and bouquets of faded silk flowers were strewn about everywhere, as if this was a long-forgotten enchanted garden, not a bedroom. Old posters depicting fabulously dressed men and women in striking poses papered every surface not already draped with velvet. The posters all bore the same imprint: STARFIRE SHAKESPEARE COMPANY, ST. LOUIS, MO. On the windowsill, sitting on a pillow placed right in a beam of sunlight as if they were the crown jewels, was a pair of silver-handled opera glasses.

I stepped into the dreamy space. Something about it drew me in like magic. I never would've guessed that Sadie—gun-slinging, lasso throwing, spit-like-a-man Sadie—would choose to retreat to a room like this.

"Shakespeare, huh?" I said, wandering over to the largest of the posters, hung prominently in the center of the wall. I recognized the scene it showed—a beautiful girl draped over a rose-covered balcony, extending a graceful hand to her pining lover below. My classmates and I had gagged and groaned our way through *Romeo and Juliet* last term despite our teacher's valiant efforts to convince us it was a masterpiece. (We'd all have been just fine to skip ahead to the stabbing parts.) I couldn't say I understood Sadie's admiration for it; she was too tough to enjoy something so sappy.

But the caption on the poster gave me a hint at why she seemed to treasure it so much. Like the others, it was an advertisement from the Starfire Shakespeare Company in St. Louis. This one announced their upcoming production of *Romeo and Juliet*, running every night except Sundays for the month of June 1873. Under the sketch of the balcony scene, it read: "Featuring principal star Ralph Wooten as Romeo, and his beautiful bride Clementine in her theatrical debut as Juliet."

"Wooten," I read, the realization coming over me. Sadie's parents were Shakespearian actors? I looked around at some of the other posters and realized the large one wasn't the only one that featured Ralph and Clementine Wooten. They appeared as Antony and Cleopatra, Hamlet and Ophelia, and even Macbeth and Lady Macbeth! Every one of Sadie's posters starred her parents in leading roles.

My enchantment with the room faded. The green velvet felt oppressive, and even the flowers looked a little sad. Poor Sadie. I knew she was an orphan…these Shakespeare relics might be the only things she had left of her family. I was trespassing on something sacred, and I felt the strong need to be elsewhere. I made for the door, but as I turned to go, my shoulder bumped against the wall, knocking out a nail and sending a small bit of paper fluttering to the floor.

I picked it up. It was a clipping from an old newspaper, and at a glance I saw it was a glowing review from a theater critic—this one about Sadie's dad's performance in *Othello*. I meant to put it back where it had come from and get out of Sadie's room, but as I bent to look for the nail, I dropped the paper again. It landed backside up. The headline staring up at me from that side of the page made my blood run icy cold:

OUTLAW GANG MEMBER 'DEUCES' DUKE HASTINGS DEAD AT 24

"Holy smokes!" I whispered. I instantly recognized the photograph printed underneath the headline. He was much younger, but he was definitely Duke. It's hard to mistake a scar like that. I snatched up the paper, scanning the article with mounting dread:

"Missouri native Duke Hastings was killed in a gunfight following an attempted train robbery, led by notorious brothers Frank and Jesse James on Saturday. Hastings, who joined the outlaw band four years ago, was shot by railway officials and left behind by fellow gang members when the robbery attempt was aborted. His body was not recovered. Hastings served as a drummer in the 15th Missouri Confederate Infantry, and is survived by his parents—"

That's where I stopped reading. I thought I might throw up. I knew—*I knew!*— there was something about Duke that bothered me! Sadie told me Duke had a history, but that was putting it nicely. I could hardly wrap my head around it: Sheriff's deputy was an ex-member of the Jesse James gang… and one who was supposed to be dead at that!

"I gotta talk to Sadie!" I said again, and started for the door. I gave up looking for the dropped nail and instead decided to leave the article on a small vanity table near the door.

The table was plain by comparison to its surroundings, with a few toiletries arranged neatly on its surface—a hairbrush, a washbasin, a pitcher. Above the vanity hung a mirror, with little scraps of paper tacked around its wooden frame. They were drawings, sketches of faces. I squinted at them for a closer look. The rough drawings, while not exactly Da Vinci, were certainly recognizable as citizens of Cactus Poke. It wouldn't have been all that odd on its own—if Sadie wanted to practice her sketching, that was none of my business. But what made me do a double take was the word jotted beneath each picture: *MOTIVATION.*

I stepped closer, eyeing the first of the sketches critically. It was Duke, even though his scar was drawn on the wrong cheek. His caption read: *"Motivation: Hiding out from his past. Wants to be sheriff himself someday."*

My heart skipped a beat. Motivation for *what?* I wasn't in a forgiving mood toward Duke, not with my newfound information about his past, so my mind jumped to all sorts of unpleasant conclusions. Was Duke planning on assassinating the sheriff? And what on earth did Sadie know about it?

The sound of the door slamming downstairs broke into my thoughts and made me jump.

"Clyde?" Sadie's voice called. "Are you up there? Sheriff said he sent you this way lookin' for me?"

"Uh, yeah," I managed to choke out in reply, my mind still reeling. "Yeah, I'm here."

Sadie laughed. "Well how 'bout you be down here instead. I'm headed to go feed the horses. Why don't you come along? You can tell me about yesterday."

"Sure, but, um," I said, not taking my eyes from the drawings. "Can you come up here for a second?"

She paused briefly, then said, "Are you all right?"

"I'm fine. But can you come?"

Boots thumped on the stairs in response.

"I'm glad you came back alive and well and all, Clyde," Sadie called, "but you should know better than make me climb three flights of stairs unless you got good reason."

She appeared in the attic doorway a second later, and despite her chiding tone she was grinning. Her freckled face glowed even fresher and rosier than usual—or maybe it just seemed like that because I'd missed her.

"So why'd you drag me up here?" she asked, pretending to pant.

I wasn't in the mood for games though.

"What's this about?" I asked, handing her the newspaper clipping detailing Duke's death.

Sadie took it, glanced at it for the briefest second, then handed it back to me.

"I already told you Duke had a past." She said. "I found it out by mistake cause it happened to be printed on the back of that clippin'. But that's all behind him now."

"But Sadie, he was with the *Jesse James gang*!" I protested, unnerved by how unconcerned she seemed by the whole thing. "That's like the most notorious band of robbers and murderers since…since the Forty Thieves! Doesn't that make you a little uneasy?"

"Listen, Clyde." Sadie put her hands on her hips and frowned at me. "Let me tell ya plain: when a man goes out West to start over, there's no sense in bringin' up what he'd rather leave behind him—or holdin' it against him, ya hear? Obviously Duke didn't want no part of the outlaw life no more. Why else would he fake his death?"

I bit my lip. She had a point…Duke had clearly cut ties with his old life—and he was even working on the right side of the law now. But something seemed off. Sadie was holding out on me somehow, I could feel it.

"Well, if you're so sure he's not an outlaw," I said, whipping my pencil out from behind my ear and pointing with it to the picture of Duke tacked to the mirror. "Then what's with the drawing? And the motive?"

Sadie looked where I pointed. A look of confusion crossed her face, followed by realization. Then she rolled her eyes at me.

"It's nothin', ya snoop," she said, giving my shoulder a light punch. "I was just doin' some brainstorm work, right after the robbery. I gathered up all the possible suspects and tried to figure out why they might have reason to take the tater." She shrugged dismissively. "But Outlaw Jack took it, and you don't need a detective to figure that out. Come on, let's go."

"Hang on," I said, still frowning at the drawing of Duke. I couldn't shake the suspicion that I'd been hunting the wrong person. "You might've been onto something here. I mean, how do you *know* Outlaw Jack took it?"

"Because he's *Outlaw Jack*," Sadie said, as if it were the most obvious thing in the world. "Honestly, Clyde, you'd be hard-pressed to come up with reasons why he *wouldn't* steal it!"

"Yeah, sure," I said, but my mind was picking up steam and moving fast. "But let's just think about it for a second. Please?"

Sadie pressed her lips together and gave an annoyed sigh through her nose, but she folded her arms and said, "Okay, but make it quick. Pinto ain't friendly when he's hungry."

It was all the encouragement I needed.

"Duke wants to make a new life for himself, right? He doesn't want the sheriff to know he's a criminal. But," I began to pace, tapping my pencil on my chin as I thought out loud. "He wants to be sheriff himself, and the only way that's gonna happen is if the sheriff appoints him his successor. I bet he plans to win the sheriff's favor forever by solving the robbery and returning the tater to him! And what better way to do that than to steal it in the first place? It's pretty brilliant," I said, seeing the clues coming together in my mind. "What if Duke staged the robbery, and is hiding the tater somewhere in Cactus Poke, waiting until the sheriff gives up all hope, and then Duke gets to come in and save the day by 'finding' it!" I smacked my forehead. "Eureka!"

"Are you quite done, Inspector Clyde?" Sadie smirked at me.

I took one look at her and realized she had information that was going to poke a hole in my theory. I deflated a little. "Yeah, I guess I'm done."

"Good. You should know that Duke was horribly sick the night of the robbery," she said. "I would know; I was the one tryin' to get him to keep some fluids down. He was throwin' up all over the place. I mean, haven't you noticed the dark circles under his eyes? I think he's still trying to recover a little bit."

"Oh," I said. "I guess I just thought that's how he looked normally."

"Rude."

"Okay, so maybe not Duke," I shook off my disappointment and turned back to the mirror. The next sketched face belonged to Kay Fay, which made me instantly doubtful, but a good reporter leaves no stone unturned. *Motivation: Secretly in love with Sheriff.*"

"What? Is she really?" I asked, mouth agape.

Sadie shrugged in response. She pulled out a stool from under the vanity and sat down with a resigned air. "This could take a while," she muttered.

"But if she's in love with the sheriff, then that means…that means…" I trailed off, trying to conjure a brilliant conclusion but coming up dry. "You know," I said after a minute, "That doesn't seem like a great motive for robbing him."

"So I ain't the best detective, okay?" Sadie threw up her hands in exasperation. "Besides, Kay Fay has an alibi too—she was the one makin' the broth for Duke that night."

"Well, you weren't with her the *whole* night," I said. "She could've easily stopped by the Town Hall and swiped the tater on her way back to the café after dropping off soup at Duke's place," even as I said it, it sounded ridiculous. "But you know what, I think we should drop Kay Fay as a suspect. If she loves Sheriff Hodges, there's no reason for her to rob him."

A little flicker of doubt crossed Sadie's face, but she hid it quickly in another eye roll.

"See, this is why I told you this wasn't important," she said. "You think I didn't go through these same thoughts before, and hit the same dead ends?"

"Who's this guy?" I asked, pointing to the third picture. It was a face I didn't recognize, and the motive underneath it said: *To purge Cactus Poke of sins and wickedness.*"

"That's Brother Parson," said Sadie, not trying very hard to mask the annoyance in her tone. "He's the circuit riding preacher 'round these parts. He's only in town every three months or so."

"Oh yeah, he's the guy who closed down the saloon," I said, remembering the sign on the door. "Was he in town at the time of the robbery?"

"No," said Sadie. "He's been gone for weeks now. But he knew about the Golden Tater and where it was kept and all, so I decided to include him. He ain't a likely suspect though. He's pretty busy doin' the Lord's work in all of Arizona Territory."

"That's a good cover story," I mused, studying Brother Parson's clean-cut, boyish face. "If he wants to purge the town of all sins and wickedness, it makes sense he'd be against the sheriff hoarding a giant gold nugget. Doesn't the Bible say gold is the root of all evil or something?"

"No, it says the *love* of money is the root of all *kinds* of evil," said Sadie. "You can't jist go around misquotin' the Scriptures, Clyde. It ain't Christian."

"Well, what about pride coming before a fall and all that," I tried again. "The sheriff seems mighty proud of that Golden Tater and it being the town's claim to fame."

"It's 'Pride cometh before *destruction*,' Clyde, 'and a *haughty spirit* before a fall.' Good grief, boy, we gotta get Brother Parson back here and learn you a thing or two about the Bible." Sadie eyed me suspiciously.

"Hey, I went to Sunday School! I'm not a heathen! But come on Sadie, surely the tater was causing *some* sort of sin and wickedness in this town! Don't you think Brother Parson would want to remove the temptation?"

"Maybe he would want to," said Sadie, "except the Bible does pretty clearly say 'Thou shalt not steal.' Even you ought to know that."

Sadie stood and pushed the stool back under the table, nodding toward the door in a "Let's go now" gesture.

"Fine," I sighed, privately tagging Brother Parson as "still under suspicion" in my mind before turning back to the mirror, but there weren't any other sketches stuck up there. "Hang on," I said, "There's people missing."

"What people?" said Sadie. "Are there other folks hiding around Cactus Poke I ain't met yet? It *is* a pretty big town, I guess, maybe I missed some."

I ignored her sarcasm. "For one thing, you don't even have Outlaw Jack up here."

"Well, duh," Sadie rolled her eyes at me. "That's because he's the most obvious suspect. The rest of 'em were only bein' considered as alternatives to the Outlaw Jack theory."

"I'm not sure your Outlaw Jack theory has enough evidence. Heck, I'm not sure he's even up there in the mountains at all," I said. "I spent all day looking for him, and the only living creature I came across that whole time was a silly old jackrabbit."

"A jackrabbit?"

"Yeah, it followed me all day," I said, annoyed at the memory. "Turned up every time I thought I saw Outlaw Jack, then vanished just as quick. Probably scared ten years off my life, sneaking up on me like that with my nerves already stretched so tight."

"Lands, Clyde, you don't think…" Sadie's eyes went wide.

"Think what?"

Sadie glanced both ways, like she was afraid of being overheard. "Do you believe in magic?"

"Magic? Look who's being unchristian now!" I scoffed. But Sadie wasn't laughing. "You're not serious, are you?"

"There are legends," Sadie insisted, but I cut her off.

"You're actually suggesting Outlaw Jack can—" it was so ridiculous I could hardly even say it aloud— *"Turn into a bunny?"*

"It's worth considering," Sadie said, drawing her shoulders up in a defensive stance. "And not any more unchristian than accusing the preacher of thievery. It was a *jack*rabbit, after all."

"That's the most absurd thing I've ever heard come out of your mouth." I shook my head in disbelief. "He doesn't have exclusive rights to the word 'jack,' you know. And on the tiniest, wildest chance that bunny actually was Outlaw Jack, why on earth would he use his magic powers to follow me around all day begging for muffins?"

"Okay, okay, you win!" Sadie laughed. "Forget the bunny."

"With pleasure. Gracious, Sadie, for a minute there I thought you were as mad as Old—"

Sheriff Hodges was on the tip of my tongue, but I caught myself just in time.

"As mad as what?" Sadie frowned at me.

"As mad as an old horny toad," I amended, a little subdued. "Let's get back to your suspects."

"Oh boy, here we go again," Sadie rolled her eyes.

"There's one obvious person missing from your list," I said.

"Me?" Sadie said, as if she'd been expecting me to accuse her all along.

"Um… yeah." Actually, I'd been thinking about myself, since I was the only suspect who'd been arrested and questioned. But I was a little embarrassed to admit I'd hoped Sadie had studied me long enough to sketch my face and analyze my motives.

"If I stole it," Sadie said, "would I be trying to solve the case, dummy? Besides, you know it's against the rules of mystery stories for the detective to be the criminal, right? It ain't fair that way."

"I guess so," I admitted. This did seem a little pointless. The people with decent motives also had alibis, and even though there wasn't any hard evidence against Outlaw Jack, he was, after all, *an outlaw*.

But just as I'd decided this was a waste of time, my eye caught on one more scrap of paper, not hanging on the mirror, but sitting on the table. It was face down with a pencil on top of it, still in progress.

"Wait a second," I said, picking it up.

"Clyde, don't—" said Sadie, but I already had it in my hand.

It was an incomplete drawing, with nothing on the face but a pair of darkly shaded eyes and long black hair. *"Motivation: Wants to be richer and more infamous than Outlaw Jack."*

"Who is this?" I asked, frowning at the picture. "I don't recollect seeing anyone like this in town."

Sadie hesitated, looking at me long and hard. "I think that's California Jackson. The drawing's a little bit of guesswork, since I'm not sure if I've seen her before or not."

"Who is California Jackson?" I asked, "And what do you mean, you're *not sure* if you've seen her?" My forehead scrunched up in confusion.

"Well," Sadie began slowly, picking her words carefully. "About a week ago, a stranger rode through town. A lady, with long dark hair." Sadie nodded at the picture in my hand. "She was nice, polite. Confident, but not too pushy. I gave her some directions and showed her to the café. I didn't see her after that, but Kay Fay told me she was asking questions about the town and its history, and about Goldwater County in general, and Outlaw Jack and his hideout, and…" she trailed off, biting her lip. "I don't know what all Kay Fay told her, but she does like to talk." Sadie sighed, then continued.

"The lady didn't stay in town; left right after lunch. Sheriff didn't meet her at all. And then two days later Duke came back—he'd been out riding a patrol around the borders of the county—and said he'd caught wind of some rumors about a lady outlaw, a newcomer in these parts who'd been stirring up trouble recently. Calls herself California Jackson." Sadie raised her eyebrows at me expectantly. "*Jack*-son, see? Like, as in Outlaw Jack?"

"I'll say it again," I rolled my eyes. "Not everything with the word 'jack' in it is directly related to Outlaw Jack."

"But this time it is," Sadie insisted. "I'm sure it is—the name Jackson is too close to be coincidence. I think it's a deliberate reference to Outlaw Jack."

"Okay," I said cautiously, chewing my lip. "So, you think this California person is Outlaw Jack's... son?"

"*Daughter*, ya beanhead," Sadie poked my forehead. "She's a girl."

"Ow." I swatted her hand away. "Yeah, daughter, whatever." I shook myself, trying to process this new information. If it was a girl who was spooking around town, that *would* explain why the footprints I'd seen were so much smaller than Outlaw Jack's feet. "So you think that lady was California Jackson, trying to scope out the place before the robbery?"

"Who else?" said Sadie. "A stranger rides through town asking a whole bunch of questions, and then a few days later the Golden Tater gets stolen—definitely suspicious!"

"Was the stranger wearing a black hat?" I demanded, annoyed that an *actual outlaw* had slipped in and out of this town unchallenged, while I'd gotten arrested on account of my choice in headgear.

"No," Sadie admitted, a little guiltily. "Her hat was white."

"Figures," I muttered.

"It all made sense once the tater got stolen," Sadie continued. "She fooled us, comin' into town all sweet and innocent like that. She had the whole robbery planned out. I even thought she might've somehow poisoned Duke so he'd be sick the night she did the job, but he told me he'd just eaten some bad grits."

"Wait, so you *do* think she stole the tater?" I said. "Then what was all that of-course-it-couldn't-be-anybody-but-Outlaw-Jack nonsense you were spouting a minute ago?"

Sadie traced a crack in the floor with the toe of her boot.

"Sheriff don't believe California Jackson exists," she quietly said after a moment. "He thinks the rumors are just myths, cooked up by Outlaw Jack to throw us off his trail. Sheriff says that lady was probably just a curious settler, lookin' for gold," Sadie said. "He told me he don't wanna hear any more fool theories about phantom lady outlaws, so proving Outlaw Jack took it is our only other option."

"That doesn't seem right," I said, running my hand through my hair. "Sheriff Hodges arrested me on the mere suspicion I might have ties to

Outlaw Jack, so why wouldn't he jump at the chance to catch a rumored outlaw who even shares his name? It doesn't make any sense!"

"Clyde," Sadie said, her eyes flashing. "The federal marshal told Sheriff that California Jackson ain't nothin' to worry about. It was them what convinced him she ain't even a real person." Sadie spat on the floor, as if the mere mention of the marshal left a bad taste in her mouth.

"That's definitely suspicious," I said.

"I told you already," Sadie said. "I'd put money on the fact that he ain't even a real marshal. He's a faker and I know it, but because he flashes his fancy badge, he's got Sheriff stuck under his dirty thumb. And jist cause he says so, we're not allowed to go after California Jackson, who by my reckoning is our best bet at ever seeing the Golden Tater again."

"Well," I said, wondering if I was about to voice my worst idea yet. "I'm kind of an outlaw hunter now, and nobody gave *me* any orders about California Jackson."

"What are you saying, Clyde?" Sadie whisked her eyes up to meet mine, and the flicker of hope I saw there was enough to make up my mind in a hurry.

"I'm saying my deal with the sheriff was to find the tater and clear my name," I said. "Not necessarily to prove Outlaw Jack took it. I reckon under those terms I can chase whatever outlaw I want." I squared up my shoulders and did my best to muster up my heroic stance again.

"I'm going to find California Jackson," I said. It would've sounded great, except my voice cracked to a higher pitch on the first syllable of Jackson. I coughed to cover it.

"Clyde, you're really something," Sadie said, and the admiration in her face as she beamed at me was enough to make me forget my squeaky voice. "But how are you planning on finding her?"

"I don't know. I wasted a bunch of time wandering in the mountains already," I said. "But I think she's still close by."

I told Sadie about the shadow that followed me up in the mountains—after all, I didn't have any proof that the shadow had been Outlaw Jack. It could just as easily have been a woman. I also told her about the footprints I'd seen in town, the ones that definitely didn't belong to a man. The California Jackson theory was gaining evidence.

"Will you come with me?" I asked Sadie. "Maybe if we're together, it won't be as easy for her to give us the slip."

Sadie hesitated, looking a little torn. I knew she wanted to find the tater and bring justice to the town as much as anyone, but to go along with my plan would mean going directly against the sheriff's wishes. I wasn't sure that was something Sadie was willing to do.

"We'll have to keep it secret," she finally said.

I nodded. I didn't like the idea of sneaking around behind the sheriff's back either, but it looked like we didn't have much choice. He would thank us later, I told myself, after we caught California Jackson and recovered the Golden Tater. My conscience poked me, saying something about ends and means, but I shushed it.

"We'll go tonight," Sadie said. "A stakeout. Midnight. Up on Goldwater Ridge."

8

WHAT THE STARS SAW

SADIE and I spent the rest of the day preparing for our midnight mission. We scavenged supplies from the abandoned General Store—a lantern, a couple of coils of rope, and a tin of shoe polish we could use to black out our faces. Sadie wrinkled her nose at that, but I told her she'd be thankful for it if it kept her from being spotted at the wrong time.

We headed to the stable to outfit Pinto for our daring excursion. I told Sadie we ought to get Abraham ready too, but she looked at me like I'd lost my mind.

"Are you crazy?" she said. "That poor old gal ain't fit to ride through a field of wildflowers, and you wanna take her out on the ridge in the dark of night? You're a monster!"

Abraham's big black eyes said she sided with Sadie on this one. I swear she even nodded her head in agreement.

"Abraham's a tough old thing," I insisted. "I mean, she got me all the way from Kansas City just fine. What's one ride up a mountain, especially after the few days' rest she's had?"

Sadie shook her head, dumbfounded at my lack of sympathy. Abraham gave me her best sad-eyes, and Pinto snorted and shook his glossy mane, as if wondering why this was even an issue when he felt more than capable of carrying us both on his own. Apparently this argument was three against one. In the end, I lost. We took Pinto.

Midnight came fast. It felt like Sadie and I had barely prepared at all before we noticed the sun going down. We parted ways at dusk, trying to snatch what sleep we could, but I had only just closed my eyes when I awoke with a start. When I struck a match and checked my watch in its glow, I found it was a few minutes to twelve. Tingling with nerves, I pulled on my boots, grabbed my knapsack, and headed out into the night.

Sadie and Pinto were waiting for me in the street. The night was moonless, so it took me a minute to pick the two of them out from the rest of the looming shadows. When I reached them, Sadie wordlessly handed me the tin of shoe polish. Her face was already smudged all over, making her look like a coal miner. I did my best to cover myself in it too. I swung up behind Sadie onto Pinto's back, and we crept out of town.

Everything was foreign in the dark. The foothills rising around us could've been on an entirely different planet than the ones I'd climbed yesterday afternoon. But Pinto moved along, confident and sure-footed—at least one of us seemed to know what he was doing. Sadie and I, on the other hand, rode in tense silence even after Cactus Poke lay far behind us.

"I think we're getting close," Sadie whispered hoarsely, finally breaking the stillness. In the darkness, I couldn't see much of the ridge and the mountains, but the ground seemed to be growing steeper and rockier, and Pinto was choosing his steps more carefully than he had in the foothills.

"Here, light your lantern, but keep it covered till I say so," Sadie said, and I struck a match. The lantern threw out a beam of light. We were nearing the crest of Goldwater Ridge. I let out an involuntary gasp. We were climbing up a narrow path—just wide enough for a horse Pinto's size— with a sheer rock wall on our left, and a drop into darkness on our right. One false step and all three of us would go tumbling down to the rocks far below.

"I said keep it covered!" Sadie hissed. I couldn't tell if she was angry or afraid.

I quickly covered the light, but my heart didn't stop pounding. With every step Pinto took, I found myself bracing for a fall. I don't think I let out a full breath until we came out of that narrow channel and into a spot where the ridge leveled out a bit. We weren't at the summit, but we were close. The air was cool and clear up here, and I breathed a deep sigh of relief. Sadie relaxed a bit in front of me, like she'd been holding all the tension of our dangerous climb in her shoulders, and only now that we were safe did she dare let it out.

"Woah, boy," she said to Pinto, reining him to a stop. Then to me she said, "I think we should take up position here."

It was a good spot. The only way down into Cactus Poke was the path we had come up, and nobody coming from the ridge could reach it unless they walked right through our stakeout. The patch of level ground meant we could comfortably stand or sit without worrying about losing our footing and starting a rockslide down the mountain.

"Keep alert," Sadie warned me as we dismounted and unloaded our gear. She drew her pistol and I did the same. "I'm not trying to scare you, but this here is the exact spot where Outlaw Jack gets sighted. I ain't sayin' he's likely to show up, but he does know this place pretty well."

It made sense that Outlaw Jack would pick this spot for his spying purposes. In daylight (or even decent moonlight) our position would have afforded the best view possible of the whole region—Cactus Poke, the desert beyond, the mountains. I bet you could even see the lake from here. The thought made me shudder. No wonder I constantly felt like I was being watched.

Without the moon, though, it was impossible to see much except what was right around us. Even with our lantern, Outlaw Jack or California Jackson could be standing fifty yards away and we wouldn't be the wiser.

"It's too bad we've only got the stars tonight," I said in a low tone to Sadie. It wasn't quite a whisper anymore, but I still didn't want to speak at full volume. "I wish we could build a fire or something, just to get more light."

"Doubt thou the stars are fire?" said Sadie. Or at least, I thought it was Sadie, but words like that sounded so strange in her voice. I turned to her in shock, but she wasn't looking at me. Sadie was staring straight up, her gaze lost in the stars.

I looked up too, and my breath caught. The stars were always spectacular out in the wilderness, but something about the darkness of the moonless night, or maybe the fact that I was standing on a mountain, made them ten times more dazzling than I'd ever seen them. Countless glittering constellations and whirling galaxies littered the whole expanse of endless space, like somebody had dumped out a treasure chest all over the Arizona sky. The stars even seemed closer tonight, like they were surrounding us. At first I felt like that was a ridiculous thought, but when Sadie reached up her hand into the blackness as if she could pluck a star from the sky, I knew she felt it too.

"Doubt thou the stars are fire," she repeated. "Doubt that the sun doth move; doubt truth to be a liar, but never doubt I love."

"Shakespeare?" I guessed, remembering the Starfire Shakespeare Company posters in Sadie's room.

"Mm-hmm," Sadie said, her voice dreamy. "And ain't it jist the prettiest thing you ever heard?"

I shrugged, shifting from foot to foot. "I guess. Seems to me he could've just said 'I love you' to get the point across clearly enough."

"Yeah, but it was Hamlet's line," Sadie said. "And he never said anything clearly." Sadie shook herself. "But we gotta focus now, Clyde. We're on a mission, remember?"

"Right," I said, tearing my eyes away from the sky. "We're looking for an outlaw."

We stood at attention for a good hour or so, our ears prickling at every tiny sound. But California Jackson didn't show up. Everything was quiet up on the ridge. Sadie and I only spoke a few sentences to each other that whole time:

"What was that?"

"Did you hear something?"

"What time would you guess it is?"

"Don't worry, it's just a lizard."

"Wish I'd thought to bring some cocoa."

Eventually, we got tired and sat down—back-to-back though, so we could watch both directions. We kept our guns in our hands, still ready.

More empty minutes crawled by. I didn't want to voice my growing suspicion that we were wasting our time, but I could feel doubt creeping up on me.

"What are we even doing out here?" I finally sighed. "We aren't outlaw hunters; we're just two kids sitting on a mountain in the middle of the night!"

"She'll come, Clyde," Sadie insisted. "And when she does, we'll be here to stop her."

"Who says? We're not heroes, Sadie. We just convinced ourselves we could be. I think we both read too many novels."

"I don't read novels."

"Yeah, well, you read too much…Shakespeare, I guess."

Sadie giggled. "Yeah, maybe so," she said, and then I laughed too. It was a little absurd: rough and tumble, spit-like-a-man Sadie Wooten, secretly a lover of poetry and drama. It was so inconsistent, so unexpected, and somehow, so endearing. As far as I knew, Sadie was the only girl in the world who could use *thee* and *thou* in the same breath as *ain't* and get away with it.

"You actually like that stuff, don't you?" I asked.

"Yep." Sadie said. "But I come by it honest. My parents were actors. Ralph and Clementine Wooten, darlings of the Starfire Shakespeare Company. I don't remember them, but if they were even half as pretty as they are on their posters, then they must've been somethin' to see."

"Yeah, I bet they were great," I agreed, even though I wouldn't know how to judge the worth of a Shakespearian actor if I saw one.

"That line from Hamlet, about the stars being fire? Well, my daddy played Hamlet, loads of times," Sadie said. "He was a legend. Half of St. Louis was convinced he wasn't acting at all; they thought he was actually as crazy as old Hamlet. That's how good he was. Crowds flocked in from all over jist to see him." Sadie's voice was rich with pride and admiration. "Then when he married my mama and they started takin' the stage together, folks said it was pure magic. That's straight from a headline clippin' I got saved—*'Pure Magic,'* they said. Starfire performed for a packed-out house every night. Every ticket sold, on account of my mama and daddy."

"So what happened?" I knew, one way or another, this story didn't end happily ever after.

"Mama died of the influenza the winter after I was born," Sadie said. "Daddy never left her side. He died of a broken heart a few days later. Ain't that so romantic? Jist like Romeo and Juliet!"

That wasn't exactly how I remembered *Romeo and Juliet* ending—I recalled more poison and stabbings and deadly lack of communication—but I wisely kept my mouth shut.

"It sounds like they loved each other very much," I replied instead. It must've been the right thing to say.

"Clyde," Sadie whispered after a few seconds. We still sat back to back, so I couldn't see the expression on her face, but her voice carried an intensity I wasn't expecting. "Do you believe in love—true love— like that?"

"I, uh," I stammered, my heart galloping. I wasn't prepared for how nervous a question like that would make me. I could tell by her voice she wasn't joking, but I shifted myself and craned my head so I could look at her. Sadie looked like an angel sitting there—a dirty, smudgy angel, glowing beneath the shoe polish rubbed all over her cheeks. There wasn't a hint of irony in her eyes; she wasn't playing around. My breath caught. Nobody had ever made me feel like Sadie did. Did I believe in true love?

"Yeah, I guess I do."

"I guess I do too," she breathed. She still didn't look at me, but her hand slipped into mine and gave it a quick squeeze. She pulled it back a half second later, but the warmth that spread over me from the spot where she'd touched my palm lingered long after she drew her hand away. I wouldn't be surprised if it lasted forever.

"You're something else, Sadie Wooten," I said. "How'd a girl like you end up in a place like Cactus Poke?"

"You can kinda blame it on Shakespeare, I guess," Sadie shrugged.

Sadie told me how after her parents died, their friends in the theater company—actors, set designers, all sorts of stage folks—couldn't bear to send her off to an orphans' home. So they adopted her. The whole Starfire Shakespeare Company became Sadie's family. She lived in the theater, and all the actors and stagehands pitched in to help raise her until she got big enough to earn her keep working in the productions.

"There's a whole lot of jobs that have to be filled in showbusiness," Sadie told me. "When I was real little, I mostly picked up trash in the auditorium after the shows, swept the stage, occasionally filled in as a stagehand, that sort of thing," Sadie said. "But later on the seamstresses started teaching me how to take care of the costumes, and I got good at sewing on buttons and hemmin' skirts and mendin' lace. Then when they needed help over on the hair and makeup team, I learned that. I was real good at it too. But I always dreamed of bein' onstage, not backstage. I wanted to be an actor, like my daddy and mama. I knew I had it in me; it's in my blood! Then one day, it finally happened. You know *A Midsummer Night's Dream?*"

I shook my head.

"Well you should, cause that's the show I got a part in," Sadie sighed wistfully. "I was gonna be Cobweb. One of them little fairies in the forest. I had a talkin' part and everythin'. You ought to have seen me in my glittery little wings and my hair all done up in ringlets with rosebuds stuck between the curls…" she trailed off.

Despite my opinion of Mr. Shakespeare and his works, I wished I'd been in St. Louis back then to see Sadie on stage.

"Was it everything you dreamed of, acting in a show like that?" I asked.

"I never got to find out," she said. "The night before the show opened, the theater caught fire. No one ever found out how it started, but the whole place burned down. I barely made it out." She sniffed. "That was probably because I went back for my trunk. It was full of Mama and Daddy's things, you know, the posters and clippings and whatnot. I couldn't lose it. It'd be like losing them all over again."

Sadie swiped at her eyes, and her hand came away black with shoe polish, which made her giggle in spite of the tears threatening to leak out.

"After the fire, the theater didn't have enough money to rebuild, so it shut down," she continued. "My friends were all out of work and most of them had to move on. The orphans' home was already full to bustin' with other kids, most worse off than me. The mission offered to find me a spot on a wagon train headed out West. They said some settlers had offered homes for orphans as hired hands on their land claims." Sadie shrugged. "I figured I didn't have much other choice."

"I'm sorry, Sadie," I said. I couldn't imagine not having any home or family. "How'd you end up here in Cactus Poke?"

"I got separated from my wagon train during a river crossin'," she said. "My wagon washed away downstream. I guess they figured I was drowned. I never did find 'em again. I tried to use the sun as a guide to keep my nose pointed west, but I ran into the desert. I got lost, ran low on water…" Sadie laughed a little. "Well, I guess you know what that feels like. And that's where Sheriff found me."

"Oh. Lucky you," I said dryly. "Did he try to arrest you too?"

"Look, I know you and Sheriff got off on the wrong foot," Sadie said. "And I know he can be a little rough sometimes. But you gotta understand something: Sheriff is a good man, good as any you'll ever come across. And he's been hurt bad in life; he's come out of some of the roughest times you can imagine."

"Yeah, I know," I said. "Duke told me about the war."

"The war took more from him than just his leg," Sadie said. "He had a family too, but…" her voice quivered. "He came out West with nothin' left to him. When he took me in and gave me a home, I think I saved him just as much as he saved me. We're all each other's got. And that's why—" Sadie stood up without warning. I fell over backwards and barely caught myself from splatting flat in the dirt. "And that's why this has *got* to work!"

"What's got to work?" I asked, scrambling up to my feet too.

"This mission, Clyde," Sadie said, clenching her hands into fists. "Finding the Golden Tater. Saving Cactus Poke. Restoring Sheriff's hope. It's the only way." She turned to me, her eyes glistening and imploring. "Do you understand, Clyde? That I *have* to do this?"

"Um, of course," I said, a little taken aback at the intensity in her voice. "But you don't have to do it alone. That's what I'm here for, remember?"

A ghost of a smile flitted across Sadie's smudgy face. She pulled at one of her braids indecisively, then said, "I'm gonna ride along the backside of the ridge, see if I can scope out anything over thataway."

"Yeah, that's a good idea," I agreed. "Let's do that. There hasn't been much action here anyway."

"No," Sadie said. "I need you to stay here and wait for Pinto and me to get back."

"What? Alone?"

I wasn't scared. Not exactly. I didn't relish the thought of being left all by myself in the middle of the night in outlaw-infested territory, that's all.

"Look," Sadie said, a bit of impatience creeping into her tone. "This is the perfect stakeout site. If anyone tries to get to Cactus Poke, they've gotta come straight through here. We can't leave this position unguarded. You need to stay and keep watch."

She was right, of course. If we both rode off and left this place, anything could get past us, and the hours we'd spent here would be wasted. I sighed in resignation.

"How long do you think it'll take you?"

"Not too long," Sadie said. She shifted nervously on her feet, biting her lip.

"Are you okay?" I asked her.

Sadie didn't answer. She flung herself at me, catching me in a tight and unexpected hug. My world spun for a long moment and I forgot the stakeout, the outlaws, and the danger we might be in. All I was aware of was Sadie holding me close, and the thump of her heartbeat against my own. My insides melted like butter as I hugged her back. Everything felt so right in the world.

"Clyde," Sadie said softly, her face pressed up next to my ear. "I want you to know I really care about you. No matter what happens, I'm truly grateful you showed up in Cactus Poke."

"I never thought I'd say this, but yeah, I'm glad I did too," I said. "You're a special girl, Sadie, and life wouldn't be the same if I hadn't met you." Sadie didn't let go. In fact, her hug got tighter.

"Um," I finally said, a warning crawling along the back of my mind. This felt an awful lot like goodbye. "You *are* coming back, right? You'll only be gone a few minutes?"

"Right," Sadie said, pulling away from me. She quickly turned away and started fiddling with Pinto's saddlebags, but she wasn't quick enough to hide the tears on her cheeks.

"Hey," I said, putting my hand on her shoulder. She flinched at the touch. "Don't be scared. If you don't want to go up around the ridge, you don't have to."

"I *do* have to," Sadie said, determination like iron in her voice. "For Sheriff." She swung up into the saddle. "Stay here, and keep watch."

She clicked to Pinto, and the two of them faded into the blackness of the night.

It got lonesome pretty quick after Sadie left. When the echoes of Pinto's hoofbeats died away, everything was far too quiet. I stood on tiptoe on the ridge for a little bit, swiveling my head this way and that, trying to keep a good lookout, but the whole night was so empty that it got to me. Shivers ran up my back, and I got the spooky feeling I was the only soul for hundreds of miles in any direction. It was such an entirely opposite sensation from the one I'd gotten used to—the feeling of constantly being followed. Now I just felt alone, a tiny speck in the middle of an endless wilderness.

"Sadie ain't far off," I reminded the darkness around me, just in case it was getting any ideas. "She'll be back soon." I counted to twenty, and when she wasn't back at the end of that I went on to a hundred. Still no Sadie. But nothing ominous happened either, so I couldn't complain.

Another ten minutes passed, and with them, the spooky feeling moved on. Now I just felt sleepy. It was long past midnight, after all. I glanced around, stretched. Shifted from foot to foot. Yawned a little bit. Well, I decided, if it was going to be a while before Sadie returned, there was no harm in sitting down.

I looked up at the dazzling stars, and at the sight of them the warm feelings came flooding back. I flopped on my back, pillowing my hands behind my head.

"Doubt thou the stars are fire," I repeated dreamily. "But never doubt I love." Surrounded by the endless beauty of the brilliant sky, with the warmth of Sadie's hug imprinted fresh on my memory, not a trace of doubt spooked around the corners of my mind. Nothing could be more certain.

I've never been too good at spotting constellations, so I made up my own by playing connect the dots in the sky. I must've spelled out "SADIE LOVES CLYDE" in a hundred different places all over the galaxy by the time my ears pricked up at the sound of hoofbeats. That snapped me right out of my daydreams. I jumped to my feet, quickly dusting off my backside.

"Nothing to report," I called, hoping my voice didn't sound as guilty as I felt. I had no idea how much time had passed. Why couldn't Sadie have come back earlier and caught me doing something right? She'd made it pretty clear this stakeout was important to her, and here I was, slacking off.

I glared at the stars, for lack of a better target for my frustration. They'd distracted me, after all. "Sadie loves Clyde," yeah right! More like "Sadie thinks Clyde is a stupid beanhead who can't even keep watch without messing it up."

I wondered if there were enough stars out tonight to spell all that out.

The hoofbeats got louder, and they didn't slow down. I guess Sadie didn't hear me call out to her the first time.

"I haven't seen anything unusual. It's been pretty quiet around—" My voice died in my throat, cutting off with an abrupt hiccup of terror.

The dark rider who crested the ridge on a glistening black horse was *not* Sadie.

The rider yanked the reins, pulling the steed up just short of trampling me. I fell backward. The horse reared on its hind legs, kicking at the air as it let loose a shrill whinny that pierced the night like a knife. I was glad for that neigh; it covered up the sound of my own scream. Choking on dust, I scrambled back to my feet. I ducked to the side, trying to dart away, but the horse wheeled around, blocking me.

The rider loomed above me like a ghost in the gloom, dressed all in black from hat to boots, except for the glistening white of the pair of pearl-handled revolvers she wore strapped to each hip. Her long loose hair trailed behind her like it was made of smoke, and she had a thick black bandana tied around her face, masking everything but her eyes. Those sharp, cruel eyes stared holes into me faster than any bullet could. After sizing me up in a single glance, they glittered wickedly in the starlight, which didn't seem so warm and friendly anymore.

I didn't need a second glance to know exactly who she was.

California Jackson.

I wanted to run. Every nerve in my body screamed at me to run, but I couldn't. It was like being in a bad dream, when you know you need to get away but you can't, no matter how hard you try. My legs felt like they didn't belong to me, and I couldn't have commanded them to move any more than I could've commanded one of those stars to come crashing down to earth and reduce California Jackson to a smoking crater. I stood there helplessly, gaping up at the outlaw with my mouth hanging open like a big, dumb catfish.

"You looking for something, City Boy?" The voice that broke the silence was smooth and cruel. Even though her face was covered, her eyes lit up with the mocking smile she wore beneath the bandana.

Her question didn't sit right with me. Looking for something? Well yeah, of course I was looking for something; I was looking for *her*! But California wasn't supposed to know that. How she figured it out, I couldn't guess, unless…my heart dropped.

"Sadie," I sputtered in a hoarse whisper. I *knew* Sadie'd been gone too long! I could've kicked myself. I should've helped her. She was my partner, and she counted on me! And while I was busy writing love letters in the sky without giving a thought to our mission, California Jackson had already found her. Sadie'd been captured—or worse.

I shoved down the panic threatening to squeeze my lungs to bits, and when I spoke again my voice was stronger. "What'd you do with Sadie?"

The slightest moment of hesitation flickered across California's face. I snatched that moment to summon every bit of heroism I had in me. I squared my shoulders and tried to look taller even though I had to crane my neck to look the outlaw in the eye. I pictured myself looking as intimidating to her as Sheriff Hodges did to me—burning with the power of righteous fury.

"If you hurt Sadie, you low-down, no-good outlaw," I said, sounding a whole lot more like the sheriff than I meant to, but hearing his voice gave me a rush of confidence. I decided to go all out. "I swear to you by the Law, the town of Cactus Poke, and the Golden Tater itself—"

"Oh, you mean *this* Golden Tater?"

My bold act crumpled fast. For all the times I'd imagined what it would feel like when I finally set eyes on the legendary Goldwater Potato, I was completely unprepared for this moment. When she whipped the gleaming nugget out of her saddlebag and held it tauntingly in front of me, its shining surface winking in the starlight, I felt like I'd been slugged in the gut.

"How did—that's—but you—give it—" I sputtered incoherently. I could hardly hear my own voice over the pounding of my heart. I grasped pointlessly for the tater, which she dangled just out of my reach.

My hand flew to my belt, reaching for Duke's gun, but it came up with nothing. I looked down in surprise, and I felt like I might throw up. My holster was empty. I must've lost my gun without realizing it. It could be anywhere between here and Cactus Poke, or at the bottom of a cliff for all I knew. I was unarmed.

I looked up slowly from the empty holster and back at the outlaw. This wouldn't end well, I knew that now. But gun or no gun, I had to do something. I raised my fists in a boxer's stance.

California Jackson smirked at me, the same sort of bored, you're-so-pathetic-I'm-almost-sorry-for-you smirk I'd seen on Duke's face a hundred times.

"You got some nerve, kid, I'll give you that," she said. She flicked her wrist, and the tater did a slow backflip through the air. I snatched for it again, but it slipped past me and landed with a muffled thump as her saddlebag swallowed it. I tried to lunge forward, fumbling for the bag, but before I'd moved more than an inch, she had both of those pretty little revolvers trained on my head. I froze.

This was it. I was done for.

"But I'll let you in on a little secret, City Boy," said the outlaw, clicking back the hammers on her guns. "It takes a lot more than just nerve to survive in the West."

I bit my lip and glanced up at the brilliant starry sky before squeezing my eyes shut tight. I didn't want the last thing I saw in this life to be California Jackson's mocking eyes.

"Well," I said through gritted teeth, and to my credit my voice didn't shake too much. "The West *is* a lawless place."

Pain blasted through my head like dynamite. Through the ringing in my ears I faintly heard a thundering whirl of hoofbeats. My face smacked the cold, rocky ground a half-second before the darkness put me out of my misery.

9

WILD NOTIONS

WAKING up came as a pleasant surprise.

I was grateful to find out I was still alive, but that's where the pleasant feelings began and ended. The far more overwhelming sensation was a horrible throbbing in my head. Every bit of me ached, but it was nothing compared with the sharp pain that pulsed from my head with every heartbeat. I didn't dare move. I was convinced there was a stick of dynamite lodged in my brain, and if I jostled it the slightest bit, my whole head would blow.

I opened my eyes—the smallest slit I could—but the bright yellow light was so piercing that I squeezed them shut again just as quickly. An involuntary moan escaped me.

"Clyde?" a voice broke through the pain. "Clyde, are you still with us?" A small, cool hand touched my cheek. A little bit of life seeped back into me. Sadie. Sadie was all right!

At the sound of Sadie's voice, I managed to get my eyes all the way open. I was in a room I didn't recognize, lying in a bed amongst more pillows than any bed had a right to. Sadie was hovering over me, tear streaks cutting through the black smudges on her face. Behind her stood Sheriff Hodges, wearing a striped nightshirt, his shiny gold badge pinned to its front.

Against all odds, I was back in Cactus Poke.

"He's awake," Sadie said, her concerned expression melting into relief. "Oh thank heavens, Clyde, you ain't dead!"

"Not quite," I croaked. The effort of talking proved too much for me. I closed my eyes again. "What happened?"

"I was gonna ask you the same thing," Sadie said. "Pinto and I went off around the backside of the ridge like we planned, but when we got back, you were all crumpled on the ground, with that big nasty gash on your head."

I gingerly raised a hand to feel for the wound, but all I found was a thick wad of bandages wrapped around my head. And pain. Lots of pain.

"I hauled you back to town quick as I could," Sadie continued. "But I wasn't sure if you'd ever wake up."

"Looks like you got hit pretty hard," the sheriff said. "Do you remember anything that happened before that?"

"Hit?" I asked, my brain feeling a little fuzzy. "Not shot?"

"Son, if you'd been shot we wouldn't be here talkin' right now," the sheriff said gently. "It was a close call as it is."

"Do you remember anything, Clyde?" Sadie asked, squeezing my hand. "Who attacked you? Did you see?"

It all came rushing back—California Jackson on her glossy black horse, her eyes flashing at me in the glittering starlight, the stolen Goldwater Potato in her hand.

"Oh!" I exclaimed, making both of them jump. Ignoring the screaming protests from my body, I struggled to sit up. I would've popped right out of the bed if Sadie hadn't grabbed my shoulders and held me down.

"Jist what do you think you're doing?" she said, shoving me back against the pillows. "You ain't in no condition to git up!"

"How long have I been gone?" I demanded, still struggling to sit despite her efforts to keep me down. "There might still be time to catch her!"

"A couple of hours, Clyde," Sadie said. "Sun'll be up soon."

I wilted back onto the bed, my sudden burst of energy dissipating and leaving me feeling weaker than before. California Jackson was long gone.

"Catch *her*?" the sheriff said, raising one wiry white eyebrow. "Catch who?"

I shot Sadie a sideways look. She bit her lip and shook her head guiltily. She hadn't told him.

"Um," I said, not sure how to tell the sheriff that we'd almost gotten ourselves killed chasing an outlaw he didn't believe existed. I decided the best way about it was to be straightforward. Facts were facts, whether he believed me or not. "California Jackson, sir. She's the one that took me out."

Sheriff's eyebrows instantly scrunched, his mouth pursing doubtfully.

"You saw her?" Sadie squeaked, her hands flying up to her cheeks.

I nodded. "Talked to her even," I said. "Sheriff, I know you think she's a myth, but I saw her with my own two eyes."

The sheriff still looked unconvinced.

"I know she's real," I said. "And what's more," I took a deep breath. "I know she's the one you're after. She's got it, sir. She's got the Golden Tater. She's carrying it around in her saddlebags as we speak."

Sadie gasped and the sheriff's eyes flashed angrier than I'd ever seen them.

"You're sure that's what you saw?" he demanded.

"On my honor, Sheriff. There was no mistaking it."

I told them everything I'd seen and heard, not leaving out even the smallest detail. When I finished, Sadie's face was flushed with excitement.

"This is good news, Sheriff, real good," she said, grabbing his hand and squeezing it. "Now that we know it ain't Outlaw Jack who has the Golden Tater, we've got a decent chance of getting it back. California Jackson can't be near as hard to catch as Outlaw Jack. And from what Duke told me, she ain't exactly tryin' to hide. There's been sightings of her all over, from here all the way to the Pacific! It'll be easy to track her down."

"And how you gonna guess which way she's gone?" the sheriff frowned.

"Only place to go from here is west, ain't that right, Clyde? I bet she's headed to California," Sadie said. She looked to me for affirmation, nodding expectantly.

"Uh, sure, I guess," I said, but I only said it because Sadie looked so hopeful, not because I agreed with her. To be honest, I couldn't be sure which direction California Jackson was headed, or if she'd been planning to leave Goldwater County at all. Maybe it was a side effect of being hit on the head, but I couldn't figure out why California Jackson had been talking to me in the first place. Something didn't seem right about any of it, but my head was too muddled and achy to sort through it.

"We should go soon," Sadie said. "The three of us. Soon as you're able, Clyde. We gotta go after her, and if we move quick we should overtake her in no time. We can leave Duke in charge. I'm sure he'll be more than capable of taking care of things while we're gone. The town'll be fine."

I looked at Sadie doubtfully. I knew she was eager to get the tater back and save the town, but this didn't seem like her best plan. For one thing, I didn't think I'd be fit to get out of bed anytime soon, let alone go on a high-speed chase across the desert. For another, I wasn't entirely sure Duke was the best person to trust with anything. After all, I hadn't seen hide nor hair of him since the marshal came to town. It wouldn't take much to convince me he had some hand in all of this.

I wasn't the only one hesitating; Sheriff Hodges didn't answer Sadie right away. I could see him silently weighing his options. It was obvious there were still doubts in his head about California Jackson, even with my eyewitness testimony. It's hard to trust the word of a person who's just taken a severe blow to the head, so I didn't blame him.

Besides, after years of hunting Outlaw Jack, the sheriff probably didn't even want to start chasing a new trail. Outlaw Jack was still out there, after all. Pulling out of Cactus Poke with the Black Hat Bandit still somewhere up in the hills would feel like leaving an enemy in command of a battlefield. But on the other hand, Sadie and I both knew the sheriff had a deadline staring him in the face, set by the marshal. Unless the tater was found in the next six days, there wouldn't be a Cactus Poke left to defend.

"I think we oughta sleep on it," the sheriff said after a long minute. He rubbed a hand across his face, looking tired and old. "It's been a full night, and Clyde here has some mendin' to do afore he's fit to go chasin' shadows again."

"Delay leads impotent and snail-paced beggary," Sadie muttered.

"Now Sadie-girl, don't you go a-Shakespearin' on me again," he scolded, but a fond smile flickered across his face. "You know I don't understand them fancy words of yours. I don't know about snails and beggars, but I do know we can't jist go a-ridin' out across the desert without thinkin' things through. I still ain't sure this whole thing ain't some trick of Outlaw Jack's. It all needs more ponderin' on. In the daylight, things get clearer."

The sheriff and Sadie left me after that, telling me to be sure to get rest and feel better. Sadie even planted a quick kiss on the spot where the bandages on my head were the thickest.

I fell into a fitful sleep, full of dreams where shadowy figures with evil, glowing eyes constantly banged pots and pans around inside my brain.

SUNLIGHT poured through my window when I opened my eyes again. My room was quiet, but someone had been here; a plate with a few biscuits and a mug of coffee, both gone cold, sat on my bedside table. My head still pounded with every heartbeat, but the pain had dulled a little—that or I was just getting used to it.

I pulled myself out of bed and stood up. I didn't immediately collapse—so far so good. A washbasin and mirror sat on a table across the room, and I cleaned up my face, taking off the last traces of dust and shoe polish. Washing up made me feel so much better that I even found the courage to risk a peek under the bandages on my head. There was a little swelling, a lot of dried blood, and a nasty bruise surrounding the gash, but my injury wasn't nearly so bad as I'd imagined.

I laughed, that's how relieved I was, but the sound died in my throat. This wasn't right, none of it. I shouldn't be here, alive and well. It didn't make sense. What kind of gunslinger takes aim, clicks back the hammer, then at the last second turns the gun into a club instead?

Maybe Sadie had come up on California Jackson too fast and scared her off. But that didn't make sense either. If that was the case, it would've been easier for her to shoot both of us. She was holding *two* guns, after all. Hitting me over the head would take a whole lot more effort than pulling the trigger. Besides, Sadie hadn't even seen California Jackson. She'd been as surprised as the sheriff when I'd told them who attacked me.

There had to be a reason why California Jackson had left me alive. From the looks of it, it seemed she wanted us to know she had the Golden Tater. It was like she wanted us to chase her. And if that's not suspicious, I don't know what is. Maybe she was working in league with Outlaw Jack. Maybe she was a decoy, trying to lead us on a wild goose chase while he made off with the real gold. Maybe it was all a trap.

My head throbbed. I needed to find Sadie and talk this through. She'd have ideas about it, I was certain. With both of us thinking about it, we'd be able to piece the clues together and get to the bottom of this story.

I opened my bedroom door and discovered the room I'd been sleeping in was one of the empty ones on the first floor of the boardinghouse. That was kind of the sheriff to put me up there; it certainly beat lodging in the jail. I left the boardinghouse, stepping out into the sunny street. I wasn't sure where to find Sadie, but I knew she often took care of the horses, so the stable seemed like a good enough place to start looking.

I was in luck. When I pushed open the stable door, I found Sadie standing with her back to me, her sleeves pushed up past her elbows and a dotted kerchief on her head. She was scrubbing at Pinto, who stood all covered in bubbles and foam, looking a little dejected. Sadie had set up a narrow table, piled high on one end with brushes, bottles of soap, and hoof-cleaning tools. On the other side of the table sat Pinto's saddlebags, Sadie's knapsack—and mine too, I noticed—along with most of our supplies from last night's mission. Several buckets of sudsy black water clustered around Sadie's feet.

"Wow, he got dirty last night," I remarked, raising my eyebrows at the darkness of the bathwater.

Sadie jumped, whirling on me with a panicked expression.

"Woah, sorry!" I said quickly, raising my hands in surrender and taking a step backwards. "It's just me. I thought you heard me come in."

"Don't you sneak up on me like that!" Sadie exclaimed, flicking her brush in my direction, spattering me with dirty bubbles. "Scared me half to death!"

"Sorry," I said again, laughing this time as I wiped a soap splotch from my cheek.

"It ain't funny, Clyde," Sadie said. "You coulda been anyone creepin' up on me. And jist what business do you think you've got bein' out of bed anyhow?"

"I'm fine, Sadie," I said. "I can barely even feel it at all this morning." That was a bit of a stretch, but I gave a careless shrug, hoping she believed me. "Look, we need to talk about what happened last night."

Sadie stiffened. "You almost died, that's what happened," she said in a tight voice. "We should never have gone out there on our own in the first place."

"Maybe, but that doesn't change the fact that we did," I said. "And I don't think it was all for nothing, either. I've been thinking a lot about California Jackson, and—"

"I don't wanna talk about it, Clyde!" Sadie cut me off. She turned her back on me and resumed scrubbing at Pinto's flanks with more vigor than necessary. "Can you imagine how awful it'd be if you'd gotten killed? I'd never forgive myself."

"It wasn't your fault, Sadie," I said, my chest tightening at the sound of tears in her voice. "None of it was. And besides that, I'm alive, ain't I? I wanna know why."

"I don't know what you mean," Sadie said stiffly, without looking at me.

"Why didn't she shoot me?" I demanded. "She had her guns out and everything. I just can't figure out why she didn't shoot."

"Well, Clyde, did you want her to?" Sadie snapped. She threw her brush down into the soapy gray water and turned on me, hands on her hips.

"No," I said quickly. "It's just…confusing. Unexpected. I'm trying to make sense of it."

"I wish you'd let it go," Sadie said, tugging at her braids. "Why can't you jist count your blessings and move on? Jist be grateful you ain't dead, and stop bustin' your brain over it. Your head needs rest, not wild notions."

"C'mon, Sadie, just think on it a little," I said. "If it had been you and not me, wouldn't you want to know all you could about the outlaw who almost did you in?"

"Fine," Sadie sighed, sitting down on an overturned bucket and crossing her arms over her chest. "Maybe she kept you alive cause she wanted someone to tell people about her. She wants to be famous, right? How's she gonna get that big bad reputation unless she gives people somethin' to talk about?"

"Maybe," I said, not convinced. "But if her goal is to raise a ruckus and gain some infamy, what's she doing in a lousy, one-horse town like Cactus Poke? No offense, Pinto."

He snorted at me, clearly offended.

"You'd think," I continued. "You'd think an up-and-coming outlaw would aim higher than a middle-of-nowhere town. There are other gold nuggets in the West, you know. And if her goal *isn't* to be famous, if she stole the tater because of its cash value, then the smart thing to do would be to make a quick and quiet getaway with the gold, and none of us would ever be the wiser."

Sadie shrugged. "Maybe she ain't that smart of an outlaw. Or she wanted Outlaw Jack to know she took it; maybe they've got some kind of rivalry going on," she said. "Okay, I've entertained some ideas. Now *please* sit down, Clyde," Sadie begged.

I did, just to make her happy, but I wasn't satisfied. Thoughts kept tumbling around in my head, stray thoughts that didn't quite fit together, like a bunch of mismatched jigsaw pieces. California Jackson, Deputy Duke and the Jesse James gang, the phantom Bitterroot jackrabbit, the federal marshal...they all meant *something*, I just wasn't sure what yet. And where did Outlaw Jack fit in, anyway? As a matter of fact, he seemed suspiciously absent in all of this. My head ached.

"Clyde? You don't look so good," Sadie said. "Can I git you something? Here, have some water." She pushed a canteen into my hands, one of the ones we'd packed and taken with us last night. I took it, but I didn't want water. I wanted answers.

"It just doesn't make sense," I said again, popping up despite Sadie's efforts to keep me settled. I set the canteen on her table and paced, holding one fist tight against my throbbing temple and wishing I could think more clearly. "It's like she *knew* we were looking for her. *She* came to find *me*, not the other way around."

"Clyde, you really oughta stop. This ain't helping your head any."

I ignored her. My mind was picking up speed, gathering thoughts like a mudslide gathers debris.

"And the way she showed me the tater—Sadie, you'd know something fishy was up too if you'd seen her. She was waiting for an opportunity to whip it out, I'm sure of it. She *wanted* me to know she had it!"

"She was taunting you," Sadie insisted. "Outlaws are arrogant people, you know."

I glanced at Sadie. She looked strained. She sat on her hands and bit her lower lip as she watched me, like she was nervous I would break. I felt a twinge of guilt seeing her so worried about me, and I forced myself to do the gentlemanly thing and drop the discussion.

"Yeah, maybe so," I sighed. I still wasn't convinced, but the look of relief that flooded her face was worth the surrender. "I think I'm gonna go lie down."

"That's a smart choice," Sadie said. Her shoulders relaxed and she rewarded me with a smile, which did help brighten my spirits a little. "How 'bout I go see if Kay Fay can whip up some soup for you? You jist take it nice and easy."

I nodded, turning to go, and a wave of dizziness washed over me as I did. Maybe it was for the best I go get some rest, after all. Maybe I wasn't quite as fine as—

"Clyde, look out!"

Sadie's warning came too late. I stumbled straight into her worktable. It crashed onto its side, spilling everything across the stable floor. Tools and supplies clanged as they scattered. Sadie's knapsack hit the ground and tipped over.

Sadie clapped both her hands over her mouth in a failed attempt to stifle a horrified squeak. Color drained from her face, making her freckles stand out starkly against her ghost-white cheeks.

I blinked hard, shaking my head viciously to clear out the cobwebs. I was hallucinating things, I had to be. That kind of thing can happen sometimes with bad knocks on the head. But no, when I looked again, it was all still there, spilled straight out of Sadie's pack.

A gleaming gold nugget shaped exactly like an oversized potato.

And beside it, a pair of pretty, pearl-handled revolvers.

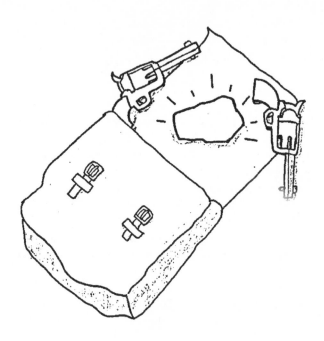

10

SADIE TAKES A BOW

"IT'S not what you think," Sadie whispered.

I didn't reply. I bent down and picked up the famed Goldwater Potato. It was cold and heavy in my hands, and it was very, very real.

"Then what is it?" I said. My voice was calm, but my world was reeling. "If it's not what I think, what is it?" There had to be some explanation. I slowly raised my eyes to meet Sadie's, but I didn't find the answers I wanted there.

The silence between us grew thicker. I waited for her to wave it away, to laugh at me for even having such a crazy notion. I wanted her to give me some simple explanation, a perfectly logical reason why *of course* it made sense why she should have the missing tater and California Jackson's weapons in her bag. I wanted so badly for her to tell me I was wrong, to laugh at me, call me a beanhead, and tell me to stop letting my imagination run so wild, for goodness sake! But she didn't.

"Sadie," I said again, taking a step back from her. "Who is California Jackson? Who is she, really? Give me the facts."

A tear slipped out of Sadie's eye and cut down her cheek. Her lip quivered. She didn't answer.

I knew, though. I knew the horrible truth, sure and certain.

"No," I choked, my chest constricting. "No, no!"

"It's fake, Clyde! It's all fake!" Sadie burst out, stretching her hands toward me imploringly, but I jerked away from her.

"*What's* fake about it, Sadie? *This* isn't fake," I shook the tater at her. Then I pointed at the wad of bandages on my head. "And *this* sure isn't either! What's so fake?"

"California Jackson," Sadie said miserably. "Sheriff is right, she ain't real. Never was."

"That's because she's *you!*" I yelled. This whole time I'd been fooled, played like a fiddle, and by a girl I'd thought was special, no less. "And the robbery, that was you, too, wasn't it?" Sadie flinched, but she didn't deny it. "What else are you hiding?" I snatched her bag off the floor.

She didn't make any effort to stop me as I rifled through it. California Jackson's black wig was in there, folded neatly so the hair wouldn't tangle. I tossed it aside in disgust. The rest of the bag contained the remainder of the supplies we'd so carefully packed, along with a case of makeup and— "Duke's gun?" I asked, pulling it from the bag. I'd thought it was at the bottom of some ravine up in the mountains, long gone. Sadie stared at her boots, shamefaced.

"You had it? You took it from me? When?" I choked. The only time she could've taken it from its holster without me noticing was…when she hugged me goodbye. Remembering how warm and content I'd felt in that moment with her arms tight around me was like pouring lemon juice on a cut. Angry tears stung my eyes, and I kicked the overturned table viciously. "Dagnabbit Sadie, I thought you liked me!"

"I *do* like you, Clyde!" Sadie wailed, burying her face in her hands.

"Well you sure have a funny way of showing it!"

"I can explain!"

"Oh, you better hope you can!" I snapped. I tossed the tater aside and planted my hands on my hips. The gold nugget landed on the ground with a heavy *thunk*. "I got arrested on account of this robbery. If it weren't for you, I'd be in California by now with my Pa, who *actually* cares about me. I've been risking my life looking for that doggone thing, and you had it all along!"

"Look, I'm sorry," Sadie said. "I'm really, really sorry. You were never meant to get caught up in this at all. You were just in the wrong place at the wrong time."

"Wrong place at the wrong time?" I exclaimed, dumbfounded. "*That's* your excuse? Sadie, you almost shot me!"

"Please stop shoutin' Clyde!" Sadie yelled, clapping her hands hard over her ears.

"Why, do the other townsfolk not know you're a thief and a liar?" I said, my voice thick with cruel sarcasm. "You don't wanna spoil that little surprise for them? Or did you plan to shoot them, too?"

"Stop it, ya hear? Jist *stop it!*" Sadie snapped. Her eyes flashed furiously at me. "I ain't never shot nobody! And don't you ever accuse me of doin' otherwise!" She snatched one of the pistols off the floor and I jumped back, afraid she'd bludgeon me again. But instead she shoved it into my hands. "Look, they ain't even real guns," she said. "Just stage props. Replicas of some fancy dueling pistols, that's all. You weren't ever in danger. Now please, calm down!"

I looked down at the pistol in my hands. She was right; there was no way this thing could ever be fired like a real gun. The barrel wasn't even hollowed out. It was heavy enough to do some damage if you swung it hard enough at someone's head, but mostly it was just a pretty fake.

Just like Sadie.

"I'll tell you everything," she said after a long minute. "I never meant for it to go this far. You gotta believe me on that, at least."

"No offense, Sadie," I said in a low voice. "But I don't think I'm required to believe anything you say."

"I shoulda told you early on," Sadie sighed, giving me a pleading look. "I jist didn't know if I could trust you!"

"*You* didn't know if you could trust *me?*" I actually laughed at how ridiculous it sounded.

"I barely knew you!" Sadie said. "And by the time I'd decided you were a good sort, I was already in too deep. What was I supposed to do? But now you're owed a full explanation."

"About the so-called California Jackson and why the girl I thought believed in true love bashed in my head like a melon last night?"

Ignoring my jab, Sadie nodded. "Yep," she said. "But there's more to it. It goes back a lot further. And Clyde, you have to promise to stay calm. Don't you yell at me, at least not till you've heard the full story. Promise?"

"Okay," I said, steeling myself for the worst. "I promise."

Sadie took a deep breath. The slightest hesitation flickered across her face, but she shook herself and plunged in. "Do you remember, up in my room, those drawings you found?"

That wasn't exactly where I'd expected her confession to start, but I nodded.

"Of course I do," I said. "Drawings of people you were trying to pin the robbery on, no doubt."

"No," Sadie said firmly. "It didn't have anything to do with the robbery case."

"Yeah, cause you knew who the robber was all along." Try as I might to keep my promise to stay calm, I couldn't stop myself from feeling angry all over again every few seconds. "What was all that nonsense you told me about how having the detective be the bad guy was cheating?"

"Will you jist let me talk? I'm gettin' to that part," Sadie said impatiently. "Look, those drawings were up there long before I ever had the idea to stage the robbery at all. I jist told you that cause you were pokin' your nose into business that wasn't any of yours, and I needed to give you a believable explanation. I didn't want you to know what they're really for."

"Which is?"

"They're character sketches, Clyde." Sadie looked at me expectantly, as if that explained all of it. I gave her a blank look. She sighed and tried again.

"I told you up on the ridge," she said. "I'm an actress. And the citizens of Cactus Poke...well, they're my role. Or, *roles*, I guess."

"WHAT?"

Sadie nodded earnestly. "I made them up. All of them, 'cept Sheriff, of course. The town was empty, so I populated it. All it took was a little imagination and creativity."

My mind was spinning too fast for me to get any words out.

"The drawings you found," Sadie continued, "were so I could get an idea of faces, so I had a firm reference point to look at when I did my makeup for each different character."

This was ridiculous. Sadie had to be making this up. But my mind flashed back to the drawing of Duke, with his long scar drawn on the wrong side of his face…a mistake that could be made from looking in a mirror. My stomach turned.

"But the motives?" I asked, grasping desperately at straws. I wanted to find a reason not to believe her. As much as I didn't like Sadie lying to me, I sure didn't want *this* to be the truth. "What about the motives for the robbery you had written down?"

"Not motives," Sadie corrected. "*Motivation*. I had to pinpoint who each character was, deep down. The first thing an actor's gotta do when approaching a new character is figure out their motivation. You have to find out why they're doing what they're doing, why they say what they say. Once you've got that figured out, then you can bring them to life."

"But they're not real," I said slowly, trying to wrap my mind around it. "None of them are real."

"Of course they're real," Sadie insisted. "They're as real as you believe them to be. That's the magic of storytelling!"

"Don't give me that," I shook my head. "Nothing but the straight facts, Sadie. What you're saying is, it's not just California Jackson. Deputy Duke and Kay Fay, too—they're just…*you?*"

"And Brother Parson, the preacher," Sadie added, nodding. "But yes, that's pretty much the long and short of it."

"That's impossible," I said, shoving my hands through my hair. "There is no way on earth you could've pulled that off."

"Ain't you never seen a stage production before?" Sadie said. "Theater runs on quick changes. It's what I do, Clyde! It's what I'm good at! I told you, I worked in hair and makeup and costumin' for years. I can turn anyone into anyone in no time flat, if I've had practice enough. Jist how do you think small theater companies put on large productions, huh? People have got to play more than one part, and be quick and clever about it."

"This isn't possible," I said again. I combed through my memories of the past few days looking for proof this was just another lie. But for the life of me I could not think of a single instance I'd seen any combination of Kay Fay, Duke, or Sadie together at the same time. And there were other things, too—the way Duke disappeared for long periods of time without explanation. The constantly red, freshly-scrubbed-clean look of Sadie's face. The shadow that ducked out of sight when I'd been headed to the boardinghouse—the shadow with Sadie-sized footprints.

"No—this is crazy," I stammered, holding my throbbing head. But then something dawned on me, a ray of hope in this madness. "And it's wrong!" I said. "The...the newspaper article! The one in your room about Duke and the Jesse James gang! It proves Duke isn't you, he's real! He's real and—"

"And he's dead." Sadie cut me off. "I based my character on the real Duke Hastings, Deuces Duke, the outlaw who was killed in the gunfight you read about in that newspaper."

"But why would you do that?"

Sadie shook her head. "You wouldn't understand."

"Try me."

"I found that article," Sadie said. "Because it was on the back of one of my daddy's stage reviews. It broke my heart to think of Duke Hastings, so young and handsome, gettin' shot and abandoned for dead. And I jist wanted to believe he could've had a second chance. I didn't want him to die alone in a ditch, ya know? So I wrote a new end to his story, where he got on the right side of the law in the end."

"Doggone it, Sadie." I shook my head in disgust. "You're such a hopeless romantic. I can't believe you'd have sympathetic feelings for, what? A *picture* of a long-dead outlaw?"

"I told you, you wouldn't understand!" Her eyes flashed in anger.

"I just—oh never mind!" I shook myself. "Dead or not, you being Duke still doesn't make sense. You can't... Duke is... I mean how did you... But he's a man!"

"Of course he is!" Sadie stomped her foot impatiently. "Don't you know nothin' about Shakespeare? Girls get away with pretending to be men all the time! Rosalind did it, and so did Viola, Julia, and Portia... heck, my own Mama wasn't just Ophelia in Starfire's production of *Hamlet*—she played Horatio at the same time! Now that's what I call impressive, doubling roles while playing a lead!"

"This isn't *Hamlet*, Sadie!" I wanted to shake her to get it through her head. "This is real life. And your audience is real people, people you're lying to. Didn't you ever stop to think about that?"

Sadie bit her lip and shrugged. "Real life and fiction overlap more than you'd think," she said. "After all, Shakespeare said, 'All the world's a stage, and men and women merely players upon it.'"

"Shakespeare was insane!" I shouted. Enough was enough. "He was insane, and you are too!"

"You promised not to yell at me!" Sadie cried, burying her face in her hands again.

"Yeah, well, I guess that makes two of us liars, then!" I threw up my hands. "Honestly, Sadie, I can't believe you. All this time you've been manipulating me, feeding me the right information right when you needed me to know it. And then having Duke back up your stories? It's sick, I tell you, just sick!"

"Look, I said I was sorry for lying to you, now if you'd just give me a chance to explain—"

"Explain what, Sadie?" I cut her off. "What, how it's so boring out here in the desert that you had to invent a fake reality for yourself? Just so you'd have something to do?" I laughed in disgust. "It's pathetic, you and the sheriff out here in the middle of nowhere, living a fake life with your fake friends, chasing down fake bandits who committed a fake robbery just so you'd feel like you were doing something with your miserable lives!"

Sadie slapped me hard across the face.

After the sharp crack of her hand on my skin, silence fell in the stable. My cheek stung. I blinked at her, dumbstruck, unable even to say "Ow."

"You leave Sheriff out of this," she said in a simmering voice. "Hate me all you want, that's fair, but don't you dare say a single thing against him."

"He…he doesn't know?" I asked, the realization chilling me. I didn't know how many more shocks like this I could take. This story was getting to be too much to swallow. My head spun, and I sat down, right on the stable floor, not bothering to look for a seat. Sadie followed my lead, sitting a yard away, facing me. She pulled her knees up under her chin and hugged them in front of her like a shield.

"You're lying to the sheriff too?" I asked after a beat or two of silence. "I thought you loved him."

"I do," Sadie insisted. "Do you think I'd go to all this trouble if I didn't? I'm trying to help him!"

"By robbing and manipulating him?"

"You don't understand a single thing, Clyde," Sadie said, her lips trembling and tears once again spilling down her face. She looked so miserable.

"Then help me understand," I pleaded. "I don't *want* to believe you're a heartless outlaw. I want you to be the good guy here, but I just can't see any way that's possible at this point."

Sadie rubbed away a stray tear. I knew I should be careful about believing anything she said, but the hope that sprung into her face was disarming. The feeling of betrayal in my chest faded, replaced by an ache of pity.

"I'm keeping up the act for the sheriff, to protect him," Sadie said earnestly. "If he knew the truth, that we were the only two folks left all alone in Cactus Poke—after all those years he worked so hard to make this town what it was—well, the truth would jist break him to bits," Sadie turned pleading eyes on me. "I'm jist trying to take care of him best I can. I've got to! He ain't right in the head, you know that!"

"Well, yeah," I replied, taken aback. "I know that. I just didn't think *you* did."

"Of course I know it," Sadie said. "I can't let him know I do, though. He's an awful stubborn man, and he wouldn't admit for a minute that he needs help. It'd break his heart if he knew I thought he was…crazy," she choked a little bit on the word, but she shook herself and went on. "That's the whole problem. That's why I've had to come up with this whole act. I need to help him without him knowin' it's me doin' it." Sadie pressed her lips together, giving me a helpless look. "I never meant anyone harm by it, least of all someone as goodhearted as you, Clyde. But I'm in way too deep now."

"I'll say," I said, rubbing the bump on my head. "I don't get it, Sadie. Sure, maybe having Duke and Kay Fay around helps Sheriff Hodges feel better about his town, I can see that. But I don't understand how stealing the tater and inventing a fake outlaw helps him at all, crazy or no."

"If you're gonna understand, I've got to start at the beginning," Sadie said, biting her lower lip. "It started out so small and harmless. And I really never meant it to go so far, cross my heart, Clyde."

"Okay, okay, I believe you," I said. "Just tell me what happened."

Sadie nodded, took a deep breath, and plunged in to her story.

"Kay Fay was my first character," she began. "She was a real person who used to live here, so I knew her pretty well."

Sadie told me how Kay Fay was one of the original settlers who came with Sheriff Hodges when he founded Cactus Poke. She was also one of the most faithful and steadfast—even when wave after wave of people left town. But about eight months ago, even she couldn't take it anymore. She closed up the café and went back East. She was the very last citizen to leave.

"When Kay Fay gave up hope, Sheriff's heart broke," Sadie said. "And I don't jist mean he was sad, I mean literally, his heart failed him. A few days after she went away he collapsed in the middle of the street and I found him layin' there looking like a ghost. I thought he was gonna die and leave me all alone out here in the wilderness."

"That's awful," I shuddered.

"Sheriff hovered on death's door for days, not wakin' up or eatin' or anythin'. I was so scared, Clyde," Sadie said. "I didn't know what to do. You get desperate at times like that, ya know? I had an idea, and I didn't even think it was a good one, but I was so fearful for his life, I was willin' to try anything. So," Sadie straightened her shoulders, tried to hold her head up high, but her lip trembled despite her brave act.

"I put on some of Kay Fay's clothes she hadn't bothered to pack up, and I broke out my old stage makeup kit, stuffed in my trunk all that time. I figured I could do a passable impersonation of Kay Fay. I nursed Sheriff back to health like that. I told him—while pretending to be Kay Fay—that I'd changed my mind, that I could never give up on this old place." Sadie sighed.

"Obviously I didn't expect that to work, so I never meant it to be a long-term solution." She shrugged. "But Sheriff made up his mind not to die. His hope came back to him. He started to recover, and of course I didn't dare stop pretending to be Kay Fay then, since her going away had nearly killed him in the first place. And he got better—mostly," Sadie said. "He was able to walk and talk and all, and seemed pretty much as healthy as he'd been before, but…" she chewed her lip. "But his mind had gone…all fuzzy. It was jist little things at first, like repeatin' conversations we'd already had or lookin' everywhere for somethin' he was already holdin' in his hand, but mostly he was his same old self. I expected his mind would sort itself out in time," Sadie said softly.

"Instead it jist got worse. He'd talk to people who weren't there. He sometimes thought he was back in the War, and he'd give me orders about where the Rebs were and what the general said or some such nonsense like that. Then he started carryin' around Ol' Trusty," Sadie shook her head. "That's when I knew I had to think of some sort of way out."

"Out?" I repeated, raising my eyebrows.

"Out of Cactus Poke," Sadie nodded earnestly. "I needed to get Sheriff somewhere he could get some help. I couldn't let him waste away out here all alone in the desert, clingin' to a dead dream, not to mention being watched night and day by a bandit up in the hills. I can't help get his mind back, and what if his heart went again? Sheriff needs a doctor, and there sure ain't one around here. So we have to go."

"You're trying to get Sheriff Hodges to leave his town," I breathed, finally understanding the enormity of Sadie's task.

"I had to find something he valued *more* than Cactus Poke," Sadie said. "And that's when I had the idea of the robbery. I figured if the tater went missing, Sheriff would have no choice but to go after it. That's when I decided to create California Jackson to steal it. I figured if Sheriff went west chasing the tater, I could string him along long enough to get him somewhere he could get some help." Sadie shrugged helplessly. "So that's my story."

Silence fell between us. Sadie looked at me expectantly, but I didn't meet her eyes. The only sound in the stable was Pinto's irritated snort as he shook his mane, still half-covered in bubbles from his abandoned bath. Sadie shifted nervously in the silence that hung between us.

"Well, what would you have done, if it was you in my shoes?" Sadie demanded, desperation gathering at the edges of her voice.

"I don't know…but not that!" I shook my head.

"I jist wanted to help him," Sadie said, blinking hard. "And I couldn't see any other way to do it without causin' him a world of hurt, and maybe even puttin' his very life in danger. This seemed like my only option." She sniffed and took a shaky breath before adding softly, "I also had a little hope that maybe chasin' an outlaw and bringin' justice to the land and all that would help his mind mend, maybe even bring the old Sheriff back. I miss the old Sheriff."

"How long have you been planning all this, anyway?" I asked, holding my head again. The throb had gone down to a dull ache now.

"It took loads of settin' up," Sadie said. "Months of plantin' ideas, spreadin' rumors, and strategizin'. There were a million ways it could've gone wrong, and I had to plan for all of them. That's why I keep that lockpickin' kit inside the jail. If Sheriff ever were to arrest Duke, I'd need a way to get out so I could go be someone else. I've got tons of stuff like that, fail-safes, ya know, all around town. Places to hide, mirrors and makeup kits stowed in secret spots. Even a couple trap doors I could disappear into if things got tight." She shrugged. "But there were a bunch of other moving pieces that needed addressin' too, not just the practical stuff." She gave a guilty half-smile.

"Like Duke, for example. He was a useful part of the plan. I knew from the start that if it all worked and Sheriff decided to chase California Jackson, he'd never be willin' to leave Kay Fay here in Cactus Poke alone. And I couldn't very well bring her along, so I had to come up with someone who could take over runnin' the town and protectin' Kay Fay while we were gone. That's where Duke came in. He wandered into town one day, and Sheriff was so excited that a new settler had chosen to move into Cactus Poke, he didn't hesitate at all to hire Duke as his deputy. Duke turned out to be real helpful in lots of ways though," Sadie said. "It was nice to have someone else Sheriff trusted who could back up my stories, especially where California Jackson was concerned. It almost worked, too, except…" Sadie trailed off, scowling.

"Except what?"

"Them no-good federal marshal pretenders got wind of it," Sadie spat on the ground. "I'm guessin' Sheriff reported California Jackson to them, and they convinced him she was nothin' to worry about. Cause they've got nefarious plans of their own for Sheriff."

"Oh," I breathed a sigh of relief. "I thought you were gonna say it would've worked, except I got in the way."

"Well, you did, a little," Sadie admitted. "With California Jackson dismissed from the picture, Sheriff was quick to pin the robbery on Outlaw Jack. I expected that, of course, so I tried to figure out a way I could convince him California Jackson was working *with* Outlaw Jack, but instead, Sheriff got his own ideas about who Outlaw Jack's partner was."

"Me," I said. "Yeah, I know that part of the story. But Sadie, I'll be honest with you—at this point I can't be sure Outlaw Jack is even real. You told me those spooky stories about him that first night to try to scare me off, didn't you? So I wouldn't get in your way?"

"No such thing." Sadie shook her head. "I was tryin' to warn you. Outlaw Jack *is* real, and he's dangerous. He's jist one more reason why we've gotta get out of Cactus Poke. Your wild determination to go after him was never supposed to be part of the plan. I almost broke down and told you everything, jist to keep you from goin' up into his mountains and gettin' yourself killed. It'd be all my fault if you did."

"You shouldn't have worried," I grumbled. "I didn't accomplish anything up in the mountains anyway."

"But you did," Sadie exclaimed. "More than you know!"

"How do you mean?"

"When you came back from huntin' Outlaw Jack," she said, her voice reverent. "Somethin' changed between you and Sheriff. I could see it instantly. By bravin' the mountains, you earned Sheriff's respect, Clyde, and that ain't an easy thing for a man to do."

"You think so?" I asked, my spirits lifting a little at the thought.

"Absolutely," Sadie nodded firmly, then she looked away, guilt stealing over her face again. "And that's why," she sighed, tracing her finger absently up and down her braid. "You became part of my plan."

Just as quickly as they'd risen, my spirits fell. She'd been using me, I reminded myself. Sadie had been using and manipulating me the entire time I'd known her.

"Sheriff trusts you," Sadie said quietly. "That's why I thought if *you* saw California Jackson, if you had eyewitness testimony that she was the one who took the tater, he might believe it after all, no matter what the marshal said."

"So our mission wasn't a stakeout at all," I said, clenching my fist. "It was an ambush the whole time, and I was the target."

Sadie nodded, tight-lipped.

"I didn't want to," she insisted. "Even right up to a minute before I did it I was still tryin' to find a way not to, but I couldn't think of anything, and there was so much at stake," she whispered. "And that's why I had to make California Jackson my best performance yet. I went up on the ridge ahead of time, after you went to bed, and stowed all her gear far away from our stakeout site so I could get ready up there."

Vaguely I remembered how sure-footed Pinto had been while he climbed the dangerous parts of the ridge. Of course it made sense that he knew just where he was going—he'd climbed that same peak not two hours earlier.

"I figured this was my one shot," Sadie continued, "So I had to make it perfect; even Pinto had to look the part. I combed coal dust over his white patches so you wouldn't recognize him, which explains..." she trailed off, gesturing vaguely toward the half-bathed Pinto and the buckets of black soapy water. "And I took your gun cause I was afraid I might be *too* convincing of an outlaw and you might try to shoot me, and then we'd be in a heap of trouble." Sadie blinked hard, but a tear squeezed out anyway. "I knocked you out so I could get you back to town to tell Sheriff what you'd seen without you being a brave fool and trying to chase after California Jackson on your own," she paused. "I know you would've done it, too, especially since you thought she'd captured me. You got more hero-type in your blood than you've a right to."

"Yeah, and a lot of good it's done me," I sighed, pushing my hand through my hair. "I always imagined being the hero would feel a lot better than this."

"Gettin' you involved was the hardest decision I had to make," Sadie said, her eyes downcast. "I knew if you ever found out the truth you'd never trust me again. I didn't want to, but I had to make a choice—risk losin' your friendship or give up on savin' Sheriff. And as much as I didn't want to hurt you," Sadie looked up at me imploringly. "When it came right down to it, I jist couldn't let him go."

Silence fell between us again. I looked at Sadie. She looked at me. She looked so defeated—an expression, I realized, I'd never seen on her face before. The Sadie I knew was used to being confidently in control of every situation, but now that was broken. She was vulnerable. I felt a pang of sympathy for her. I wanted to put my arm around her and tell her everything was going to be all right. But I couldn't do it. I had no idea if anything would be all right ever again.

"I'm so sorry I hit you, Clyde," she finally said. "Honest, I am. I jist really needed you to believe in her. For Sheriff."

"My head's the least of my worries," I said, swallowing hard. "What we need to figure out is where this leaves us. What do we do now?"

"We?" Sadie repeated, cocking an eyebrow at me. "There ain't no question about *we*. You git on outta here, Clyde. Go to California and find your Pa. Your horse is right here. I won't stop you."

Abraham whinnied to me from across the stable, poking her head out from her stall.

"There's nothin' for you here," Sadie said. "Go. We've held you up too long already."

"But," I stuttered, my heart torn. I knew I should jump at the chance to get out of town. Wasn't that what I'd been fighting for this whole time? I looked from Abraham to Sadie and back again. She was right, there was nothing for me in Cactus Poke, at least not anymore. The entire population of this town was either crazy, lying, or a ghostly shadow. My more reasonable self told me to jump in the saddle and ride like the wind, and not look back till I hit the Pacific Ocean. But when it came right down to it, I couldn't. I looked back at Sadie and made up my mind. Like it or not, Cactus Poke had a claim on me now, and I had to see this through.

"I'm not leaving you here," I said firmly. "I can't. Not with the marshal and his lackeys hanging around, not to mention Outlaw Jack. You aren't safe here, and I'm not okay with that. Besides," I added, nodding decisively. "What would Sheriff Hodges think of me, running off without fulfilling my end of our bargain? You just said it wasn't an easy thing to earn his respect."

"Except you *did* fulfill your end of the bargain," Sadie shook her head. "You solved the robbery, recovered the tater, and found the bad guy. Hooray for you, Mr. Noble Hero," she sighed. "But that won't save the town, and it won't help Sheriff. It sticks us right back where we started, and time's runnin' out. We're getting shipped off to Tombstone at the end of the week, remember?"

"I hate to say it, since it feels like giving up," I said, "but would that be such a bad thing after all? I mean, Tombstone's no Philadelphia, but I've heard it's decent sized. Maybe the sheriff would be able to get the help he needs there. I'm sure they've got a doctor, at least."

"You don't get it, do you?" Sadie snapped, jumping to her feet. "Sheriff would never make it there. It's four hundred miles across desert and wilderness, and he'd be carryin' the weight of failure and the grief of losin' his life's work the whole way there! He'd die of a broken heart before we'd got fifty miles. We can't go, Clyde, we jist can't! I won't let him go out like that."

"Well you can't lead him on some wild goose chase after a fake outlaw, either!" I scrambled to my feet too. "You want to take care of him so bad, why not try actually respecting him a little? That's what he really needs from you, not your protection!"

Sadie looked stunned, like I'd slapped *her* this time. "What do you mean?" she whispered.

"Look, I think I understand why you did all this. I get the heart behind it, at least." I stepped forward, putting my hands on her shoulders and looking her straight in the eye. "But this is *wrong*, Sadie. You're controlling Sheriff Hodges as much as you're trying to control everything else around you. That's not love."

Sadie's faced crumpled, but I went on.

"Real love is built on honesty and trust, and that goes both ways," I said. "How can you say you love someone you constantly lie to? You aren't worthy of his trust, and what's more, *you don't trust him*. How do you even know he can't handle the truth? Ever asked him? You assume he's weak without giving him a chance."

I didn't know how I expected Sadie to respond, but if I had to predict it, throwing herself in my arms wouldn't have been one of my first guesses.

"I know it's wrong," she sobbed, clinging to me. "But I thought it was the only way. I jist wanna help him be okay, Clyde."

"Hey, hey, it's all right," I said, trying to make my voice comforting rather than shocked. I hugged her, cautiously at first, but she held me so tight and her shoulders shook so hard, my heart broke for her. "Don't cry, Sadie, it's all gonna be okay."

"How can you say that? You don't know!" Sadie's voice was muffled against my shirt, which was growing pretty damp by this point. "I've messed it all up good, haven't I? And you know what the worst part about it is? I never did feel guilty about it before. I actually enjoy bein' such a good liar! It's real dark and selfish and I know it, but…I like the way foolin' people makes me feel. I always did wanna be an actress," she added in a small, sad voice. She dropped her head, burying it in my shoulder. "You can feel free to hate me now."

"I don't hate you, Sadie," I said, and I meant it. My arms tightened around her, hugging her shaking shoulders close. "In fact, I forgive you, for all of it. Every last bit. You did what you thought you had to do. You have a good heart, that I'm sure of."

"But what are we gonna do now?" Sadie pulled away, looking at me with red, puffy eyes. "I'm relieved you know the truth, I really am. But that don't change our troubles. We're still in the same pickle—only now neither of has a plan to fix it. I don't like being without a plan, Clyde."

"Well," I said. She was right, if we were going to do anything—save the town, help the sheriff, not get booted off to Tombstone in a matter of days—we needed at least the start of a plan.

"Um," I stalled, staring up into the rafters and hoping some brilliant idea would fall from above in the next ten seconds or so. When that didn't happen, I looked back at Sadie and tried to appear confident. "We'll think of something. Besides, you're not in this alone anymore. We're working together now, and two heads are better than one. Especially when we've both got all the cards on the table and we aren't keeping secrets from each other. That part's got to be over now, okay?" I said. "We can't work together on this unless I can trust you. No more lying. No more pretending. Not for me, not for Sheriff. And not even for yourself. Just be plain old Sadie. I always did like her best, you know."

"You mean take a bow, pull the curtain, and exit stage right?" Sadie sniffed, wiping her eyes and giving me a ghost of a smile.

"Something like that," I said.

"It's a deal," Sadie said. "I'm jist plain Sadie, nice to meet you." She stuck out her hand to me.

"Billy Bob Clyde," I said as I shook it. "Let's be friends."

The smile Sadie gave me was the most genuine one I'd ever seen on her face.

II

DOWN THE RABBIT HOLE

THE mouth-watering smell of frying bacon filled the café, making my stomach rumble. I tapped my fingers against the half-empty coffee cup in my hand.

"Is it done yet?" I called over to the stove, for probably the fifth time.

"Only if you like it raw," Sadie shot back. "Didn't nobody ever teach you not to pester a cook? It's a good way to git yerself poisoned."

A shouting match, especially one immediately following a sleepless night and a bad shock or two, can leave a person feeling mighty hungry. At least that's what Sadie and I decided. We'd quickly finished up Pinto's neglected bath, stashed the Golden Tater and other incriminating evidence under a pile of hay in Abraham's stall, and left the stable to find something to eat. Sadie claimed food would help us think up a decent plan of action, and I didn't argue. I always found it difficult to think clearly when I was hungry.

The café was an entirely different place without Kay Fay in it, I realized. While she'd been calmly and deftly in control, just-plain-Sadie was much louder and more haphazard, now that she wasn't performing.

She moved around the kitchen like a whirlwind, slapping things together without ceremony, and with a certain air of carelessness that Kay Fay never would've allowed. Already she'd almost capsized the coffee pot and briefly set at least one dish towel on fire.

Even though I knew in my head they were the same person, there was such a gulf between Sadie the actress and Kay Fay the character that it was hard to believe. Every movement Sadie had made while pretending to be Kay Fay must've been carefully rehearsed and calculated. The real Sadie slapped the bacon onto a plate, wiping up a bit of the extra grease with a dishrag as she came over to the table where I waited. She even walked differently than she had as Kay Fay. There was no doubt about it: Sadie was good at what she did.

"*Now* it's ready," Sadie said, plunking down a heaping plate of bacon on the table between us. She didn't bother getting out the faded checkered napkins; we licked the hot grease off our fingers instead. Manners don't matter where bacon is concerned, anyway. I grabbed myself a piece, not even flinching as it seared my fingertips, and crunched away happily. As different as their methods were, I realized with satisfaction, Sadie and Kay Fay had one thing in common: the food they prepared was beyond delicious.

"Don't just eat," Sadie reminded me, sipping at her mug. "You gotta think at the same time. We need plans, remember?"

As we munched, we weighed our options. We decided our most pressing issue was the deadline set by the federal marshal. Under his terms, we needed to catch Outlaw Jack by the end of the week, or Cactus Poke would be history. If we could get the marshal off our backs, it would buy us a little more time to think of a way to help the sheriff and put Cactus Poke back on the map. The only thing standing in our way was Outlaw Jack.

At the mention of the Black Hat Bandit, Sadie's eyes sparkled like she'd just remembered something. But before she could tell me, a familiar *step-thump-step-thump* came from right outside the door of the café.

"It's the sheriff!" I hissed, freezing like a panicked mouse. "What are we gonna do?"

"Nothing, of course," Sadie whispered back. "Just act natural."

The door burst open and Sheriff Hodges poked his head in.

"Duke? *DUUUKE!*" He bellowed into the tiny room, so loud I nearly jumped out of my skin. "Where in tarnation has that boy gone off—well, hey there, Sadie, Clyde," he stopped short when he saw us. He nodded at me. "Yer head feelin' any better this mornin', son?"

"Yes, sir," I gulped, nodding quickly. "I haven't noticed it hurting at all for a few hours."

I smiled, trying my hardest not to look like a kid with his hand caught in the cookie jar, even though that's exactly how I felt. I sneaked a glance at Sadie, but her face, all innocent and placid, betrayed nothing. Oh, she was *really* good.

Sheriff Hodges gave me a funny look, and I swallowed again, then smiled even wider. I grabbed the last piece of bacon off the plate and stuffed the whole thing into my mouth at once, just to have something to distract me from his scrutiny. It was a bad call; I accidently inhaled a shard of bacon and ended up choking and sputtering and gulping scalding coffee just so I could breathe again.

"Uh, okay," the sheriff said, once I'd gotten myself in a place where I was sure I wasn't about to suffer death by bacon. He still eyed me critically from under those bushy white eyebrows of his. "You two talkin' about anything I should know about?"

"Just, uh, jackrabbits?" I gasped, my eyes still watering, but I forced a smile—a grin that was growing increasingly desperate. Sadie kicked my shin sharply under the table. "Ow!" I exclaimed.

"Oh, don't strain yourself, Clyde," Sadie said, leaning forward and putting her hand on my forehead with a look of concern. "Everything's all right, Sheriff. I was helping Clyde talk through his memories from the last few days, jist to make sure nothin' got too damaged in his head." She smiled sympathetically and lowered her voice. "Between you and me, Sheriff, I think that bump on the head may have got him more muddled up than I'd hoped."

"C'mon, Sadie, I'm sitting right here," I said.

"Well, carry on, I s'pose," said the sheriff, still frowning quizzically at me. But Sadie seemed to have assured him there was nothing to worry about. "Sadie, you seen Duke anywhere about? I need to git his take on this California Jackson business so's I can put a report together for the marshal."

"I ain't seen him this mornin'," Sadie replied, "but you might check round back of the stable. I think he'd mentioned he was lookin' to fix that bit of fencing on the corral that blew down a while back."

"You think I'm gonna catch Duke in the middle of doing *work*?" Sheriff Hodges said, his blue eyes twinkling. "Well, I guess there's a first time for everything, ain't there?"

"If you don't find him there, you might also check the saloon," Sadie said, laughing. "I heard a rumor he keeps a spare key to the back door and sneaks in when nobody's lookin'."

"Sounds more like it," the sheriff harrumphed, stumping over to the door. "You young'uns git back to your jackrabbits."

The door closed, and his uneven footsteps faded away, off to search for a deputy who wasn't there.

"You just did it again," I said to Sadie once he'd gone, a little spooked by how naturally she'd slipped back into the charade.

"Did what?" Sadie asked. Apparently she hadn't even noticed.

"Lied to the sheriff."

"Well, you sure weren't any help," Sadie shook her head at me. "Seriously, what part of 'jist act natural' was hard for you to understand?"

"Yeah, I was pretty terrible," I admitted. "I can't imagine how you've kept that up eight months. I didn't even last eight seconds. Um…do you actually keep a spare key to the saloon?"

"That ain't no business of yours," Sadie grunted, but it was Duke's voice that came out, and even without her face done up in Duke's stage makeup, I recognized his signature smirk. My eyes widened in astonishment.

"It's impressive how good at that you are," I said. "Scary, even. But I thought we weren't gonna deceive Sheriff Hodges anymore, remember? Wasn't that the plan?"

"I know, I know," Sadie said, and now she was Sadie again. She tugged at her braids. "I'm gonna stop, I promise. It jist wasn't the right time."

"The right time? And when's that gonna be, Sadie?"

"When we can offer him some real hope alongside the hard truth," she said, nodding firmly. "And not a minute before."

"Hope," I sighed. "Where are we gonna find any of that? There seems to be a scarcity of it around these parts." I rubbed my head. It was starting to ache again. "And we still got no plans!"

"I was jist about to say, I think I know a good place to start," Sadie said, lowering her voice. "There's one more secret I ain't told you yet."

"You know Sadie," I said, a sense of dread creeping over me. "I'm getting real tired of all these surprises. Please tell me this one's good."

She took a deep breath, glanced over her shoulder, and leaned in close. "I know where Outlaw Jack is," she whispered.

A chill ran up my spine.

"You…you do?" I squeaked.

"Yes," Sadie nodded solemnly. "And before you get mad about me not tellin' you earlier, you should know I jist discovered it last night. Up on the ridge."

"What happened?"

"I was puttin' the finishin' touches on my California Jackson getup, and was about to start on Pinto's disguise," Sadie said in a hushed voice, "when I looked up and I *saw* him."

"You actually saw Outlaw Jack?" I gasped. "I thought nobody ever saw Outlaw Jack!"

"I thought so too," Sadie said. "That's why it shook me up so bad to see him up close like that. He stood there, all shadowy in the starlight, not twenty feet away from me, stock still."

"Wait, you don't think he saw you too, do you?" I asked.

"I can't be sure," Sadie shook her head. "I'm pretty sure he was faced toward me, but I couldn't see his eyes or nothin'."

The realization that Outlaw Jack's eyes didn't actually glow with an evil white light disappointed me more than it should have.

"But he didn't try to kidnap you or shoot you or anything?" I asked in disbelief.

"No, and that's what's so strange," Sadie rubbed her forehead. "He just stood there, lookin' at me all quiet-like, and did nothin'. Ain't that odd and unsettlin'?"

"Very," I agreed, shuddering. "But what happened? What did he do? Where'd he go?"

"After a minute or two of standing there," Sadie said, "And I know this sounds crazy, Clyde, but I'd swear it to you on a stack of Bibles— Outlaw Jack up and disappeared...*into* the mountainside."

"Into?" I repeated in disbelief. "You're sure that's what you saw?"

"I'm sure," Sadie nodded firmly. "He went straight down into the ground. Jist like a trap door in a stage. Once he was gone, I waited for a few minutes, to make sure he wasn't comin' back, and I went over and poked around the spot where he'd vanished."

"That was beyond dangerous, ya beanhead," I said. "What if he'd been waiting for you to do just that, and was about to jump out at you or something?"

"I know, it was pretty dumb," Sadie admitted. "I realized that as soon as I did it. But it shook me up so much to see him up close like that, I wasn't thinkin' straight." Her eyes sparkled a little. "But I *did* find out somethin' worth knowin'. There's a hole in the ridge, Clyde, a little thing all hidden by some boulders, and you wouldn't think anything of it if you came across it, not unless you were lookin' for it."

"A hole?" I asked. "All this time, Outlaw Jack's been hiding in a hole?"

"Not jist a hole," Sadie corrected. "I peeked down it, and didn't see him, even though there was nowhere else he could've gone. I think it might be the entrance to somethin' a lot bigger. A cave or somethin'."

"That sounds a lot more promising than a hole," I said. "Either way, it's the only lead we've got."

"You're plumb crazy if you think we should jist mosey on up there and knock on his front door," Sadie knocked on the table. "S'cuse me, Mr. Jack, do you have a minute to chat about why you've been hauntin' Cactus Poke for years?"

"Maybe I am crazy, but you are too, so I'm in good company," I shrugged. "Look, I'm not saying he isn't dangerous. And yeah, maybe we are crazy to think we can go up there and confront him on our own." I frowned thoughtfully. "But he hasn't made any hostile moves on us so far. Maybe he's waiting on the right timing, or maybe he's playing a different game entirely. We won't know until we go find out. Without

Outlaw Jack, none of our plans work." I said, standing up from the table. "Are you with me?"

Sadie nodded, and I put on my hat.

"We're coming for you, Outlaw Jack."

"I THINK I prefer taking this trip in the dark," I gasped as the ground finally leveled out. I let out a breath I'd been holding all the way up the ridge.

"You're safer in the daylight," Sadie called from where she and Pinto walked behind me and Abraham on the narrow trail. "Since your horse can see where she's steppin'."

"Yeah," I gulped, risking a glance back down the steep cliffs and the sharp rocks far below. One false step and we'd have been history. "But at least in the dark I don't have to look down at a drop to sudden death the whole way."

Abraham snorted and shook her mane, offended I didn't trust her to carry me safely.

We kept climbing, passing right through the level spot where we'd camped last night. Hoofprints, footprints, and the signs of a scuffle were still evident in the dirt, but I didn't mention it. We rode on past and left it behind us.

The ridge got steeper and rockier the farther we got from our stakeout site. Abraham picked her way along daintily, putting each hoof down like she was trying to tiptoe on a squeaky floor.

"I think we're getting close now," Sadie whispered. I guess she felt the need to be quiet, too. Everything around us was hushed. Even the wind seemed more subdued than it should've been. The back of my neck prickled in apprehension. We were in Outlaw Jack's territory. I could feel it.

Sadie slowed Pinto as she scanned the ground for landmarks. "There," she said after a minute or two. "That's the rock I stashed my stuff behind."

Sadie dismounted and jogged over to the spot, and I followed suit. "Which means," she murmured thoughtfully, standing on the rock and looking intently around her. I could see her reconstructing the memory in her mind. "Outlaw Jack was to my right, about twenty feet away, so that should be..."

I wandered a few yards in the direction Sadie pointed, studying the ground as I went. There wasn't a trace of any sort of cave entrance, at least not that I could see. Just rocks and dust and some dry, scrubby plants poking up from between them. I frowned. Outlaw Jack couldn't have disappeared straight into the side of a mountain. He *couldn't!*

"I don't believe in ghosts," I said to the empty mountain air.

"No one said you did," Sadie replied, shooting me a confused look. "Come on, we're real close, I know it. Help me look around, okay?"

I did, but it didn't help much. Neither one of us found any sort of cave near where Sadie thought she'd seen Outlaw Jack vanish last night. I was about to suggest we move on, go a little further up the ridge— maybe we weren't in quite the right spot—when an all-too-familiar eerie feeling crept over me.

We were being watched.

A slight movement caught the corner of my eye. I froze, held my breath. There it was again. Something dark and shadowy was moving around up here. Something that was watching us. Trying not to draw too much attention to myself, I turned, slowly.

"Sadie!" I hissed. "Don't move! It's *him!*"

Sadie whirled to see, her eyes wide and wild. Her pistol was in her hand in an instant, and her freckles stood out starkly on her ghost-white face. Her alarm only lasted a second though; she looked where I was pointing and lowered her gun.

"Seriously? Clyde, that's a rabbit."

And so it was. The jackrabbit regarded us calmly from its perch atop the boulder, one of its fuzzy, oversized ears twitching slightly.

"I know!" I whispered, still frozen to the spot. "Not just any rabbit. It's that same phantom jackrabbit that followed me all over the Bitterroot Mountains the other day!"

"So what?" Sadie snapped in annoyance, apparently no longer worried about keeping her voice low. "Ooh, I oughta smack you good, Clyde. You had me scared stiff. I thought you'd seen Outlaw Jack!"

"But what's it doing way up here? You gotta admit it's creepy!" I insisted. "How come it always shows up? What's that supposed to *mean*?"

"Who cares?" Sadie threw up her hands in exasperation. "You're letting your nerves get to you. Focus, Clyde! We've got bigger things to worry about. Shoo, bunny. Go on, git outta here. Git!"

The rabbit's ears drooped. He twitched his nose in my direction hopefully, but I shook my head.

"Nope. I'm with her," I told it.

The jackrabbit gave one dejected little sniff, then looked away sadly. He jumped off the boulder and disappeared.

Right into the mountainside.

"Hold up, where'd you go?" I yelped, running to the boulder where the rabbit had vanished. There was a dip in the ground, right at its base; the angles and shadows made it impossible to see unless you were pretty much right on top of it. And down in the dip, mostly obscured by loose strands of dry grass, was a dark, round opening.

"Sadie, I think that rabbit knows something we don't," I called to her. "Look over here."

"That's it, Clyde!" Sadie exclaimed, coming up behind me. "That's the hole I saw Outlaw Jack go into!"

"Are you sure?" I squinted at it doubtfully. "It doesn't look like the entrance to a cave. Outlaw Jack must not be a big fella."

"No, it opens up down there, I'm sure of it," Sadie said, shoving past me. "This is what we've been hunting for. Are you coming in or not?"

Now that it came right down to it, jumping right into Outlaw Jack's hideout struck me as a very, very bad idea. But Sadie had already wriggled halfway down the hole, feet first, her face fairly glowing with the thrill of it. What sort of a noble hero would I be if I chickened out now? I gave her my hand and helped lower her down the rest of the way.

"It's about ten feet to the bottom," Sadie called softly to me from in the hole. "You'll have to drop down, so be careful."

I took one last sweeping look at the ridge, the blue open sky, and the tiny town of Cactus Poke nestled far below, praying this wouldn't be the last time I saw it. I slid down so that I was sitting with my legs dangling over the edge of the hole.

"Take care of each other," I said to Abraham and Pinto. Then I jumped.

Sadie and I blinked hard, trying to get our eyes to adjust to the sudden darkness inside the hill. Above us, we could see a patch of blue sky through the hole, but that was the only source of light. Palpable darkness enclosed us on all sides.

"Should we light our lantern?" I asked Sadie in a whisper. This was no place to speak aloud.

She shook her head. "We don't know if there's any sort of gas or fumes in here," she said. "That's the sort of thing that causes explosions in mine shafts and such. We'll have to deal with the dark. Let's see what we can find out here. Stay close to the entrance."

We both felt blindly around for a minute or two, and discovered we weren't in a cave at all; we were in a tunnel, and the hole we'd come down through was the light at the end of it. It came to a dead end a few feet beyond the hole. There was a rickety makeshift ladder leaned up against the wall of soft earth, which meant good news and bad news— the good news: with the ladder's help, we could climb back up and get out of here when we needed to. The bad new: this tunnel was definitely inhabited, and by something much more dangerous than a jackrabbit. Sadie and I looked at each other, wide-eyed.

"I guess we go that way, then," she whispered, pointing into the tunnel's yawning blackness.

"Right," I said. "Let's do this. Keep your hand touching the right-side wall at all times; that way we won't get turned around and lost down here."

"Good idea," Sadie said appreciatively. I allowed myself a small smile. Who said reading adventure novels wouldn't help out in real life?

Sadie took my hand and gave it a quick squeeze, then we started into the tunnel, leaving the light behind us.

We shuffled along through the darkness, not speaking, barely breathing. I was convinced if Outlaw Jack was down here, he'd hear our hearts pounding long before we were able to sneak up on him. More than once, my imagination populated the blackness with slits of glowing white eyes, peering at us through the gloom. But nothing—not even the rabbit we knew was down here with us—jumped out to spook us, and we crept along, undisturbed and undetected.

My fingers traced lightly along the dry wall, getting gritty with dust. Sometimes the tunnel got narrower, and we had to shimmy through the tight spaces. In other spots it got low, and we had to crouch. It was erratically windy, and went uphill in some places and downhill in others, but there weren't any side channels or weird openings—just the one path. My worry grew the longer we were underground. There'd be no way to run and nowhere to hide if we needed to make a quick getaway.

"How long do you reckon it goes on for?" Sadie finally dared to whisper.

"Can't be much longer," I said, mostly to make myself feel better. No wonder nobody had ever found Outlaw Jack. If anyone had ever made it this far, chances were they never made it back out again.

"Clyde, do you see that?" Sadie asked a minute or two later.

I blinked hard, and found that I did see something. I could distinguish the walls of the tunnel around us.

"Light," I whispered. "It's getting lighter in here."

"And wider, I think," Sadie added.

A few more yards of shuffling through darkness and we found ourselves at the end of the tunnel, but it didn't open into daylight like we'd assumed. The end of the tunnel was a small arch, like a doorway, and it opened into the back corner of a long, low cave. We could see the mouth of the cave far away, and the light filtering through it revealed a rocky, domed ceiling.

"Ready?" I asked.

Sadie nodded, her hand on her gun. We crept forward into the cave, crouching low and keeping close to the rock walls as we headed for the cave's mouth, and daylight beyond.

"Clyde, look," Sadie whispered, grabbing my arm. I followed where she pointed and saw none other than the jackrabbit, sitting in the middle of the cavern, regarding our sneaking progress with amusement. It cocked its head toward the entrance of the cave, as if its big ears had picked up on something ours hadn't, and then it bounded away, out of the cave and out of sight.

Sadie and I exchanged nervous glances, then kept on. The closer we got toward the mouth of the cave the fewer shadows there were to hide us. It was getting warmer too, and louder. We could hear running water, and I guessed there was a stream gurgling away close by. I could smell woodsmoke and... coffee?

"He's here," I whispered to Sadie. We stalled one last moment, staring wide-eyed at each other. Then we stepped out of the safety of the cave.

If I hadn't been scared out of my mind, the view from the hideout would've taken my breath away. The cave opened up onto a narrow shelf that jutted out over a sheer cliff, forming a paradise only reachable to hawks. The Bitterroot Mountains spread out in a striking panorama in every direction, a pure and untouched wilderness. To the left of the cave mouth, a mountain stream tumbled down from somewhere far above the cave, crossed the shelf, and went plummeting over the cliff's edge in a waterfall that threw shimmering rainbows through the air.

A few yards away from the mouth of the cave, close to the edge of the cliff, a lone figure crouched, tending a small campfire and scratching behind the ears of a certain traitorous jackrabbit. The figure's back was to us. My mouth went dry. This was it. This was our hero moment.

"Do something," Sadie mouthed at me, her eyes big as saucers and every freckle on her face standing out like ink splatters.

I took a shaky breath and drew my gun.

"Outlaw Jack," I squeaked, my voice coming out far higher than I wanted it to. "We have you surrounded! Surrender peacefully, and we won't hurt you."

Outlaw Jack stood, took one last swig at his tin coffee cup, and tossed it aside. Then he turned to face us, and Sadie and I got our first look at the bandit who had haunted the dark corners of our imaginations all this time.

Jack had the look of a rugged outdoorsman, with shaggy hair and a few days' stubble on his chiseled face. He was dressed all in black— dusty trousers, worn boots, faded woven poncho, and...no hat.

My heart skipped a beat. Holy smokes, the Black Hat Bandit wasn't wearing a hat because...because...

My hand flew involuntarily to my own head and the black hat sitting on it.

I was wearing his hat!

"Hey, son," Pa said, a smile splitting his tanned face as he nodded proudly at me. "I see you got my message."

12

FRIEND OR FOE?

IT had been five long years, and he looked a lot different than I remembered, what with his newfound ruggedness and all. But there was no doubt about it. Outlaw Jack was my long-lost father.

I stared, wide-eyed and open-mouthed.

"Good to see you too, kid," Pa chuckled. He put a hand on my shoulder and gave it an affectionate squeeze. I wanted to flinch away from his touch—after all, by all accounts, he was supposed to be a heartless outlaw—but I found I couldn't. This was all so wrong, so confusing. Pa was the last person I expected—or wanted—to find up here in this bandit hideout. But outlaw or no, when Pa put his hand on my shoulder, I felt like I'd come home.

"Hey Pa," I choked around the lump in my throat.

"Glad you made it," he said with a smile that made his eyes crinkle up, just like I remembered. "Are you with her?" Pa said, turning and cocking a suspicious eyebrow at Sadie. "Ya know, Billy Bob Clyde, you gotta be careful who you trust out here. I wouldn't have recommended this thievin', connivin' little troublemaker."

I tried to reply, but Sadie found her voice first.

"You're with *him?*" she gasped, her face going impossibly white. She took a step away from me, trembling. "All this time, you were with him?"

"Course he's with me," Pa said before I had a chance to open my mouth. He said it like it was the most natural thing in the world. All at once I realized how bad that was, to be "with" Pa. That was to be "with" Outlaw Jack! The surge of happiness I'd felt at seeing Pa again evaporated. I thought I might be sick. My father—my own Pa—was the Black Hat Bandit! I couldn't believe this was happening.

"What? No! No, nobody's with anybody," I said desperately, but I could tell by the look of betrayal on Sadie's face that she didn't believe me. She kept her gun trained on Pa.

"Well, why wouldn't he be with me?" Pa said, seemingly unfazed by Sadie threatening to shoot him. He looked more confused than scared. "He's my boy, ain't he?"

"Ain't he just!" Sadie whirled on me, pointing her gun in my direction. It wasn't a fake stage pistol this time. Her eyes were wild with anger. I ducked, fearing for my life.

"What sort of game are you playing?" Sadie yelled at me. "I knew I shouldn't have trusted you! I knew it as soon as I saw that doggone hat! But I fell for it! You no-good two-timer! How could you do it? Leadin' me on, makin' me think you cared about Sheriff, and this town, and me, and all the while you were jist bidin' your time, waitin' till the right moment to turn me over to *him!*"

"Sadie, please calm down and don't shoot me," I pleaded, putting my hands up in surrender. "I swear I had no idea, none at all!"

"Hang on now, you had no idea about what?" Pa interjected, frowning. "You wouldn't be standin' here if you hadn't got my letter."

I opened my mouth to protest, but then shut it again. He wasn't wrong. This whole thing *had* started with that letter.

"Funny how you jist forgot to mention one little detail," Sadie said, not lowering her gun. "That your letter was from OUTLAW JACK!"

"I DIDN'T KNOW!" I shouted back at her. But she was right—my letter should've said something about this. Come to think about it, my letter was wrong about everything. I wheeled on Pa. "Pa! What are you even doing here? You're supposed to be in California!"

"California?" he repeated, his forehead scrunching up. "Says who?"

"Says you! In your message!"

"Well I dunno whose mail you were reading," he said, rubbing a hand over the rough stubble on his face. "But I've never been to California in my life. I wrote you pretty clear instructions about where to find me." His eyes brightened. "And lookee here! You found me, didn't you?"

"I came here by mistake," I insisted. "I never even meant to stop in Cactus Poke at all." I dug in my pocket and pulled out the well-worn letter. "Look here," I slapped it into Pa's hand. "Isn't this what you wrote me?"

Pa studied it for a second, then nodded. "Yep," he said. "Sure 'nuff."

"So why aren't you in California?" I demanded.

"This note don't say nothin' about California, son," Pa said. "You sure you can read?"

"Of course I can read!" I yelled in exasperation. "And I figured out the part about the hat too. I found the message inside…" I trailed off as realization dawned on me. I got a sinking feeling in the pit of my stomach. The missing letters in the hat message—never once had I considered that I might have guessed them wrong.

"Look, Pa," I cleared my throat awkwardly. "Some of the message might've gotten rubbed out, so I couldn't read it all," I said. I pointed to the bottom of the note where I'd copied down what was left of the message. "Here's what was written in the hat when it got to me."

COME   GOLD   TER RI   CA   OK

"Rubbed out?" Pa frowned at the fragmented message. "Well that's too bad," he said. "Thought it'd be the safest spot for a secret message."

"Why'd you write it in chalk, ya beanhead?"

Pa crouched and picked up a rock, and his fingers came away white with chalky dust. "You use what's available," he shrugged. "But I see how it might not have been the best idea."

"So you mean to say," I said, "This isn't supposed to tell me to come join you in Terrieville, California cause you found gold?"

"Nope," Pa shook his head. "Good guess, though. Here, you got a pencil?"

I pulled my pencil from behind my ear and handed it to him mutely. He sketched in the missing letters, then gave the note back to me. I blinked at it. For the first time, I read Pa's full message:

COME **FIND ME** GOLD**WA**TER RI**DGE** CA**CTUS P**OK**E AZ**

"So," I rubbed my head. "I was supposed to come to Cactus Poke all along? Even though I've been trying to leave this whole time?"

"This ain't important!" Sadie snapped. I jumped. I'd completely forgotten she was standing there. Pointing a gun at me. "All it means is Outlaw Jack wanted you to come here."

"And it's *not* my fault!" I added. "See, there was no way I'd have known that letter came from here. You gotta believe me on that at least, Sadie! I'm not your enemy!"

"Maybe so," she said. Her pistol whipped from me back to Pa. "But *he* is!"

"Depends on whose side you're on," Pa said, crossing his arms and looking at Sadie thoughtfully.

Sadie threw her chin in the air. "I'm on the side of Sheriff Lawrence Hodges!" she declared. "And I'm the enemy of *anyone* who takes up arms against him and our town!" She darted a meaningful glance at me when she said "anyone." I got the message, loud and clear.

"Is that so?" Pa said. "Then it looks like we're on the same team."

"You take that back!" Sadie snapped, her eyes flashing. "You're Outlaw Jack—the Black Hat Bandit, Terror of Goldwater County, Ghost of the Bitterroot Mountains…and Sheriff's sworn enemy!"

Pa threw back his head and laughed, long and hard. Sadie and I both jumped. It was such a merry sound, so out of place in this tense moment, that it made my skin crawl. I'm surprised Sadie didn't pull the trigger right then.

"Hoo boy, those are some good titles!" Pa said, wiping his eyes. "Almost wish I could claim them."

"Wait, are you saying you're *not* Outlaw Jack?" I asked, hoping too much of my relief didn't show on my face.

"I guess I'm him all right," Pa said, still chuckling a little. "But I think you'll find Outlaw Jack ain't all he's cracked up to be."

"Look here, we didn't come all this way to play riddle games with you," Sadie snapped. "Keep it simple, mister. Are you or are you not Outlaw Jack?"

"It ain't as simple as a yes or no," Pa said. He looked wistful as he gazed out over the mountains. He kicked a pebble, which went skittering over the cliff's edge and plummeting deep into the ravine far below. Pa watched it go, silently, but once it faded from view he shook himself back into the moment. "While I am the man people mean when they talk about Outlaw Jack, I ain't him, not really. Now, I don't wanna disappoint you or nothin', but the Outlaw Jack you've got in your head there, the spooky shadow sittin' on a pile of gold up in the mountains, well, I hate to break it to you, but," Pa shrugged, "he ain't real."

"Not real?" Sadie repeated, dumbfounded. Her gun wavered a little bit, but she didn't put it away.

"Doesn't feel so good, does it?" I muttered to her.

"But," Sadie said to Pa, narrowing her eyes and deliberately ignoring my comment. "But you've got this hideout, and you watch the town all the time, and you're dressed like Outlaw Jack, and you've got wanted posters and…and…if you ain't Outlaw Jack, who are you?"

"Albert Jackson," Pa stuck out his hand. "Explorer, prospector, cartographer, geologist, and proud father to Billy Bob Clyde here. But most folks jist call me Jack nowadays. I dropped the full name soon as I crossed the Mississippi. Seemed to me the West wasn't no place for an Albert." Pa wrinkled his nose a bit as he said it. I knew that feeling.

"Actually, Pa," I coughed, feeling shy all of a sudden. "I just go by Clyde now."

"Oh, do you?" Pa nodded encouragingly. "That's good! He always was my favorite brother."

"*Jackson?*" Sadie demanded, glaring at me. She didn't take Pa's handshake. She didn't lower her gun either. "All this time, your last name was *Jackson,* and you didn't say anything?"

"Aw, come on Sadie, you can't blame me for that!" I said, rolling my eyes. "I got arrested on account of sharing the color of my hat with Outlaw Jack—can you imagine what the sheriff would've done to me if I'd admitted to sharing part of his *name*? Especially considering the California Jackson rumors? Admit it, you wouldn't have trusted me for a second. Heck, you accused a rabbit of being evil just cause he's a *jack-rabbit!*"

"Well I was *right* to be suspicious of him, wasn't I?" Sadie snapped, nodding at the rabbit. "He's with the bad guys!"

"Oh, you got no reason to fear Hermit here," Pa interjected, patting the jackrabbit between the ears. "He's a friend. Led you here, didn't he? I told him to keep an eye out for you."

"Hermit?" I repeated. "You…you named the bunny?"

"Yup," said Pa. "I call him that cause he's a reclusive little feller. Likes his privacy. This here hideout's his own little getaway, but he's been lettin' me stay here a while."

"Um, Pa," I said. "How long have you been living all alone up here, exactly?"

"Oh, 'bout three years now, I reckon," he said. I grimaced. Three years all alone…no wonder he'd started making friends with the wildlife.

"Where are you keepin' the Cactus Poke gold?" Sadie demanded. "And how come you ran off all the settlers in these parts?"

Pa smiled sadly at Sadie.

"Long story," he said, but that's all he offered. He turned his back on Sadie, completely unfazed by her gun. Pa put his hands in his pockets and rocked back and forth on his heels, staring out over the mountains.

"Hawk," he said after a moment, pointing off into the distance somewhere.

"What?"

"Oh, I jist, uh," Pa glanced back over his shoulder, and I swear he looked almost surprised to see me. He shrugged a little sheepishly. "Um, there's a hawk out there. Hermit and I, we like to count 'em."

Sadie and I looked at him blankly. *This* was Outlaw Jack, the infamous, dangerous bandit? What's more—*this* was my Pa, the rugged gold-hunting adventurer? A cliff-dwelling loner who spent his days counting hawks, with only a rabbit for company? I shifted uncomfortably on my feet.

"That's number thirty-four this morning," Pa offered into the awkward silence. When nobody answered, he gave a one-shoulder shrug and turned back to the view. He shoved his hands back in his pockets and whistled a few bars of "The Bonnie Banks," sending the tune echoing out over the cliff.

"Outlaw Jack," Sadie cut in, her voice firm and a little too loud. Apparently she'd had enough. She took a threatening step forward. "By my authority as Deputy Sheriff of Cactus Poke, I'm puttin' you under arrest. If you got a story to tell, you can testify in a court of law."

"You ain't a deputy right now, missy. Not if you ain't wearin' the costume," Pa said, giving Sadie no more than a chuckle for her trouble. He didn't even turn to look at her. "It ain't time for me to talk to Hodges yet," he added, running a hand through his shaggy hair.

"Courts are rigged, anyway," I muttered, kicking at a pebble.

"Clyde, help me out here!" Sadie whispered to me. Her face was growing frantic. "We gotta do *something!* We came out here to find Outlaw Jack and bring him to justice. I'm sorry for the way it turned out, I really am, but we can't jist walk away!"

If Pa was hearing any of this, he didn't show it. He stood with his back to us, still as a statue, staring deep into the distance. The wind tugged at his hair and the fringes of his poncho. Even up close, he looked a little shadowy, like that wanted poster back in town.

"He says he's not an outlaw," I said. And boy, I wanted that to be true. I wanted it so bad it hurt. "Look, Sadie," I said slowly, wondering if my next words would turn out to be a big mistake. I took off my troublesome hat and rubbed my sore head thoughtfully. "Earlier today, I gave you a second chance when all logic and reason screamed at me not to. Maybe…maybe you could do the same for him."

Sadie looked at me like I'd completely lost my mind.

"This is different!" She protested.

"Yeah, you're right, it is different. Cause he's *my father.* And I love him, and I trust him, no matter what." I swallowed hard. "Please, Sadie, give him a chance, for my sake. Just hear him out."

Sadie looked at me long and hard, her lips pressed tight together. She flicked her eyes over to Pa, then back at me. Several agonizing seconds crawled by. The only sound was the tumbling of the waterfall behind us. But then, Sadie let out a tight breath and finally lowered her gun.

"Okay," she whispered. I reached out and squeezed her hand in thanks. She frowned at me, pursing her lips. "But if this crazy scheme of yours winds up gettin' us killed, Clyde," she added, "I swear I'm never speakin' to you again!"

13

THE LEGEND OF OUTLAW JACK

"ALL right Out—I mean, Mr. Jackson," Sadie said, squaring up her shoulders and taking a deep breath. "What've you got to say for yourself?"

Pa finally turned around. He blinked at us as if he was seeing us for the first time. He looked around a few times, like a man trying to get his bearings after waking up from a dream.

"Bit of a long story," he said. "Care to sit down?" Pa motioned toward his campfire. Sadie and I followed his lead. I noticed Sadie took care to be on the opposite side of the fire from Pa, with me situated between the two of them. She looked like a rabbit, tense and poised to run at the first sign of danger. The actual rabbit among us showed no such instinctual alarm. When Pa sat down, cross-legged by the fire, Hermit nuzzled up to him, resting his chin on Pa's knee, and was rewarded with an absentminded scratch between his ears.

"Coffee?" asked Pa.

"Sure," I said.

"No thank you," Sadie replied quickly, darting suspicious eyes toward me.

"That's good," Pa chuckled. "Since I've only got one cup."

He picked the tin cup off the ground and squinted into it, gave it a good shake, then dusted the rim of it off on his pant leg. He bent and grabbed the pot that hung over the fire, filled the cup, and handed it to me.

"Now then," he said, settling back in. But that's all he said. Sadie and I looked at him expectantly, but he just stared into the campfire. His eyes stayed wide and blank for far too many seconds than was comfortable for anyone.

I sipped at my coffee to break the awkwardness, then immediately wished I hadn't. It tasted so much like dirt that I wouldn't have been surprised if Pa had run out of real coffee long ago and was now contenting himself with drinking hot mud in its place. I gagged and set the cup down. Pa didn't seem to mind—or even notice, for that matter. He kept on staring into the fire, still as a statue except for his fingers, which kept rubbing one of Hermit's velvety ears.

"Um," Sadie cleared her throat, breaking the silence. Pa didn't respond. "Mr. Jackson?" She tried again. "Clyde told me you went off lookin' for gold. How did you become Outlaw Jack?"

"*Known as* Outlaw Jack," I corrected. "We know you're not really an outlaw."

"Do we?" Sadie mouthed silently to me.

"Hmm?" Pa said, coming back to us again out of his distant stare. "Sorry. Been awhile since I've had anyone to talk to." He patted Hermit's head and added, "Anyone who cares to listen, that is. Guess I'm out of practice." Pa pushed a hand through his hair and blinked at the sky, collecting his thoughts, then he began his story.

"It all started pretty soon after I left Philly. Crossed paths with some rookie prospectors in St. Louis who were lookin' to try their fortunes too. We decided to travel west together." Pa glared into the fire. "Worst doggone decision I ever made," he muttered under his breath.

"You had partners?" I asked. "You never mentioned that in your early letters."

"They were more like traveling companions than partners," Pa said. "Wouldn't want my name associated with the likes of them. I wouldn't have thrown in my lot with them at all except I figured there was safety in numbers. After all, the West is a lawless place."

"So I've heard," I said wryly.

"What about these partners of yours?" Sadie pushed. "Who were they, and what happened to them?"

"A set of brothers—surnamed Pasadena." Pa spat into the fire, like the name left a bad taste in his mouth. "And a more rotten, black-hearted bunch of scumbags you never did come across. There's three of 'em, Clint, Bud, and Epaphroditus."

"Bless you," I said. Pa and Sadie gave me blank looks. "Um," I said. "That wasn't a sneeze? Oh, sorry to interrupt. You were saying something about an epidermis?"

"*Epaphroditus*. It's a name," Sadie shook her head at me. "Lands, Clyde, you really never have read the Bible, have you?"

"I have too!" I sputtered. "Bible names are names like David and Moses and Matthew! I'd be willing to bet money that Epap…eppy-doritus isn't even in there and you're just making it up to spite me!"

"Book of Philippians," Sadie said without missing a beat. "Look it up. And you owe me two bits." She turned back to Pa. "You'll have to excuse Clyde; he's a heathen," Sadie said, waving my protests away. "So what about these Pasadena brothers? Where'd they go?"

"Nowhere, they're still pretty close by," said Pa. "They camp out near the ravine most nights. You've met 'em, in fact. They were in Cactus Poke a few days ago."

"The federal marshal!" Sadie growled, her eyes narrowing into angry slits.

"Sadie! You were right about those guys!"

"I told you," Sadie replied. "I can always spot a liar a mile away. It's jist bad acting, Clyde, and those three fellas stink of it."

"Oh, so they're marshals now?" Pa smirked. "They've been any number of characters over the past few years…settlers, postmen, surveyors, anything they can think of to have an excuse to creep around Cactus Poke. But Clint's gettin' bolder if he thinks he can pretend to be a marshal and actually get Hodges to take orders from him."

"It's workin' out for him fine," Sadie sighed. "Sheriff's good'n fooled. He'd jump in Goldwater Lake if the marshal ordered him to. He…he ain't quite himself anymore."

"Which one's Clint?" I asked Pa. "Is he in charge? Big guy, built like a bull?"

"No, that's Bud," Pa said. "Bud's always the face of the operation, since he's big and has all the charisma. But don't be fooled. Clint is the mastermind. Nasty sort, but he puts up a proper face on the outside."

I remembered the soft-spoken deputy with the swashbuckling look, quietly getting the "marshal" to do whatever he wanted. I shivered.

"So the skinny one must be Epaphroditus," Sadie said. Pa nodded.

"Explosions expert," Pa said with a grimace. "Not real smart, but likes to make things go boom."

My mind conjured up an image of that shifty-eyed little weasel of a man, and my imagination garnished his image by putting a stick of dynamite in his hand. It wasn't a pleasant thought at all.

"They're looking for you, Pa," I said. Panic tightened in my stomach. "These brothers, they've ordered Sheriff Hodges to find you and turn you over to them."

"Course they are," Pa said, waving away my worry. He didn't seem fazed by it at all. "What else would they be after? Not *California Jackson*, that's for sure." He winked at Sadie, and she stiffened. "They've been tryin' to git their revenge on me for years."

"Revenge for what?" I asked.

"Our gold hunt didn't turn out so good," Pa said. "Like so many others, we thought we'd try our luck here in Goldwater County, seein' as how the name's so promisin'." He rolled his eyes. "But it didn't take me long at all to figure out whoever named it didn't know what he was talkin' about."

Sadie prickled. "That's hardly fair," she said. I had a pretty good guess who had named the county—Sadie couldn't stand hearing a word spoken against the sheriff.

"But it's true," said Pa with a shrug. "I'm a geologist. I know the land. And this here land is not the sort that hides gold. Why do you think nobody ever found any, even with a whole town full of settlers out lookin' for it, huh? You'd think maybe jist a couple of 'em would get lucky, but no one ever did. Why do you suppose that is?"

Sadie stuck out her chin defiantly. "Word around town is cause *you're* hoardin' it all up here somewhere, keepin' it all to yourself."

"You wanna check?" Pa laughed, gesturing behind him towards his cave. "Be my guest. But it'll save time if you take my word for it. There ain't no gold. Never was, never will be. That's just how it is."

"But...but..." Sadie stuttered. I could tell she didn't want to believe him. "But the Golden Tater, how do you explain that? It was found right here, in these very mountains, on the shores of the lake!"

"A curious thing, that tater," Pa said. "For a while I couldn't make heads or tails of it—a nugget that big, out here all on its own, jist sittin' on the lakeshore to get picked up. For a while, I thought it wasn't much more than an interesting bit of local lore."

"But it is real Pa," I said. "I've held it in my own two hands. So where'd it come from?"

"Not sure," he said. "But not here. It couldn't have formed anywhere in this whole area. I figure it's got a past of its own. Must've been brought here from elsewhere long ago—maybe hundreds of years even—and then it got lost, buried, and forgotten. It's possible it got unearthed in a flood or somethin' jist in time to git picked up by Hodges and prompt the Cactus Poke Gold Rush."

"Oh," said Sadie, her voice hollow.

"Believe me, I was jist as disappointed as you are," said Pa. "Nuggets the size of potatoes poppin' up under every cactus sure would be nice."

"The town's done for, then," Sadie said with a resigned sigh. "No one will ever move out here without the lure of gold."

"I didn't say that," Pa said, lowering his voice to a conspiring whisper that made Sadie and I both perk up and lean forward expectantly. "Gold ain't the only valuable thing that hides underground."

"What'd you find, Pa?"

"Black gold—oil. The fuel of the future," Pa's dark eyes sparkled. "By my assessment, Cactus Poke is sittin' right on top of the biggest deposit of the stuff in all of Arizona Territory. This patch of desert is destined to become the biggest boom town this side of the Mississippi. A center of industry, the thrivin' heart of the West. Fella who owns this dusty old scrap of earth is gonna find himself rich as a king. All we gotta do is tap into it!"

"Pa," I said, trying to wrap my head around it. "You mean there'll be an oil rush here? Like what happened back in Pennsylvania in the fifties?"

"We're talking ten times that," Pa said. "Maybe fifty times, hard to be certain."

I sat back, stunned. If Pa was right, this meant millions of dollars, bubbling away right under the sheriff's boots. Millions! It'd make the Golden Tater look like pocket change! And what a story too:

BURNED-OUT GHOST TOWN BECOMES HEART OF THE WEST

Forget the *New York Post*, that kind of headline would make the front page of the *London Times!* And just think what Cactus Poke would become—I could already see thousands upon thousands of settlers flocking here, full of life and hope and thriving community.

"Oh my stars," Sadie breathed, wide-eyed. "Wait till Sheriff hears this!"

"Pa, this is incredible!" I exclaimed. "You'll be the hero of Arizona Territory! Heck, we might even get statehood! Why didn't you say something before?"

"Well, it didn't all go as planned. Took me a while to be sure of the discovery," Pa said, rubbing his chin thoughtfully. "And in the meantime, my gold-hungry partners were gettin' mighty impatient. They seemed to think I'd promised them we'd all be rich in a matter of weeks, and they were tired of bein' empty-handed. 'So where's all the gold at?' they kept naggin' me. I told 'em to be patient. But time didn't do anything for their tempers, and then they started givin' me sidelong glances. Started gettin' suspicious that I was holdin' out on 'em. Eventually they decided I'd found gold myself and was hidin' it from them, squirrelin' it all away somewhere afore they had a chance to git at it themselves. After all, I was supposed to be the one who knew the land. And I was the only one who still seemed happy to keep up the hunt in Goldwater County even when we hadn't seen so much as a flake of gold for months."

Pa went on to tell us he never did share his discovery with the Pasadena brothers. Frankly, he didn't want anything to do with them.

He'd always had his suspicions about them, but hadn't been able to prove it. They never wanted to talk if Pa started asking about what they'd been doing before they went west. But eventually they got careless, and Pa picked up the details bit by bit. He was right—the Pasadena brothers had made a living for themselves in St. Louis as burglars and petty crooks, but they'd botched their biggest job and were on the run from the law.

"I didn't know any of this when I joined up with 'em, mind you." Pa wagged a finger at us. "And if I had, I never would've gone a single mile west with 'em—I don't affiliate with outlaws, even sloppy ones."

"What'd they do?" I asked.

"Burned down a theater, a little Shakespeare company right in the middle of St. Louis." Pa shook his head sadly.

Sadie gasped, clapping her hands to her cheeks. She looked like she'd seen a ghost.

"Oh, Sadie." I inched closer and slipped my arm around her shoulders.

"I *knew* I hated them nasty no-goods!" she whispered in a broken voice, dropping her head into her hands.

"I think they just meant to burgle it, ya know—take all the cash from ticket sales," Pa went on, too caught up in his story to notice Sadie's reaction. "But they're sloppy robbers—left a bunch of evidence all over the place that would've been easy as pie to trace back to 'em—so they went back and burned the whole place down jist to cover their tracks." He shook his head mournfully. "Ain't that awful? I mean, what sort of rotten, no good, poetry-hatin' scumbag do you have to be to rob and ransack a Shakespeare company? Shakespeare is culture, and art, and learnin'. That sorta thing oughta be respected!"

"You...you really mean that?" Sadie peeked up at him through her fingers.

"Course I do!" Pa smacked his knee for emphasis, sending a cloud of dust billowing up from his pants. "I even had tickets to the opening night of *A Midsummer Night's Dream*, at that very theater too. I used to read that story with yer Mama, Bill—I mean, Clyde. Always thought she reminded me of the queen of the fairies."

"Oh, Outlaw Jack," Sadie whispered. "Ain't that jist the most romantic thing?"

155

"Uh, sure, I guess?" Pa said with a grin that was a little bit shy but mostly confused. Pa didn't know it, but just like that, he'd won Sadie's heart for good. I could see it written all over her face. It was as certain as if he'd said magic words—all her suspicion and distrust of him melted away like snow in April. He could've ended his story right there and she'd have been satisfied.

But I wasn't. I needed the rest of the story.

"So your partners turned out to be outlaws," I prompted.

"Evil, wicked, monstrous outlaws," Sadie put in viciously. "Scum of the earth, the... the...rankest compound of villainous smell that ever offended nostril!"

"Shakespeare knew how to craft an insult," I said, letting out a low whistle and finding I had a new respect for the old Bard. "So what happened, Pa?"

"Eventually, I overheard Clint plotting with his brothers to turn on me," Pa said, his face darkening. "I knew I had to escape. I packed up my gear and tried to slip away late one night...didn't make a clean getaway though. I'll spare you the details, but there was a whole lot of shootin'. Barely made it out. Took two bullets, and that nearly did me in. I did manage to git away into the mountains," Pa looked around him at the cliffside hideout with an expression of unmistakable fondness. "That's when I found this here place, all tucked away and secret-like. Best spot in the Bitterroots for a fella lookin' to disappear."

"But you were shot," Sadie said. "How'd you survive? Did you get to a doctor or somethin'?"

"Nope," said Pa. "I knew they were watchin' the whole area, so I had to make do with what I had as far as medical supplies, which wasn't much more than basic field dressings and whiskey."

"You nursed yourself back to health from two gunshot wounds," I said, rubbing my sore head, "In the middle of the wilderness, using only *bandages and whiskey?*"

Pa nodded. "And a good supply of the most potent medicine in the whole world: hope." He smiled at me, a proud, warm smile. "I kept myself alive with the hope of seein' my boy again someday, and of buildin' this town into a place where we could make ourselves a good home."

"That's beautiful," Sadie breathed. The admiration in her face was radiant.

"Once I healed up enough to walk," Pa went on. "I tried to slip into Cactus Poke for help. I managed to come down off the ridge without the Pasadenas knowin' about it. But it'd been a month or so by that point, and the damage had already been done." He shook his head. "I walked into town and came face to face with a wanted poster with my name on it. Turns out those no-good scumbags had spread stories all over town that I was a dangerous bandit livin' up in the hills. They had the whole population of Cactus Poke out huntin' for me. I tried two or three times to make contact with the citizens and explain myself, but it was too late. I was infamous—seems ol' Hodges authorized a 'shoot-on-sight' policy concernin' me." Pa chuckled, brushing his shaggy hair off his forehead. "Hodges is a real spitfire, ain't he? The world needs more folks like him in it, that's a fact."

I frowned. If a crazy one-legged lawman wanted me dead, I wouldn't be laughing about it like Pa was. And I certainly wouldn't be wishing for *more* people like him! One Lawrence Hodges was trouble enough, thank you very much!

"I never meant to hide out so long up here," Pa said. Hermit nuzzled his hand, and he rubbed the rabbit's head. "But while I'd been tryin' to recover from bein' shot, I'd been turned into an outlaw and a fugitive against my will. I betcha it wasn't even hard for the Pasadenas to do. The poor old town of Cactus Poke was already strugglin' bad; they jumped at the chance to point a finger of blame rather than admit defeat—that there ain't any gold to be had. 'Of course there's gold,' they all said to each other. 'It's jist he's keepin' it all for himself up there!'" Pa looked up at Sadie and me and shrugged. "And that's how the legend of Outlaw Jack was born."

Pa fell silent, and his gaze traveled back out over the mountains. The waterfall behind him kept rushing noisily on, endlessly spilling over the cliff. The lonesome screech of a hawk floated by on the wind.

"Thirty-five," said Pa, a half-second before I spotted the bird, soaring across the valley below us.

My head spun, whirling with all the new information: an oil discovery, millions of dollars, bloodthirsty revenge-bent bandits. And in the center of it all, my father—potentially one of the most influential men in the history of the West— hiding here all alone on a cliff.

"Why didn't you come home?" I asked. "We could've helped you if we'd known." Guilt burned in my chest at the knowledge that my father had been living all alone in the middle of nowhere without a soul to help him. "We weren't even sure if you were alive, Pa."

"Believe me, I wished every day that I could just give it all up and get home to you. But how would I do that?" Pa smiled sadly. "I've got a band of outlaws ready to gun me down the minute I dare show my face. I probably never woulda gotten out of the Bitterroots. Even if I did manage to sneak past 'em, I got no horse and no money. And who knows how far Hodges has spread my warrant? How could I know if it's safe to travel—I very well could be wanted in every county from here to the Mississippi."

"That's pretty likely, knowin' Sheriff," Sadie admitted.

"The man's good at his business." Pa nodded. "That's why I reckoned the only way I was gonna get outta here alive was if I could somehow convince Hodges I wasn't an outlaw. But talkin' to him directly was suicide."

"Well, you never did try to explain yourself to me," Sadie said. "I might've listened."

"Sadie, you almost shot him ten minutes ago."

"Well, yeah, but maybe I wouldn't have."

"Oh, you'd have shot me, no question," Pa said, casual and unconcerned about it. "And it's no fault of yours, Sadie. You'd been taught to believe in the Outlaw Jack story, so I knew you'd never trust me. And to be honest," he added. "I didn't think I could trust you either. I never could tell whose side you were supposed to be on. All the sneakin' about and playin' games had me confused about your loyalties. No offense, a'course."

"None taken," Sadie nodded. "I guess it *would* look mighty suspicious if you didn't know the whole story."

"The way I saw it, there was only one person who could git us all outta this mess," Pa said.

But that's all he said. I waited for him to expand on his statement, but he didn't. A few blank moments passed before I realized he and Sadie were both looking at me.

"What, me?" I sputtered. Pa nodded, beaming at me in fatherly pride. "Wait, what can *I* do about this?"

"You're the missing piece. The only person in the world I figured would trust me enough to risk throwin' in your lot with Outlaw Jack," he chuckled. "Thinkin' back though, maybe I shoulda warned you about the whole outlaw business. Course that ain't the sort of thing you want to put in writin', in case it falls into the wrong hands."

"How'd you even send that message?" I asked. "I don't suppose you just waltzed into Cactus Poke and asked to use the post office?"

"We ain't got one," said Sadie.

"Railroad runs through Flagstaff," Pa said. "I figured if I played my cards right, I might be able to sneak outta town without the Pasadena brothers noticin', and maybe get that far on foot."

"Pa that's…" I squinted, tried to picture my old map in my head, but the memory was long gone now. "That's pretty far away, isn't it?"

"Bout a hundred miles or so," he nodded. "Lucky for me, I didn't have to go that far. I ran into some lumberjacks out in the badlands on their way to Flagstaff—timber's the big business there, ya know—and they agreed to git my package where it needed to go. Sorry if the message was confusing. I had to be all secret-like in case the Pasadenas somehow followed me or intercepted it. Didn't want to put you or Helen's family in danger. I knew it was a gamble, that it might never reach you, but it seemed like my best bet. And I had a hunch you'd figure it out." He smiled at me again. "You got a good head on your shoulders, son. And you came through, you really did. I'm so proud of you."

"But I haven't fixed anything yet, Pa," I said. His praise should've warmed me, bolstered my courage, but instead it made me feel small and useless, destined to let him down. "The town's all but dead. Sheriff Hodges doesn't know you're on his side. You're not a single step closer to getting the oil. And what about the Pasadenas? They're still out there, you know. And I'm…" I hesitated. "Well, I'm not exactly a hero."

Pa looked at me blankly. "Course you are," he said. "What are you talking about?"

"I wish I was as brave as you think I am," I said, chewing my lip. "I wish I was more like you."

"You came this far, didn't you?" Pa said, putting a heavy hand on my shoulder. "Not many grown men, let alone boys your age, would up and leave everythin' they know to strike out into the desert by themselves. And look at you right now!" Pa laughed. "You and Sadie came up here to a deserted spot, ready to take on a fearsome outlaw all on your own. Foolhardy, maybe, but no one can argue that ain't heroic! What's more," he continued, his voice growing gentle. "You're brave enough to trust in people. You trusted my letter, even though you hadn't seen me in years."

"I guess I did."

"And you're gutsy enough to trust your partner," Pa nodded at Sadie. "Even though she's a little bit of a snake."

Sadie made a face, but she didn't contradict him.

"And Hodges trusts you, don't he?" Pa asked.

"Well, yeah, I guess," I said. "But only because I agreed to help him arrest you."

"That ain't gonna matter here pretty soon," Pa waved my worry away with his hand. "As long as you get him to believe in me, and in this town's future, this'll work. If we get him on our side, we can get that oil and run the Pasadenas out of town for good!" Pa smacked his knee emphatically. "But unless we work together on this, we can kiss the future of Cactus Poke goodbye."

"And Sheriff's chance at hope along with it," Sadie added. "Don't you see, Clyde? This is the answer—this will save the town, and Sheriff, and your Pa won't have to be a fugitive anymore! And," her face hardened in determination, "We'll see some long-delayed justice served up to some no-good theater-hatin' scoundrels. All we gotta do is talk to Sheriff."

"Easy for you to say," I muttered.

"Is it?" Sadie asked quietly, her voice laced with sadness. My heart sank as the realization hit me: this was my chance to offer Sheriff Hodges hope. Which meant Sadie was the one who had to tell him the truth now. The whole truth.

"It's okay Clyde," she said, smiling bravely, despite the fact that her voice broke. "He needs to know. And I'm sure...I hope he'll understand."

"It won't be easy, but we can do this." I nodded, reaching out to squeeze her hand. She gripped mine back, so hard I almost jerked away. "We can do this together."

Sadie got to her feet, determination etched in her face. I stood too.

"We'll come get you when the coast is clear," I said to Pa, handing him my untouched coffee mug and dusting off my pants. He sipped at the brown sludge.

"Hodges will listen," Pa said, though if it was to reassure us or himself, I couldn't tell. "He's a good man. He'll come around."

"Let's just hope he does that *before* he shoots you dead or turns the town over to a gang of ruffians," I said grimly.

"I'm real glad we found you in time, Mr. Jackson," Sadie agreed with a grimace. "Clyde's right, if we'd waited any longer, we might never have known the truth about you, or about Cactus Poke and the oil. The marshals—I mean, the Pasadena brothers—were gonna force us to relocate to Tombstone at the end of the week."

"Tombstone?" Pa asked. He jolted upright, his eyes wide. "Did you say *Tombstone*?"

"Sure did," Sadie nodded.

"Then we got no time to lose," Pa jumped to his feet, sending a startled Hermit scurrying away. He snatched up my hat—his hat—from where I'd set it on the ground between us and shoved it onto his head.

"Wait, aren't you staying here?" I frowned. "You know, so Sadie and I can talk to the sheriff about you first?"

"We ain't got time to break it to him gently anymore," Pa said. "We gotta get to Cactus Poke, *now*. This'll be more dangerous than I thought."

"What do you mean, Pa?" I asked, unnerved by his sudden agitation. "What's so bad about Tombstone? I hear it's a decent sort of town."

"That's jist the problem. I know Clint Pasadena," Pa growled, "And he ain't got a single decent bone in his body. When he says the word *tombstone*," Pa straightened the hat low over his eyes. "He ain't referring to the town."

14

BITS AND PIECES

OUR journey back toward Cactus Poke was quicker than our trip to the hideout had been. Pa didn't bring any lights into the tunnel, but he walked with surefooted steps even in the pitch darkness. It was the sort of confidence that comes from having walked a path about a million times; his feet knew every inch of this tunnel whether his eyes had ever seen it or not. Sadie and I had to scramble to keep up, and even though he called back from time to time with instructions—"Watch your step now; it veers left here a bit"—both of us ended up with stubbed toes, scraped hands, and more bumps into Pa and each other than we cared to count.

In no time, we spotted the sunlight streaming in from the hole in the ridge, marking the end of the tunnel. Thankfulness surged through me at the sight of it. When we'd jumped down here an hour ago, I wasn't sure I'd ever get the chance to climb back out.

"Okay, up we go," said Pa, grabbing hold of the makeshift ladder. Sadie sent a hesitant look my way, but the flimsy thing didn't turn to dust or anything when Pa touched it. If it could hold him, I figured it wouldn't collapse under my weight, or Sadie's either. But I didn't want to push its limits, so I waited till Pa disappeared out of the hole before I started up the ladder. I didn't get far though. A sound froze me with my foot hovering halfway to the first rung.

It was the unmistakable click of the hammer of a gun.

"Hello, Jack," said a smooth, calm voice. "Did you miss us?"

A dark silhouette flashed across the small circle of sky as a burly arm grabbed Pa by the throat and jerked him out of sight. There was a strangled shout, then a heavy thump as a body hit the ground. Dust and loose pebbles shook down from the roof of the tunnel, and Pa's black hat came tumbling back down the hole, landing at my feet.

"Back, get back!" Sadie hissed at me, grabbing my arm and tugging me deeper into the tunnel. And not a moment too soon, either. We'd barely melted into the shadows before a pinched, ferret-like face appeared in the hole, blinking blindly against the dimness. I recognized him instantly as the marshal's skinny deputy—or, more accurately, Epaphroditus Pasadena. Sadie and I flattened ourselves against the tunnel wall.

"Ooh boy, no wonder it took us so long to find ya!" he crowed. I flinched as his shout echoed and bounced down the tunnel. "Lookee here, boys, it goes right into the hill!"

"Git your noggin out of the ground, you idiot," a third voice grunted. That would be Bud, the one we knew as the marshal. The same big hand that had grabbed Pa appeared again and yanked Epaphroditus out of the hole by his shirt collar. Sadie sagged in relief once he was gone, but I was still frozen with fear. They had him. The Pasadena brothers had Pa.

"You plannin' to kill me, Clint?" Pa's voice sounded a little rough.

"Oh, you bet I am," Clint answered with relish. "No doubt about that. Jist not right away. You made me wait three years for this moment, so you'll have to forgive me if I enjoy it for a bit." He punctuated this with a kick, and by the sound of Pa's sharp gasp I guessed it had caught him right in the stomach. The other two brothers laughed.

That was about all I could take. My blood boiled, and I lunged for the ladder, ready to take on Clint Pasadena with my bare hands if I had to. But Sadie pulled me back, her arms pinning mine to my sides.

"You tryin' to get yourself shot?" she hissed in my ear.

"They've got my Pa!" I whispered back. "Let me go!"

She didn't. I was tempted to kick her in the shins.

"You can't help him if you're dead!" Sadie said. "Hold on, and we'll wait for the right moment."

I balled my fists in frustration. She was right; it wouldn't help anything if I went up there and got myself captured too. But standing here helplessly, doing nothing, might just kill me. My heart pounded faster and faster and I chewed my lip so hard I tasted blood.

"Besides," Clint's suave voice went on above us. "I can't get rid of you jist yet. You ain't given us what we want."

"Yeah, where's the gold at, Jack?" chimed in the nasal whine of Epaphroditus. "We *know* you found some. Don't bother denyin' it. You wouldn't still be here if you hadn't."

"So lemme see if I've got this straight: you're gonna shoot me once I talk?" Pa asked. I couldn't believe how calm he sounded, especially in light of my own growing panic. "You know, that ain't great incentive for me to help you boys out."

"Don't make me shut that smart mouth for you, Jack," growled Bud.

"Why, you scared you won't do a good job or somethin'?"

The smack of a fist against a face made Sadie and I both flinch. Pa grunted, but he didn't cry out.

"Bud, please," said Clint with affected politeness that made my skin crawl. "We know Jack to be a man of reason, don't we? I'm sure he can be persuaded."

"Psh, unless your bargain involves the three of you maggots jumpin' in the lake, I ain't takin' it," said Pa. His words were a little muddled, like his mouth was swollen.

"Where are the kids, Jack?" Clint asked without preamble. He'd dropped the smooth act entirely. His voice sounded hungry. Sadie and I exchanged a wide-eyed look and involuntarily shrank back further into the darkness.

"Kids?" Pa said, and for the first time, there was an edge of fear to his tone. "There ain't no kids. I don't know what you're talkin' about."

"Maybe I can jog your memory." Another kick, this one followed by a groan. "Two young'uns—the sheriff's little spies. The orphan girl and that skinny kid who pokes his nose into business that ain't his own. We know they came ridin' up here not too long ago, on them two horses, right there. How do you think we woulda found you if they hadn't led us right to you?"

"Well, I dunno, cause I ain't seen 'em," Pa insisted. "They couldn't have come down this hole without crossin' my path. It's no more than a little burrow; dead ends about fifty feet back," he said. "If any kids came by this way they're most likely way farther up the ridge by now. Probably dismounted and left the horses here cause the ground got too rocky to ride."

Sadie and I held our breath through the silence that followed.

"You swear you ain't been conversatin' with anyone down there in that little burrow of yours?" Clint asked. "Anyone who might know things they ought not? Who might share those things with other people if left to their own devices?"

"You're more'n welcome to look," Pa said with a forced laugh. "But I'd save myself the effort if I was you. Nothin' down there but some dried-up worms and a whole lot of dust."

"Hmm," said Clint. A space of a few heartbeats passed where I almost let myself believe he was going to walk away and let us go. But then he chuckled. "Is that so? Then I'm sure it won't bother you a bit if we go ahead and close it up, then. Epaphroditus? Care to help Jack lock up his front door?"

What? Lock up his front door? Sadie gave me a confused frown and I shrugged, but we didn't have much time to wonder about it. We heard the scratch and hiss of a match being struck. My stomach flipped as the realization hit me. Epaphroditus. The *explosions expert.*

"Wait!" Pa yelled. "The lake! Gold's at the lake. Got a big ol' stash of it. More gold than you could spend in ten lifetimes! I'll take you right to it, I swear!"

"I knew you were a reasonable man." We didn't have to see Clint Pasadena's face to know there was a triumphant smirk on it. "Get him up."

We heard the three men mount their horses, and one of them— probably Bud—dragged Pa up into the saddle with him.

"So, I can't blow the hideout?" came the thin, whiny voice.

"All this talk of gold has put me in a generous mood," said Clint. "Aw, go on and have your fun, brother."

Sadie and I watched in horror as a thick stick of dynamite sailed down through the hole, landing inches from our boots.

"No!" screamed Pa, but his shout was lost in the thunder of hoofbeats.

The fuse was bright and hissing and not long at all. There wasn't a single second to think through what I planned to do.

I snatched it off the ground and ran.

"Clyde, don't!" Sadie shrieked, but I couldn't hear her over the pounding of my heart. I had to get as far away from her as I could, and fast. I stumbled into the darkness of the tunnel, the glowing fuse growing shorter and shorter until I knew I didn't have even one heartbeat left. I threw the dynamite as hard as I could.

It exploded a half second after it left my hand. The whole mountain roared, and the tunnel shook. The shockwave flung me backward. I inhaled a burning lungful of smoke and sparks and dust. A wave of heat engulfed me, and for a second the whole tunnel flooded with light as a huge fireball blazed like an underground sun. Then the roof caved in and smothered it, sealing it into the mountain—and me along with it.

SOMETHING touched my hand. It was rough and hard and heavy.

The only thing I could hear was a constant, high-pitched ringing in one ear. I could feel myself fading, smothering under the weight of the warm earth that covered me. I was unable to force enough air into my scorched lungs to keep my mind from going black. *Lie still,* my body told me. *Sleep. Let go.*

But then that something was back. It nudged my hand…no, it was pawing at it. Repetitive. Insistent. Then a cool rush of air washed over my hand. I stretched my fingers and found they were no longer trapped in dirt.

My fuzzy mind barely had time to process the fact that something was digging me out before a large, leathery hand closed around mine and pulled. Hard.

For a second nothing happened except that pain screeched along my shoulder. But then the earth around me started to give way, and I found myself being yanked from the rubble of the collapsed tunnel like a bone from the jaws of a hungry dog. The ground seemed reluctant to give me up, but my rescuer was even more stubborn than the mountain itself. My head broke through the earth, born out of darkness into brilliant sunlight, and I gasped fresh air like a drowning man.

My rescuer let go of my arm, and I collapsed onto my back, eyes shut tight, taking gulp after gulp of the mountain air. It burned against my raw throat, but I didn't care. All I could feel was gratitude: I wasn't buried alive or blown up.

Something large and soft and rather wet nudged my face. I cracked open a slit of one eye.

"Abraham?" I croaked, the effort of that single word scraping painfully against my scorched throat. I barely heard my own voice through the ringing in my ear. But it was Abraham, dear old thing, pushing against my face with her nose.

"That may be the oldest horse I ever seen in my life," said a voice. "But she's also the most loyal. I never woulda found you if she hadn't already been diggin' you out."

I don't know how he got there or how he'd known to come, but I'd have recognized that voice anywhere. Besides, there was only one person I'd describe as more stubborn than a mountain.

"Thanks for saving me, Sheriff," I rasped. "How'd you know where to find me?"

"Followed your trail. When I couldn't find you in town, I thought you'd probably come up here again. And that didn't seem too wise, considerin' your head and all."

"Oh, right." I'd forgotten I was recovering from a head injury.

"I was about halfway up the ridge when the explosion went off, and somehow I knew that was none other than your doin'."

I grabbed onto Abraham's harness, and she pulled me to my feet. I rubbed her snuffly wet nose and planted a kiss on her velvety forehead. She whinnied softly—or maybe it just sounded soft to me, since I wasn't sure if my ears were working all right. I was relieved to find that my legs still worked, at least, even if they were a little shaky. I shook rubble and dust from my hair and blinked. The area around me was unrecognizable: overturned earth and scorched shrubs made the quiet patch of mountain look like a war zone.

Sheriff Hodges regarded me from underneath his bushy eyebrows, his arms folded across his chest.

"You gonna tell me what fool thing you did to git yerself buried alive?" he asked.

"I..." I began, but trailed off immediately as my fuzzy mind cleared. The events of the last half hour plowed back over me like an avalanche. "Holy smokes, *Sadie!*"

"Sadie?" The sheriff repeated, his stony face shifting to wild alarm in no time flat. "What in the blazes is Sadie doing—!"

I didn't hear the rest of his sentence.

"Sadie!" I yelled, sprinting on wobbly legs across the broken ground to where the hole had been. "Sadie, where are you? Can you hear me?"

"Sadie!" Sheriff Hodges bellowed, not half a step behind me. "Look here, kid," he said, grabbing me by my shirt collar and forcing me to look right into his icy blue eyes. "If you've gone and involved my Sadie in some fool scheme that's gotten her hurt in the slightest, I swear I will break you in half!"

"Let me go!" I kicked his good knee. "We gotta find her!"

"Sheriff?" Sheriff Hodges and I both froze at the sound of the weak voice that cut in. The ringing in my right ear had faded a little, and even though I still couldn't hear a thing out of my left one, I was sure I'd heard Sadie's voice.

"Sheriff, is that you?" she called again.

He dropped me.

"Sadie!" he called, running in the direction of her voice. I stumbled after him. "Where are you? I'm coming, sweet girl!"

"I'm down here, in the hole," Sadie replied, her voice shaky with tears. "Ladder's broke and I can't get up. And oh, Sheriff," Sadie sobbed. "Clyde's dead!"

"Sadie, I'm all right," I said as I reached the hole. Sadie was huddled down at the bottom, her dirty face streaked with tears. She held something tight against her chest, which on second glance I realized was my hat. Sadie looked up at me, startled, but her face melted instantly in relief.

"Oh, Clyde!" she cried. "I thought you were a goner!"

"Hang on, we'll get you out." I turned to the sheriff. "Can you get me down there?"

I laid on my stomach on the edge of the hole and the sheriff anchored himself, holding my ankles, and lowered me into the hill.

"Here, grab on," I said. Sadie scrambled to her feet, but she jerked her hand back instead of grabbing onto mine.

"Clyde, your hand," she gasped, her eyes wide with horror. I followed her gaze and saw, to my surprise, that my right hand was burned—badly. The skin was a nasty mess of raw, angry red.

"It doesn't hurt, honest," I said, trying to sound brave even though I thought I might throw up at the sight of it. "Come on, grab on. I can't hang like this forever."

She hesitated another half second. She put my hat onto my head, then took my hands. I braced myself for pain when she touched the burned parts, but I didn't feel anything other than a dull pressure. I'm no doctor, but that didn't seem like a good sign.

The sheriff grunted, yanking on my ankles, and heaved Sadie and me back up to the surface. We sat there for a second, panting and blinking in the sunlight. Then Sadie turned on me.

"What were you thinking?" She demanded. "You grabbed a lit stick of dynamite! Why do you have to be so doggone heroic?" Sadie's face crumpled up. "You could be dead right now and you...you saved me." She grabbed me by the collar and kissed my cheek. "Thank you, Clyde," she whispered.

"Do you two young'uns wanna tell me what's goin' on here?"

I certainly didn't want to be the one to explain to the sheriff why *his* Sadie was kissing me, but when I looked up at the sheriff, I realized that wasn't what he was talking about.

"Dynamite?" Sheriff Hodges asked. His eyes were solemn as he took in the smoke in the air and our dirty, ash-smudged faces.

"Yes, sir," I gulped.

"How did you manage to git yerself caught in an explosion like that way up here on the desolate ridge?"

"We came up here hunting down Outlaw Jack," I offered.

"And jist why would you do that," Sheriff Hodges asked, narrowing his eyes, "When you knew full well *this* was hid away in your horse's stall?" He slid the strap of a backpack off his shoulder and plunked it on the ground in front of me.

I recognized it instantly. Sadie and I had hidden it there just this morning.

"Go on, open it," the sheriff said, in a voice that left no room for argument. I obeyed, unbuttoning the bag's flap and reaching in. Cool, hard metal brushed my fingers.

"Here goes," I murmured to Sadie, and she nodded solemnly. As Sheriff Hodges watched with smoldering eyes, I pulled out the Goldwater Potato.

"Now, I don't know what kinda story you got to explain yerself," he said. "But all I can say is it better be good." He put his hand on his holster and leveled me with a piercing glare from his glowing blue eyes. I knew nothing in that holster could hurt me, but it was impossible not to shrink back under that kind of a look.

"Clyde didn't take it, Sheriff," Sadie said firmly, snatching the Golden Tater from my hand. She stood, stepping between me and the sheriff. "I did."

His face transformed from menacing to stricken as quickly as if he'd been shot.

"It's true, sir. That's *my* backpack. I staged the robbery, and I've been keepin' it from you."

"Sadie, sweet girl?" The sheriff's voice was cautious, like he was afraid to believe her. "Now why would you go and do a thing like that? If you'd wanted the tater, all you'd have to do was ask."

Sadie hung her head, her cheeks burning.

"I jist wanted to help you, Sheriff," she choked. "I thought it was the best way, but I was wrong. And now I've gone and made a mess of everything. I'm so sorry."

The rest of the story came tumbling out, all at once. Sadie's words came faster and faster as she confessed it all: the Town Hall robbery, her plot to leave Cactus Poke, the truth about California Jackson, Kay Fay, and Duke—she hardly stopped to breathe. If this was Sadie trying to break the news gently, I'd hate to see her trying to be blunt.

As Sadie talked, I watched the sheriff. He didn't collapse instantly like Sadie had feared; he just looked stunned as one truth after another came to light. He took off his hat and mopped his bald spot with a red handkerchief, but other than that he didn't even move. The sheriff's face went from shock to hurt to resignation. His shoulders sank, losing the rigid military posture he always kept. The intensity drained out of his face. Even his eyes dimmed from their vibrant icy blue to a dull slate color.

"It was wrong of me to lie, I know that," Sadie finished, her tears leaving pale tracks through the dirt on her face. "It was wrong not to trust you. I'm sorry. I'm so very, very sorry. But you ain't your old self, Sheriff," she squeezed his hand. "And it makes me so sad to see you like this. I wanna help you come back. But I knew there was nothin' dearer to you than this town and…and I didn't wanna lose you. I jist couldn't bear it, Sheriff."

Sadie bit her lip as she waited for him to respond, her fists balled up so tight I could see her knuckles turning white. When he didn't say anything, I though Sadie might fall apart. Full minutes passed, but in that nervous silence they felt more like years. The sheriff turned away from us and looked out over the mountains, the desert, and the town. He sighed deeply as he studied the distant rooftops of Cactus Poke.

"You were wrong," Sheriff Hodges said finally, turning back to us. "There *is* something dearer to me than this town."

He placed his hands tenderly on Sadie's shoulders and waited for her to look up at him. When she did, her lip trembled, but he smiled at her.

"I do love this place. It was a home and a purpose when I needed one most," Sheriff Hodges said, with a smile that was almost wistful. "I've worked hard to make it what it is, and I've fought for it when things got tough. But a town's jist a thing, Sadie," the sheriff brushed a tear from Sadie's cheek with his thumb. "And that gold nugget's no more than a hunk of metal. It's people that matter, when you lose everythin' else. Trust me, I know. If it came down to a choice between this place and family, I'd pick family every time. And you're the only family I've got, Sadie-girl."

"Oh, Sheriff," Sadie said, collapsing into his embrace. His arms closed around her. I stepped backward and turned away, feeling like an intruder in this moment.

"I love you, sweet girl," the sheriff said. "I forgive you for the wrong you did me. And I'm sorry for the hurt and worry I've caused you. It's an awful big burden for one girl to carry, even if she *is* the cleverest girl in the West." He tugged playfully at Sadie's braid, making her smile despite her tears.

"It ain't right for you to feel solely responsible for takin' care of me. It's true," he hesitated, as if the words were difficult for him to get out. "I ain't been too sure of myself in recent days. My head gets fuzzy and I don't know what's goin' on sometimes. I can't think straight, like something's broke inside me, but I don't know what..." he trailed off, frowning at nothing. Then he shook himself and continued, in a much stronger voice. "But I feel clear right now, so I'll tell you plain: if you think we ought to move on, get to somewhere with more folks about, I'll go with you. Maybe it's time we start again, after all." Sheriff Hodges shrugged and gave a half-smile. "I figure I ain't too old to put down new roots."

"But you don't have to!" Sadie's head snapped up, her face brightening like a sunrise after the darkest of nights. She broke away from the sheriff and grabbed my arm. "Cactus Poke ain't done for yet! Clyde! Tell him our good news! About your pa and the oil and all that!"

As soon as the words left her mouth, Sadie realized her mistake. "Oh lands," she breathed, her hands flying to her face in horror. "Your pa."

"Ain't he in California?" the sheriff asked.

"No," I said, feeling like I'd been punched in the gut. I'd been so relieved Sadie and I had lived through the explosion that I'd forgotten about Pa. "He's here, at the lake. If he's even still alive," I added grimly. "I don't think Clint Pasadena's patience will hold too long once he realizes there's no gold."

"Pasadena?" the sheriff frowned, like the name was distantly familiar but he couldn't place it.

"The so-called federal marshal and his deputies," Sadie said, spitting on the ground. "They ain't who they say they are. They took Clyde's Pa and tried to blow us up with dynamite. They're imposters of the worst kind!"

"I'm going after them." I said, straightening my hat and squaring my shoulders. "I've gotta save my Pa."

"Well you sure ain't goin' alone," Sadie said.

"Sadie, you saw what those guys can do. I can't ask you to risk your life for my sake."

"Well, I didn't ask you to jump into a fiery explosion on my account either, but you did without a second thought." Sadie put a hand on my shoulder. "It's what partners do for each other, Clyde."

"And if you two think you're goin' after murderous outlaws without me, you've got another thing comin'," the sheriff put in. His eyes flashed with righteous fury. "No one gets away with disgracin' the title of federal marshal in *my* town. That's like spittin' in the eye of the Union itself! No sir!" He puffed up his chest, and the gold badge on his vest gleamed in the sunlight. "This sounds like a job for the Law!"

As he said it, Sheriff Hodges looked so strong, so determined, so full of purpose and power. The mere thought of bringing criminals to justice had breathed new life into him. Sadie's face brightened.

"Then we'd better get going," I nodded. "We might be too late already."

"So what are you thinkin' we should do? You've gotta have a plan, Clyde," Sadie said. "You ain't gonna get far if you just walk up and ask nicely for them to let your Pa go."

"I know that. But I don't think we can go in guns blazing either. There's not enough of us. One more well-aimed stick of dynamite and we're all history." I rubbed my sore forehead, willing an idea to hit me...wait, *hit me.*

Hang on, that might just be it.

"Sadie! How hard could you punch me in the face?"

"I could break your nose," she answered without a blink of hesitation.

"Oh," I said, a little taken aback. "Well, don't do that, exactly."

"What's this got to do with anything?" Sadie asked. "Have you got a plan?"

"Sort of. Bits and pieces. But it's coming together," I started to pace. "Here's the deal: if we're going to get Pa out of there without getting anybody shot, we'll need to be clever. We've got to get the Pasadena brothers to let their guard down. Maybe even make them trust us. Then we'll steal Pa back and take them down from the inside."

"*Trust* us?" Sadie laughed skeptically. "And jist how do you plan to do that?"

"Well first of all, we'll need an outlaw," I said, running my finger along the brim of my battered black hat. "And I think I know just the man for the job."

15

ENCORE PERFORMANCE

"**ARE** you sure you want me to do this?" Sadie said, turning to me.

I almost jumped out of my skin. She'd only been sitting in front of the little mirror for five minutes, but she was barely recognizable as herself. Her braids were tucked under the shaggy black wig and all her freckles were gone, replaced by tired gray circles under her eyes. Even her jawline looked sharper.

"Yikes, Sadie," I cringed. "That's downright unnatural."

"You never thought Duke was creepy before," she said.

"I'm not sure that's entirely true."

Sadie rolled her eyes at me. She didn't look *exactly* like Duke as I'd first met him, but the disguise would have to do. We'd only had what was in Sadie's bag that the sheriff brought with him—the bag with the Golden Tater—and that had mostly been full of her California Jackson getup. We'd toyed briefly with the idea of featuring California Jackson in our plan instead of Duke. But after some thought, we decided against it, due to California Jackson's rumored relation to Outlaw Jack. We didn't want to give the Pasadena brothers any extra reason to be suspicious. This was going to be risky enough as it was.

Even without her regular Duke gear, Sadie seemed confident she could work with what costume pieces she had. She'd cut California Jackson's wig short with my pocketknife, and hid the ragged edges of the hair under my black hat. Sadie kept the same coat and bandana from California's costume, and traded boots with me to make her feet look bigger. The result was a pretty passable Duke, if a little darker and more outlaw-like. Which was just fine, for our purposes.

"I've just got the scar left to do, then I'll be ready." Sadie said, turning back to the mirror.

"Make it a little gnarlier than normal, okay? We really gotta sell this."

"You mean *I* really gotta sell this," Sadie corrected. "Your job is to *buy* it. Cause if you don't believe it, they won't either." Sadie shuddered. "And if they don't believe it, we're in deep trouble."

"Don't remind me," I grimaced. "But I don't think I'll have any trouble with the pretending-you-hate-me part." I traced my finger along my swollen jaw. It was already starting to bruise.

Sadie shot me daggers with her eyes through the mirror. "You can't ask me to punch you in the face and then give me a hard time when I do it!"

"I didn't expect you to do such a good job!"

"Whenever you two young'uns are done with your bickering," Sheriff Hodges cut in, his voice laced with impatience. He was already in Pinto's saddle, ready to get a move on.

"Right, sorry sir," Sadie said. She dabbed a few finishing touches on her chin, then rubbed her hands in the dirt and patted her face deftly. The result was Duke's smudgy appearance, which I'd always thought was due to his lack of proper washing, but now I saw was deliberate. To my satisfaction, the scar that split Duke's face did look a little bigger and angrier than usual. Sadie swept her makeup, mirror, and tools into the backpack and stowed it behind a boulder.

"Ready," she said.

I swung up into Abraham's saddle and Sadie jumped on behind me.

"Deputy?" the sheriff said. "Duke, is that you?" Sadie and I turned to see him giving us a bewildered stare. He blinked at Sadie, his eyes looking lost and cloudy.

"Jist me, Sheriff," Sadie said gently. "Remember?"

"Right, a'course," the sheriff murmured, nodding. He shook himself a little and nudged Pinto into a walk. "Not Duke, he ain't real. I remember now." But he still eyed Sadie with a suspicious squint, as if unsure he believed it.

I felt Sadie's posture slump a little behind me. But her voice was still resolute as she said, "Come on; let's go."

We rode down the ridge in silence, then through the foothills, retracing the steps I'd taken a few short mornings ago. But with everything that had happened since then—everything I knew now— the very landscape seemed like a different place. I almost laughed at the memory of how nervous I'd been then, scared spitless that Outlaw Jack was going to jump out from behind every scrubby little bush I passed. But then I jolted as the realization hit me—something *had* been watching me that day. I remembered the camp I'd stumbled into and the lone figure I'd seen from across the lake. And it hadn't been Outlaw Jack— he'd been up in the hideout on the ridge. I'd been one step behind the Pasadena brothers all along. The thought made me shudder. I'd been in more danger then than I even knew.

Danger, I realized with a flinch, that I was willingly headed right back into. And I was taking my friends with me. Questions dogged me as each of Abraham's plodding footsteps took us closer to the lake. Were we going to be too late? Were we even going to make it out of here alive?

"We're getting close," Sadie said in a low voice, breaking into my nervous thoughts. "I think we should dismount here and go the rest of the way on foot."

I nodded, reining in Abraham. The sheriff did the same, pulling Pinto to a stop and swinging his wooden leg over his flank in a flawless dismount. We'd already agreed on leaving the horses behind, but it still made my chest constrict to separate from Abraham, after all we'd been through together.

"Take care of yourself, old girl," I murmured to her, stroking her nose. "And Pinto, too. He's just a young whippersnapper and doesn't know what's what, not like you."

Pinto snorted at me, but Abraham nosed my shoulder solemnly, as if to remind me that of the two of us, I was the one who needed to be careful.

"Thanks for saving my life back there," I said. "You're the best horse a man could ever wish for."

"Don't say goodbye," Sadie interrupted, putting a hand on my shoulder. "We're coming back, you'll see. We're winning this."

"Right," I nodded, wishing I believed it. "Yeah, we'll be back soon."

"Okay, Sheriff," Sadie said, turning to him. "Clyde and I will go on ahead from here. You scout along the perimeter, make sure we're not walkin' into a trap. Don't let anyone see you if you can help it—you're too recognizable. If they see you up here, they'll know somethin's up. But if anyone tries to get away, stop 'em."

"Be careful, Sadie-girl," the sheriff said. He touched her cheek softly, then he turned to me.

"Clyde, I want you to have this."

Sheriff Hodges offered me a well-worn piece of wood, vaguely curved in the shape of a gun. Ol' Trusty. I hesitated, reluctant to take it, but he pushed it forward into my hands.

"Ain't much to look at," he said, "but she won't let you down. You stay strong and aim straight, and you won't lose a fight with that gun in your hand."

"Thank you, sir," I said, taking the battered piece of wood. I knew the meaning of such a gift was huge. Even if the weapon was useless, his faith in me should've bolstered me. But as I tucked Ol' Trusty into my belt, all I felt was the sinking sensation that this whole thing was hopeless. Our enemies had guns and dynamite, and I was going into battle armed with a stick.

The sheriff, on the other hand, looked stronger than I'd ever seen him. He gave me a satisfied nod, then his eyes flashed as he snapped a sharp salute. "Now let's hunt some outlaws!" He declared, sounding for all the world like a general about to lead a charge.

"This way," I said, and Sadie followed me, leaving Sheriff Hodges behind us. We kept low as we got closer to the lake, ducking behind boulders and zigzagging through the dips and ravines. Then Sadie stopped me.

"I think we should start it now, in case anyone spots us," she said. "We don't want to look like we're sneaking in."

"Okay," I agreed. "But this is my acting debut, so go easy on me."

"You've got one job," she said. "Just pretend like you don't want to be here. Drag your feet a little—jist a little though, you don't *actually* want to make this hard for me—and maybe struggle against my hold a few times. It looks like I had to beat you up to get you here, remember?"

"Oh yeah," I said, rubbing my sore jaw.

"Here, give me your hands." Sadie dug in her pack for the rope.

"Not too tight now, remember?" I warned her. "I've got to be able to get out of it without a problem, even with this hand all mummified."

"I remember," Sadie said. We'd practiced my escape a few times already. I'd been able to pull free of the rope without too much effort, even with the awkwardness of my burned right hand, all bound up in field dressings from the sheriff's bag. When Sadie finished tying it, I tugged a little and was relieved to find the knot had plenty of wiggle room.

"I think that'll work just fine," I said. "I'm ready. Let's do this."

"Right," Sadie repeated. "Let's do this."

She closed her eyes, folded her hands in front of her, and took a deep breath. A count of three passed, and when she opened her eyes again, she wasn't Sadie anymore.

I sensed the change the instant she became him. It was uncanny how entirely she shifted. Her whole posture morphed; her shoulders slumped, her eyes narrowed, and the rhythm of her steps fell into Duke's loping gait. She sniffed, rubbing under her nose with the back of her hand, and spat on the ground. I sneaked a glance at her and found myself looking at Duke, no less real to me even now that I knew the truth about him. It was downright spooky.

"All good?" I asked Sadie.

"Shut yer yap," Duke growled back at me. He grabbed me roughly by the elbow and half-dragged, half-marched me forward at a quick pace. He smacked the back of my head. "What, you excited to be here or somethin'?" he sneered at me.

I got Sadie's hint, and hung my head, trying to look like I'd been cowed and defeated.

We were close; the glimmering waters of Goldwater Lake were visible when we crested the next rocky rise. I could hardly remember the peaceful feeling that had enveloped me the last time I saw this lake. Sadie-Duke shoved me down the incline toward the lakeshore. Loose pebbles and dirt skidded out from under me and I struggled to keep my footing. I couldn't shake the feeling that we were walking straight into our doom.

We spotted the Pasadena brothers before they spotted us. Clint was nowhere to be seen, but the other two sat on the shore of the lake, exactly where I'd stood a few days ago. They had their backs to us as Bud spat a sticky brown stream of tobacco and Epaphroditus tossed rocks into the water; apparently they weren't expecting company. They'd propped Pa up with his back against the Golden Tater monument and tied him there, but one look at him told me the ropes were unnecessary. Pa wasn't going anywhere. He slumped limply to one side, gagged with a dirty bandana. His battered face was still, and though his chest rose and fell a bit with each painful, shallow breath he took, that was the only sign of life he gave. My blood boiled. I wanted to throw our plan out the window right then and there, to charge in and take down those dirty scumbags with my bare hands. Sadie must've sensed me stiffening, because she breathed an almost imperceptible "Steady, Clyde," into my ear, even as she gave me a rough shove forward.

"Hey, boys," Sadie-Duke called. "How come nobody invited me to this here Sunday School picnic?"

Even though we'd talked our plan through about a million times on the way over here, I still jumped when Sadie launched it into action. I wasn't ready, I knew that. I also knew if I waited till I *was* ready, we'd never act at all.

But there was no going back now. Bud and Epaphroditus scrambled to their feet and whirled to face us, looking guilty. But as soon as it registered with them that Sadie and I were intruders, and not Clint coming to make them sorry for goofing off on the job, they rallied.

"Who are you?" Bud demanded, his gun in his hand instantly.

My heart started galloping and I instinctively shrunk away, but Sadie held me firm.

"Relax," she drawled, not acknowledging the gun as she fixed them with a smirk. "I'm on your side here."

"You better make it plain what you mean by that and quick," Bud said, pulling back the hammer on his gun.

"Well I ain't with Hodges, and I sure ain't with Outlaw Jack," Sadie said. "So whose side do you think I'm on, ya beanhead?"

Bud frowned.

"Beanhead?" he repeated, squinting suspiciously at Sadie. "What kind of insult is that supposed to be?"

The kind a twelve-year-old girl would use, I realized, cold sweat streaking down my back. Sadie's grip on my elbow tightened. If she was making slipups like that, I knew she had to be scared.

"Think we oughta call for Clint?" Epaphroditus asked Bud in a whisper that probably could've been heard a hundred yards out.

"I'd vote for that," Sadie answered before Bud had a chance to open his big mouth. "It's him I wanna see, seein' how he's the one callin' the shots around here."

Sadie had touched a nerve. Bud stiffened, then drew himself up to his full towering height and glowered down at us.

"He ain't the boss of me," thundered Bud, narrowing his eyes. "Anything you say to me's same as if you said it to him."

"An equal partnership, huh? How very modern and advanced of you fellas."

I kept my head down to hide the growing alarm on my face. *Dangit Sadie*, my mind screamed. *Why'd you have to make Duke such a cocky character? His smart mouth's gonna get us killed!*

"Look," snapped Bud. "You gonna say yer piece, or am I gonna be obliged to put a bullet in ya?"

"Fine, if you're in such a hurry," Sadie shrugged, unfazed. "Look, I'll tell you plain: you've been duped. You're wastin' your time out here. You ain't gonna see a single speck of the Cactus Poke gold if you don't listen to *me* instead of that two-timer there." She jerked her head toward Pa.

"Listen to you? Jist who did you say you were again?"

"Name's Duke Hastings. We've met a couple times, down in Cactus Poke. Sheriff Hodges thinks I'm his deputy." Sadie laughed a nasty sort of laugh. "Jist like he thinks *you're* the federal marshal."

"Hastings? *Duke Hastings?*" Bud repeated. "Hang on, you can't mean old Deuces Duke, who used to ride with the James gang in Missouri way back after the War?"

Sadie hesitated just a beat too long. Neither of us had counted on Duke getting recognized. I made a mental note to advise her against basing characters on real people, assumed dead or otherwise.

"I'm impressed." Sadie recovered, hiding her surprise with a smirk. She dipped her head, touching the brim of my black hat. "You know your outlaws."

Bud narrowed his eyes. "Thought you was long dead," he said.

I gulped. He wasn't buying it. We were about to get called on our bluff, and then what? It'd all be over then. But while I teetered on the verge of panic, Sadie kept her head.

"Well, how *else* are you s'posed to get out of the James gang?" she shrugged, like it was the most obvious thing in the world. "Can't jist walk up to a whiner-baby like Jesse James and say 'Adios, and thanks for the memories.' Not unless you jist like gettin' shot."

"You sayin' you faked your death?" Bud squinted at her. "And what, you've been hidin' out in the wilds of Arizona ever since? What's that been, twenty years or so?"

"Bounced around a bit before I settled here." Sadie nodded. "But I ain't stupid, Bud, and neither are you." I could tell she was trying to steer the conversation back where we needed it to be, and I prayed with all my might that it worked.

"Jist spit it out, Hastings, or quit wasting my time," Bud snapped. He didn't lower his gun, but when I sneaked a glance at him, he looked far less confident than before. A trace of uncertainty flickered across his face, bordering on nervousness. Apparently riding with the James gang gives you some clout in the outlaw world.

"I know as well as you there's somethin' to be had here in Goldwater," Sadie-Duke said. "Why do you think I cozied up to old Hodges for so long? Thought maybe he knew a thing or two about the gold's whereabouts. But that old coot's crazy as a horny toad." Sadie flinched as she said it, but covered it in another harsh laugh. It was the first time I'd heard her—or any of her characters, for that matter—say a word against the sheriff.

"Course we know that," Bud said. "Anyone with eyes can see he's mad. But we got no use for Hodges anymore. We were only usin' him to get at Jack, anyway."

"And now you got him," Sadie nodded towards Pa. "But somethin' tells me he's bein' less than helpful. What'd he tell you? That the gold's at the lake?"

"*Under* it," Epaphroditus grinned, but Bud smacked the back of his head.

"Quiet you," he hissed.

"Under the lake?" Sadie laughed easily. "That's rich. That'll keep you busy a good while."

"Whaddaya mean by that?" Bud's gun wavered, and he glanced at his brother uncomfortably.

"Jack knows you're keeping him alive till you got the gold in hand, jist in case he's lyin', right?"

"Well yeah, but—"

"So it makes sense he'd tell you the gold was in the most inconvenient spot so you'd waste loads of time tryin' to git at it while he thinks up a way to escape."

"'Cept he didn't ever say the gold was at the bottom of the lake," Bud countered. "We figured that part out ourselves. Jack ain't talked since the ridge. Not a word since we blew up his hideout. And let me tell you, we tried. All he said was there were mountains of gold at the lake, and there ain't any place he could've hid it here 'cept underwater."

"Well, he lied," Sadie shrugged with a disdainful sniff. "He's conning you again. Probably waiting for the right moment to slip away and go get his *real* stash himself."

"How'd you know that?" Epaphroditus whined.

"You've only got half the puzzle," Sadie said, shoving me forward. "I've got the other half."

"A kid?" Bud raised a doubtful eyebrow.

"*His* kid." Sadie grabbed my hair and pulled—harder than was necessary, I thought—forcing me to look up at Bud. "Lookee here and tell me that ain't the same face as Ol' Jack over there. They've even got matching shiners."

The outlaw brothers leaned in close, eyeing me critically. I didn't dare meet their eyes for fear they'd see right through me and read the whole truth. They looked from me to Pa and back again, and it didn't take more than a glance to convince them.

"Does Clint know about this?" Epaphroditus said, grabbing Bud's elbow. "That Jack's got a son?"

"Who cares if Clint knows?" Bud shook him off. "He ain't here, is he?" He shoved his brother away and refocused on Sadie. "What you're tellin' me is, Jack had a partner he managed to keep secret from us?"

"Yep," Sadie said. "And it don't seem to be his best idea neither. This kid knew everything."

"He talked?"

"Squealed like a stuck pig," sneered Sadie. "If you want the whereabouts of the gold, I'm your man."

"What's in it for you?" Bud frowned, suspicious. "Why tell us any of this at all, when you could jist as easily slip off and git the gold on your own?"

"I want Hodges." Sadie said. "You can have all the gold you want, but when this is all over, you're gonna turn the old man and his pathetic little town over to me."

Bud and Epaphroditus exchanged a doubtful glance.

Sadie and I had debated this point of the plan—she argued it wouldn't be believable enough that Duke would just hand them the location to a treasure without requiring a cut of it. She thought it would raise suspicion if he was willing to give that kind of information away in exchange for next to nothing. But I was more concerned with getting the Pasadenas to take our bait than I was with telling a watertight story. I didn't want to give them any reason to refuse Duke's help, or worse, agree to his terms and then double-cross him once they got the information they wanted. Besides, if it all went south, at least we'd be sure the sheriff didn't fall into the wrong hands. In the end, Sadie gave in and decided to do it my way. Now we got to find out if I was right. I held my breath.

A long moment or two passed where my heartbeat pretty much doubled in speed.

"I think we can make that happen, *Sheriff Hastings*," Bud finally said.

"No!" I grunted, struggling against Sadie's hold. "You'll never rule Cactus Poke, you no-good, two-timing—*Ow!*"

"Pipe down, you!" Sadie smacked my ear. My cry of pain wasn't acting at all—I'd forgotten to warn her my ear had been damaged in the explosion. I still couldn't hear a thing from it, but I could feel a warm trickle of blood running out of it.

"So what about the kid?" Bud jerked his chin toward me.

"It's nice not to have loose ends, ya know?" Sadie-Duke grinned wickedly. "'Specially loose ends who like to talk."

It flickered across my mind that once the Pasadenas got what they wanted, Duke would be a loose end too. I shoved down the lump of fear that formed in my throat. If all went according to plan, we wouldn't let it get to that point.

Bud grunted in agreement. "Put him there with the other, then," he said. "And tell us where that gold is."

Sadie dragged me over to the stone marker and shoved me to the ground beside Pa.

"Work fast," She whispered before turning back to the brothers on the lakeshore.

"Gold's hid real good. Here," she said, grabbing a stick and tracing it through the soft mud. "I'll draw you a map so you can git an idea of what we're lookin' at."

Sadie had the brothers' full attention as she started sketching out the map on the ground. As soon as no one was looking my way, I pulled at the ropes on my wrists. They came free easy, like we'd practiced.

"Pa," I whispered, shaking his shoulder. "Pa, can you hear me?"

Sadie kept explaining her map, louder than she probably needed to, but I was grateful for the cover as Pa groaned. He opened his swollen eyes just a slit, but when he saw me they widened.

"Don't make a sound," I whispered. "It's okay. We're getting you out of here."

"Billy Bob Clyde!" Pa choked as soon as I untied his gag. "I thought I'd lost you, sure and certain. How'd you get out of the tunnel alive? What happened to Sadie?"

"She's fine, but I can't explain it all now." I worked at the ropes tied around his chest. It took me longer than I liked, but I got him loose. "We have to get you somewhere safe. Can you walk?" I reached down to help him to his feet, but he grabbed my wrist and pulled me close.

"There ain't anywhere safe. They're crazy, Clyde," Pa hissed, his eyes feverish and wild. "They've got it in their heads the gold's at the bottom of the lake. They're gonna blow it up—drain the lake, flood the whole valley, and destroy the town."

"They're gonna *WHAT?*" I gasped, shock streaking up my back.

Sadie threw a warning glance over her shoulder that told me she'd heard me, even if the Pasadenas hadn't. *Hurry it up!* She mouthed at me.

"They've already set the charges," Pa said. "See there?" he pointed to a little box a few yards beyond us. A plunger handle stuck out of its top, and a dark cord ran from it and disappeared off into the woods beyond the shore. "There's a heap of dynamite on the other end of that fuse. When they push the handle on that blasting machine, it'll blow the whole low shore. Clint's gone round to check the charges before he fires a signal shot. You've gotta stop him, Clyde. If the lake goes everything will be lost—the town, the oil, all of it. And probably all of us with it."

"The low shore?" I said, my eyes widening. "But the sheriff's out there. He'll be caught in the blast if he's anywhere nearby when it goes off!"

"Go, Clyde," Pa urged, pushing me to get up even though he grimaced with every movement. "You've gotta stop him."

"I can't leave you here," I shook my head. "And Sadie, we can't abandon Sadie. She can only hold them so long."

Pa glanced over at Sadie-Duke, and understanding crossed his face.

"I'll cover for Sadie," Pa grunted, getting painfully to his feet.

"No offense, Pa, but you don't look like you oughta be covering for anybody."

"We got no choice, son," Pa put his hands on my shoulders and looked me square in the eyes. "If you've ever wanted to be the hero, now's your moment. Without you, we ain't got a prayer."

Now's your moment.

I took a deep breath. "Okay," I said with a resolute nod. "I...I love you, Pa."

He opened his mouth to respond, but instead his eyes focused on something far away, across the lake.

"What now?" Pa murmured.

I followed his gaze and saw, to my surprise, a lone, black-clad figure standing in the gap between the mountains where the river filled the lake—exactly where I'd seen one a few days ago.

The figure took off his hat and waved it back and forth.

"Is it Clint?" I choked. "Is that the signal?"

"No," Pa said. "Clint's signal would be a gunshot."

"So who is *that*? And is he signaling *us*?"

We didn't have to wait long for answers.

A sharp whistle split the air from somewhere in the trees to our left, followed by an answering one from the trees to our right. Sadie and the Pasadenas startled from their study of the map-drawing in the mud. Sadie's hands flew to her face in a very un-Duke-like gesture. Bud whirled toward me and Pa, drawing his gun again.

"Hey!" he barked. "Jist whaddaya think yer—"

But he didn't have a chance to finish his sentence. From the trees rang out a shout:

"*Te tenemos rodeado! Mantén tus manos a la vista!*"

We have you surrounded! Keep your hands in sight!

16

CACTUS POKE'S LAST STAND

WE didn't have a chance to react before a thundering roar of hoofbeats surrounded us. Nine riders burst out from the trees—five from one side, four more from the other— and encircled us. Bud's gun went off, but he didn't hit anything; he just added to the sudden confusion.

I didn't get a good look at any of the riders before they started attacking. One jumped from his horse and took down Epaphroditus first, wrestling him to the ground and shoving his face in the dirt. I didn't have time to celebrate though, because the next rider grabbed Sadie. She screamed, kicking at his shins. She broke away from him as he curled over in pain. But she only ran a few steps before another one threw a lasso around her, pinning her arms to her sides and yanking her down into the mud.

"Sadie!" I yelled, but my shout was lost in the chaos.

They took Pa without a fight. He was hardly able to stagger to his feet before they had him down again with his hands cuffed behind his back.

"Please, he's hurt!" I yelled. I tried to run to him, but one of the riders jumped off his horse and landed squarely between me and Pa. He came at me, but I ducked away before he could grab me. He gathered himself and lunged forward again, and this time I got a good look at his face.

I stopped dodging. I knew this man.

"Marco?" I panted. "Marco Casado? Is that you?"

Marco froze and blinked at me. The shock on his face lasted only a second before it broke into a wide grin.

"Jovencito!" he exclaimed.

I looked around. The attack was over as quick as it had begun—and I was the only one left standing. Bud and Epaphroditus Pasadena were down and bound, but so were Sadie and Pa.

"Marco, what's going on? Who are those guys, and why'd they attack us?"

Marco didn't answer. "Look, amigos!" he called to the other riders. "It's our little *Jovencito*, popped up again from nowhere!"

The other eight riders turned toward us at Marco's shout, and smiles broke out all around. At the sight of them, my own spirits shot through the roof. I couldn't believe my eyes! It was the whole band, the Mexican bounty hunters who'd taken me in and let me travel with them from West Texas all the way up to the edge of the desert. There wasn't a man among them I wouldn't count as a friend.

Marco reached out and ruffled my hair. "I am very glad to see that you did not die in the desert, my friend!"

"Not this time," I replied, laughing in relief. "You have no idea how happy I am to see you! Sadie! Pa!" I called. "Don't worry, these are the good guys! We're saved!" I turned back to Marco. "What are you doing here? I thought you all were headed down to the border!"

"We got a better offer," Marco said. "A federal marshal was looking for a posse to ride with him to confront some suspicious behavior up here in the Bitterroot Mountains." Marco gave my shoulder a friendly slap. "The men and I thought of you often on our ride through the desert—all of us prayed you made it to California all right."

"Well, I didn't make it to California," I said. "But I definitely got where I needed to go, no mistake."

"Clyde, help me out here, would ya?" Sadie called to me. I turned away from Marco to find Sadie seated in the lakeshore mud, smushed between Bud and Epaphroditus. "If these fellas are the good guys like you say," she groaned. "They've got a funny way of showing it."

"It's a misunderstanding. We'll get it all sorted out, Sadie," I said, stepping towards her, putting out my hand to help her to her feet. But Marco stopped me.

"Perhaps we will wait for the marshal before we make any decisions, friend," he said, putting a firm hand on my shoulder. I frowned at him.

"But Sadie's my partner," I protested. "Those are your bad guys, right there." I pointed to the Pasadenas.

"I am sure you are right," Marco said, but he sounded unconvinced. He didn't release his hold on me. "We will wait for the marshal, though."

"Well he better get here soon, cause we ain't got much time at all before—" I didn't finish before I caught sight of the *real* federal marshal coming toward us. He was a dark-clad man, definitely the same figure I'd seen on the lake's far shore. He broke through the trees and strode across the beach.

"Well, Señor Casado," he said in a gruff, gravelly voice. "Looks like you and your men got more than you bargained for here."

"Nothing we could not handle, sir," Marco replied with a businesslike nod. "I think you will find we have made good on our promise."

"Is that our man?"

"It is." Marco nodded again. "*El Bandido del Sombrero Negro.* The Black-Hat Bandit, Outlaw Jack."

All my hopes turned to ash. These men, my friends, weren't here to help us. They were here to arrest Pa!

"No, you've got it wrong," I said, but nobody was listening to me. One of the bounty hunters pulled out a wrinkled wanted poster of Outlaw Jack and handed it the marshal.

"You boys oughta be proud of yourselves," the marshal said, nodding grimly at the posse. "This fella is wanted in every county between the Mississippi and the Pacific. Worth more than twice his weight in gold. I'll see you're well rewarded."

The bounty hunters cheered. Even Marco let out a celebratory whistle, the traitor. Pa, looking like anything but a heartless criminal, barely conscious and bloodied beyond recognition, didn't offer any defense.

"All due respect, señors." Bud Pasadena cleared his throat. "But my brother and me here are jist a couple of petty crooks, not near on par with the likes of Outlaw Jack."

"And we ain't worth nothin' to you by comparison," Epaphroditus piped up. "Hardly even worth the cost of the trip to St. Louis to fetch the reward for bringin' us in."

"Even callin' it a reward is a bit generous," Bud agreed. "It'll be pocket change compared to what you'll git from Jack here. Not even worth the effort, I say."

"I bet you do," Sadie growled. "Don't listen to him, Marshal, sir! He's lying!"

"And jist who are *you* to be tellin' *me* what to do?" demanded the marshal, narrowing his eyes at Sadie.

"Well, I'll be darned, Mr. Marshal, sir," Bud answered before Sadie could open her mouth. "I forgot to tell you the best part. As it turns out, your day jist got luckier. That there is Deuces Duke Hastings! Me and my brother here did you the service of trackin' him down!"

"What?" the marshal gasped. His eyes widened. "Hastings? Duke Hastings? Not the one from the James gang?" He shook his head in disbelief. "There were rumors every now and again that maybe he survived and escaped out West, but that trail's been cold twenty years."

"It's Deuces Duke! The very one!" Epaphroditus nodded, too eagerly. "Said so himself. He came in here braggin' up a storm 'bout how he faked his own death to give Jesse James the slip, and how he wants to take down Ol' Sheriff Hodges so he can run this town himself!"

"I am not either Duke Hastings, you illiterate skunk," Sadie snapped, using her real voice this time. She wiped the side of her face on her shoulder, and Duke's scar rubbed right off her cheek, leaving a ghastly smear. I could make out a few of her freckles peeping through the ruined makeup mess. It gave Sadie a repulsive likeness to a wax sculpture left too close to the fireplace. The Pasadenas—and the marshal too, for that matter—drew back with horrified stares.

"Honestly," Sadie continued, rolling her eyes. "It's hard to imagine how much of a pea-brain you have to be to confuse a full-grown man with a twelve-year-old girl!"

I don't know if Sadie realized she'd lumped me and the sheriff into that same pea-brain category, but I held my tongue.

"Hold up," Bud said, recovering himself. "If you ain't Deuces Duke, who *are* you, anyway?"

"Like I'd tell you, scum," Sadie hissed, turning away from Bud. "Would thou wert clean enough to spit upon!"

"Was that...Shakespeare?" asked the marshal, looking more confused with each passing second.

"Look here," I interrupted, grabbing the marshal's arm and forcing his attention off of Sadie and Bud. "It's a long, convoluted story. But there's no time! No time for any of this. We can sort it out later, but right now we have a serious problem, and we've got to act now!"

"Señor Casado?" The marshal shook my grip off and turned to Marco without even acknowledging I'd spoken. "Who is this kid and why didn't anyone arrest him? I thought you had orders to take down any suspicious persons."

"I can vouch for him, señor. He's one of us."

"One of who? One of you? He don't look much like a bounty hunter, Casado." The marshal jerked his chin toward Pa, giving me a significant look. "And he *does* look an awful lot like the bad guys, if you get my drift."

"But he is not, I swear it," Marco insisted, putting a protective hand on my shoulder. "Ask any one of these men. He's one of us."

"Then what's he doing involved with the likes of these fellas? If those really are the Pasadena brothers out of St. Louis, then there's three confirmed outlaws here, counting the notorious Outlaw Jack, and—" the marshal cut his eyes toward Sadie "—one shady character of unknown loyalty or origin."

"I cannot speak for the rest of them, señor," Marco shrugged. "I am sure he has a story to tell. But this I can tell you for sure: there's not an outlaw bone in Jovencito's body."

"I told you, I *can* explain, sir," I said. "But not right now. Right now, you've *got* to help me! These guys you've got here are just the lackeys; the real criminal—his name's Clint Pasadena, sir—he's still on the loose out there somewhere, and—"

"We'll get to that, boy," the marshal said, waving away my protests. "He can't get far. And I need to sort through..." he gestured vaguely at

Sadie, Pa, and the Pasadenas. "Whatever the heck is going on here, first."

"Go, Clyde," Pa whispered, his rasping voice weak, but urgent. "He said you ain't under arrest. So go, now! We'll be fine!"

I looked from Pa to Sadie. She nodded earnestly at me, wide-eyed.

"Go on, Clyde," Sadie whispered. "It's up to you now!"

"Now hang on one minute—" the marshal said, stepping toward me. I didn't wait for him to finish.

I ran.

"Hey! Kid! I didn't say—" but I didn't hear the rest as I sprinted into the trees.

Apparently I did have a little bit of outlaw in me, after all.

I KEPT on running, hard and fast as I could, my feet pounding the shoreline as I darted through the trees. I followed the fuse, which ran like an infinite, deadly snake along the ground. At the end of it, I knew I'd find enough explosives to blast us all to the moon and back. And somehow, someway, I had to stop it.

I was panting and my side was aching by the time I came to a little clearing. The lake trickled out into a narrow stream, which ran off away toward the foothills, and Cactus Poke beyond. Sure enough, right at the stream's mouth sat a pile of dynamite, staring menacingly up at me.

My heart pounded. If this thing blew, it wouldn't just cause a flood— it'd be a mudslide of epic proportions, followed by all the water in the lake. It would sweep up every tree and stone and living creature in its path until it became an oozing monster only a nightmare could conjure. When it reached Cactus Poke, it would level the town in the time it took to blink.

I couldn't let that happen. I knelt beside the dynamite, taking care not to jostle it at all, or breathe on it, or even look at it wrong.

"How the heck am I supposed to disable this?" I demanded of the woods. "I don't know a doggone thing about explosives!"

I remembered the blasting machine back on the far shore. Marco and his men had the Pasadena brothers tied up. As long as no one could get to the plunger handle, no one could detonate the charges. Surely the bounty hunters wouldn't let Bud and Epaphroditus get loose…right? But was I willing to bet my life—not to mention the whole town and millions of dollars in oil—on that? Besides, there was a third Pasadena brother still on the prowl out here somewhere. If he got near the blasting machine, we'd all be history.

"Come on, Clyde, think!" I couldn't stand there doing nothing forever. At any minute, the situation could go south, and I sure didn't want to be standing next to a pile of explosives when it did. I looked down at the ground and spotted the fuse, trailing away through the woods.

It stood to reason that without the fuse, the dynamite wouldn't detonate. So if I cut the fuse, that would disable it, right? I wasn't sure if it would work—I wasn't sure about anything, other than that a heck of a lot was riding on this dynamite not exploding. I had to try. I patted my pockets for my knife, but came up empty. I groaned, remembering I'd loaned it to Sadie so she could give California Jackson's wig a haircut. Without my knife on me, I'd have to get creative.

I looked around, feeling for any sharp rocks I could use to saw the fuse. It was useless; I was in a stream bed. Every single stone nearby was worn smooth and polished by years of trickling water. Not a sharp edge in sight.

In a desperate attempt, I grabbed a length of the fuse off the ground and yanked on it with my teeth. That was hopeless from the start. I might just as well have tried to chew my way through the mountain itself. The fuse was sturdy, and my teeth weren't made for gnawing though fibers.

"The *one* time having a jackrabbit around would actually be helpful, and he's nowhere to be found!" I grunted in exasperation, spitting out the fuse.

"Too bad, really," a smooth voice answered. I about jumped out of my skin.

Clint Pasadena grabbed me by the collar and hauled me up out of the stream bed.

"Best not to stand too close, kid," he sneered as he dragged me away from the charges. "But I'll make sure you get a good view."

"You're insane!" I shouted, swinging blindly with my fist. Somehow I landed the punch, directly on his jaw. His head jerked back, but he didn't release his grip on me. Blood trickled from the corner of his mouth.

"That wasn't wise," he hissed at me, grabbing at my throat.

"Put the boy down, outlaw scum," a commanding voice rang out over us. Clint paused. It was the first time I'd ever seen him look surprised. His head swiveled in the direction where the command had come from. I could've cheered.

Sheriff Hodges stood on a rocky ledge overlooking the shore where Clint held me. He stood tall and strong, his shoulders square and his head held high. He looked for all the world like a general in a painting, charging toward certain victory. That little star pinned to his vest could've been a Congressional Medal of Honor and it wouldn't have made him look one speck more grand and noble than he looked in that moment.

"I don't know if you've heard or not," the sheriff said, his voice firm. "But this here lake falls under the lawful jurisdiction of the town of Cactus Poke. And in case you didn't realize, the Law is respected in Cactus Poke." The sheriff's brilliant blue eyes glowered at Clint from underneath bushy eyebrows. "So I'd kindly suggest you and your motley bunch turn tail and crawl back into whatever slimy stinkhole you came from."

"Where's the gold, Hodges?" Clint demanded, releasing me. "I know you know. You wouldn't stay in this forsaken patch of desert if you didn't know where it was!"

"Nah." The sheriff shook his head. I could swear it almost looked like he pitied Clint. "What you don't git, what none of you money-grubbin' gold-hunters git," he said, "is that this town don't need gold to make it worth defendin'. This place matters cause the people who live here say so. This is our home, and we'll fight you for it down to the very last speck of dust!"

"You're lyin', Hodges!" Clint shouted back. Every remnant of his usually calm exterior was gone. He looked like a wild man, with his blazing eyes and blood running from the corner of his mouth. "You're lyin' and you're a fool! I've spent too many years huntin' the famed Cactus Poke gold, and I ain't leavin' a single tumbleweed unturned till I git my hands on it!" He snarled. "I'll git my gold if I have to level every single building in that miserable little dump you call a town. And not you, or Jack, or anyone else can stop me!"

"Oh, you want gold, do ya?" Sheriff Hodges smiled a knowing little smile, and he pulled from his bag the famous Goldwater Potato. Sunlight glinted off its shining surface as he held it up above his head. "This here is the only confirmed piece of gold in all of Goldwater County. Probably the only gold for a thousand miles in any direction. You want it?"

Clint stepped forward, greedy hands outstretched.

"So go and git it, why don't ya?" the sheriff yelled. He drew his arm back, then flung it, hard as he could. The Golden Tater sailed through the air like a meteor, sparkling all the way as it streaked across the sky. It landed with a satisfying splash in the center of Goldwater Lake, leaving behind only ripples.

Then Sheriff Lawrence Hodges laughed, long and strong.

"Boy, that was worth the tater's weight in gold jist to see the look on your face!" He said. "Like a kid who dropped his candy in the dirt! Ha! Still want my gold now? No? Well, all right then." His grin dropped instantly, and he leveled Clint with the sort of stare that could make enemy soldiers surrender on sight. Clint must've felt like he was staring down the barrel of a cannon.

"If gold's all you wanted," the sheriff said. "You'll kindly take note that it's gone now. So I suggest you git outta my town, for good and ever, ya hear?"

I didn't even see Clint draw his pistol. The crack of the gunshots— two in rapid succession— bounced over the calm waters and echoed off the mountains.

Sheriff Hodges crumpled. His body fell limply, tumbling off the rise where he'd stood so grand and glorious just moments ago. He landed hard on the rocks that bordered the lake below. There was a horrible splintering crack as his wooden leg split in two. He lay unmoving, half on the shore, half in the shallows. The water lapping around him began to stain red.

"No! Sheriff!" I screamed.

"Blow the charges!" Clint roared, his shout drowning out mine as he fired the signal shot into the air. "Do it now!"

There was no answer from across the lake.

"Blow the charges, you idiots!" Clint screamed again.

"You can't win this!" I shouted at him. "There's a federal marshal and a whole posse of bounty hunters over there—they already arrested your brothers, and I bet they heard those shots you just fired. They're probably headed this way now. Give up!"

Clint turned on me, his eyes wild, as if just then remembering I was there.

"I gotta do all the work around here myself, don't I?" he growled. He raised his pistol and fired again. I flinched, too late to brace myself for impact, but the shot missed, grazing the dirt several yards beyond me.

Clint spat a curse and took aim again, this time sidestepping me, getting me out of his line of fire. He wasn't aiming at me.

"No!" I shouted, diving at him as he pulled the trigger. I caught him around the knees, taking him to the ground with me. His shot skewed wild—I didn't see where it went, and I didn't care. All that mattered was that he didn't hit the dynamite.

"You're crazy!" I yelled. Clint thrashed in my grip, trying to shake me off, but I managed to keep hold of him. It was like trying to wrestle a crocodile—and the consequences if I let go would be no less devastating. "If you shoot those charges, we all blow up!"

Clint writhed, spewing a string of angry words I can't repeat, but I didn't let go. I grappled at him and he kicked at me and I clawed back. It was a desperate few seconds. Then Clint's boot connected with my jaw, and I lost my grip on him. Stars flashed in my vision as I tumbled away and came to a rolling stop in the soft lakeshore mud.

My head was reeling, but I forced myself back to my feet. I wasn't the only one who'd gotten back up though. Clint was panting, and he looked a little worse for the wear, with deep scratches marring his clean-cut face, but the madness in his eyes burned brighter than ever. His gun was still in his hand.

"You can't stop me, kid!" Clint rasped. "I intend to blow up this here lake and wipe the miserable little town of Cactus Poke off the map!"

I wasn't quick enough to stop him this time. He fired.

I blinked. No deafening explosion followed his shot. The dynamite didn't blow, and the lake was still intact.

But something wasn't right. I wasn't sure what, but something felt wrong. A long, frozen second passed where all I could hear was my own ragged breathing, and all I could see was Clint Pasadena's smug smirk.

Then my body caught up with what had happened. Searing pain tore through my side, and I staggered back a few steps, gasping at its sudden intensity. Something ominously warm and wet soaked through my shirt, spreading fast. I pressed my good hand over the spot where the pain was the sharpest.

It came away slick with blood.

"Holy smokes," I whispered, staring wide-eyed at my red-stained hand. Logic informed me that I'd been shot, but my own thoughts seemed to be coming from somewhere foggy and far away.

"Now git outta my way," Clint growled. He put a hand on my shoulder and shoved me down hard. I didn't—couldn't—resist. I went down to my knees.

He turned his back on me, took a clear aim at the pile of dynamite, and pulled the trigger.

I closed my eyes, waiting for the valley to start shaking, for the deafening roar that would tear through the mountains as the lake exploded. But all I heard instead was a hollow, empty *click*.

Clint spat a curse.

"Huh," I said, my voice sounding far away and tired, very tired. "Six-shooter, I guess?"

Clint didn't answer, but he didn't need to. The hatred that contorted his face when he looked at me spoke volumes all on its own.

"That makes this," I continued, flinching as I touched my bleeding side, "bullet number six, am I right?"

"I s'pose that's so," Clint growled at me. His voice sounded strained, as if he was working hard to keep his cool composure, but could explode any second. "And if my aim had been a bit better, we wouldn't be havin' this here talk. Looks like I just grazed you. Very clever," he spat, "making me waste shots like that. But you shouldn't have bothered. It'll all come out the same in the end." He holstered his empty gun and narrowed his eyes. "After all, there's more than one way to skin a cat."

And then, to my surprise, he started walking away, toward the woods.

"Wait," I croaked. "Where are you going?"

"To light this fuse myself," Clint snapped at me. "It'll be easier without you gettin' in my way, anyway."

I wanted to follow him, to stop him, but I couldn't move. I curled up in pain and said nothing.

"I suggest you start runnin', boy," Clint said, smiling at me with that unnervingly suave, controlled face of his. "If you don't fancy a one-way ticket to the moon, that is."

I could only manage a whimper by way of an answer.

"Oh, that's right. You can't run. You're hurt. Hm. Too bad, really," Clint sneered in mock pity. "Well, I hope you enjoy the fireworks, at least. I'm sure they'll be real pretty from up close." He grinned wickedly at me. "Hold tight now. The show starts in about two minutes."

Clint laughed at his own cleverness and strode away into the woods. Through the trees, I could hear him whistling.

Two minutes. That's all I had. Two minutes till Goldwater Lake shot sky-high and Cactus Poke was history. Two minutes till a million-dollar future was lost forever. Two minutes left to breathe.

Come on, Marco, where are you?

But Marco didn't come bursting through the trees to my rescue. Neither did Sadie. Or the federal marshal. Or Pa. Or anybody.

Ninety seconds.

Clint would be cutting off the fuse now, making a new end he could light…now he'd be kneeling beside it, his crazy eyes sparkling with nasty delight as he pulled out his matchbook… now he'd be striking a match down near the frayed edge of the fuse, humming a satisfied little tune to himself as a small flame blazed up with a sulfuric hiss…any second now…

"No," I grunted through gritted teeth. This story needed a different ending than the one Clint had planned. It took every ounce of strength I had, but I pulled myself to my feet, ignoring the screaming pain in my… well, my everywhere.

Sixty seconds.

There wasn't time to think about the pain. Gasping, I forced myself to move. I staggered straight toward the creek mouth, where the pile of dynamite leered at me menacingly. I struggled to scoop it up, filling my arms with huge bundles of charges, and stumbled into the lake's shallows. The icy mountain water snatched my breath away, but I didn't stop. I splashed on forward.

It was a strange moment to laugh, and maybe loss of blood was making me feel lightheaded, but as I caught sight of my bandaged hand once again clutching dynamite, I actually giggled a bit.

"You know, Clyde, this can't become a habit," I mumbled to myself. I could just see the headlines now:

LOCAL IDIOT PICKS UP EXPLOSIVES NOT ONCE, BUT TWICE IN ONE DAY

The water was at my waist now. I stopped. This was as far as I could run. I started to swim as best I could with my arms still hugging my deadly burden tight against my chest. It was all but impossible to keep my face above the icy water, which stung my cheeks and burned my lungs. I thrashed my legs furiously, trying to put as much distance between me and the shore as I could. My boots filled with water and tried to drag me down, so I kicked them off. They sank immediately.

Thirty seconds.

Finally, just when I felt I couldn't swim another stroke, I let go, shoving the explosives forward. They disappeared into the depths, still trailing their long fuses like deadly tentacles. I could only pray I'd gotten them far enough away from shore.

"Clyde, get out of there! Swim, Clyde!" somehow Sadie's scream from the opposite shore reached my ringing ears, and I snapped back as if waking from a fuzzy dream.

Ten seconds.

"Holy smokes!" I gasped. I was in the middle of a lake, treading water directly above enough dynamite to blow up a mountain! I took a deep gulp of air and tore through the water towards the shore as fast as my arms could pull me.

Two seconds.

I was a few lengths from shore when the lake exploded. I felt the charge go off before I heard it. Every individual drop of water around me seemed to stand perfectly still, then begin to rumble all at once. I pulled myself up onto the shore, shaking and panting, just in time to see a huge tower of water shoot skyward, exploding with a roar like an upside-down waterfall. The whole valley shook. Then, as the water crashed back to the lake where it belonged, a massive wave radiated from the explosion site and came charging to shore.

I barely had time to hold my breath before the wave crashed over me. It catapulted me far up out of the lake and onto the shore...straight toward where Clint Pasadena stood, shaking with rage.

By the time the wave caught Clint, it was still at waist-level, and it hit him hard, pushing him backward with a force impossible to withstand. He stumbled, then landed on his backside on the shore. He was soaked straight through to his chest.

As the wave retreated, he was up again in an instant, snarling like a mad dog.

Displaced lake water fell around us like soft rain. It was a strange moment to be struck by how peaceful it felt. Maybe I was losing it, maybe the loss of blood and the rush of adrenaline had gone to my head—but I could've sworn the droplets raining down on us glittered. Almost like they were infused with tiny shards of gold.

"You'll pay for that, kid!" Clint shrieked at me. His eyes held the wild look of a rabid dog. "This whole miserable town will pay!"

"No. It's you who's gonna pay," I snapped, drawing myself to my full height and raising my chin defiantly. "You, Clint Pasadena, will pay for what you did to Sadie's theater. You'll pay for spreading lies about my Pa. And most of all, you'll pay for what you did to Sheriff Hodges!"

Sheriff Hodges.

Of course! He'd already given me everything I needed. I reached for my holster, and my hand grasped smooth wood. I drew out Ol' Trusty, a slow smile spreading across my face.

"Ain't much to look at," the sheriff's words came back to me, *"but she won't let you down. You stay strong and aim straight, and you won't lose a fight with that gun in your hand."*

"Oh, I'll pay, will I?" Clint scoffed at me. "And who's gonna make me, you? What are you gonna do, shoot me?"

Stay strong. Aim straight.

"Lucky for me," I said. "My gun doesn't run out of bullets."

I swung Ol' Trusty as hard as I could at Clint's head, California Jackson-style. I landed the hit with a solid *thunk* against his skull. Clint's eyes went wide in shock for half a second before he crumpled at my feet.

Finally—*finally*—I heard the thunder of approaching hoofbeats.

I looked down at the piece of wood clutched in my shaking hands. "Thanks, Sheriff," I choked.

The federal marshal, flanked by Marco and another rider, burst through the trees toward me. They all had their guns drawn and looked ready for a fight, but they stopped when they saw me, still standing, and Clint, sprawled out on the ground in front of me.

"The sheriff needs help," I said without preamble to the closest of the riders, and I hoped with all my heart that it was still true. He nodded at me wordlessly, and galloped off to where the sheriff had fallen. Marco picked Clint up out of the mud, handcuffed him, and slung him—none too gently—across the back of his saddle.

I sank down weakly, sitting in the mud. My head felt airy, and I realized faintly that I was still bleeding. But we'd done it. We'd actually done it. I closed my eyes and breathed a deep breath. The fight was over, and we'd won.

"Clyde!" Sadie's voice brought me back. I opened my eyes to find her standing right over me, looking like a total mess. Tears and mud streaked through her makeup, and her Duke wig was gone, leaving her ratty braids all askew. But she couldn't have looked any prettier to me in that moment, not even if she'd been Cinderella in her glittering ballgown.

"You're all right!" I said, choking on the words.

"*I'm* all right? *Me?*" Sadie snapped, her face incredulous. The Cinderella illusion vanished instantly. This was just-plain-Sadie, through and through. But somehow that didn't make me any less happy to see her.

"Look at you!" she yelled at me. "Who do you think you are, some sort of hero or something? You've been shot, ya beanhead, and near well blown to bits, and half-drowned, and you're happy to see that *I'm* all right?"

"Yeah," I said, laughing weakly. "I guess I am."

Sadie's lower lip quivered for a second, then she threw her arms around my neck and held me tight. That hug hurt like the dickens, but I wouldn't have let her stop, not for all the gold in California.

"Hate to interrupt, but we need to get you some help," The federal marshal said, placing a heavy hand on my shoulder. "The bounty hunters have a medic, and he's with your father now. We'll get you to him. And here I was thinkin' nothing ever happened in Goldwater County." He ran a hand through his graying hair and looked at me with a little bit of wonder. "That was some quick thinkin', kid, takin' the explosives out into the lake. Plumb stupid, but brave. And then taking down an outlaw…with a *fake gun,* of all the wild notions! Now I've seen everything." He shook his head in disbelief at Ol' Trusty.

"Oh, that?" I shrugged, rubbing the fading bump on my own head and slipping a teasing smile at Sadie. "Just a little trick I picked up from an outlaw."

EPILOGUE

IT was a beautiful spot, up at the crest of Goldwater Ridge. The best for miles around. Behind us, the mountains rose up, their peaks and dips all golden in the setting sun. Goldwater Lake glimmered like a jewel dropped into the valley. Below us, at the base of the ridge, the town of Cactus Poke stood, pretty and perfect as a doll village staged against the backdrop of the wide-open desert beyond. Streaks of brilliant orange splashed across the pink Arizona sky in one of the most breathtaking sunsets I'd ever seen. It was perfect.

"You'd like it here," I said to the fresh grave in front of me, tears threatening to choke out my voice. I knelt, resting my hand on the headstone. "Prettiest little spot in all of Goldwater County."

"Peaceful, too," Sadie added softly, putting a comforting hand on my shoulder. "Exactly as it should be."

I sniffed and blinked hard up into the sky.

"Goodbyes are hard," I said finally. "So I won't say one. I'll just say thanks. You did more for me than save my life. You helped me get on the right path, helped me see what was really important. Life won't be the same without you, but it'll be forever better for having you in it. I'll never forget you."

"Nobody will," Sadie said, squeezing my shoulder. I put my hand over hers, grateful for her strong and steady presence, even though I knew she was grieving too.

"I'll…say a few words, if I can," Pa said, clearing his throat, as he stepped forward. "I'll never be able to thank him enough for all he did for my boy," he nodded solemnly, his old black hat clasped in his hand. "He was faithful, brave, and good. Without him, I'd never have gotten my family back. I'm glad I got the chance to call him my friend."

"Her," Sadie corrected him quietly.

"Oh yeah, right." Pa coughed, rubbing the stubble on the side of his face. "I'm glad I got the chance to call *her* my friend," he corrected.

Despite the tears in my eyes, I had to smile. In the whole fifteen years since we'd first come to Cactus Poke, Pa had never once been able to get his mind around the fact that Abraham was a girl.

"There's no truer creature than a man's horse," Sheriff Hodges said. "You were lucky to have such a good one, son."

"Daddy?" said the little girl with sandy braids and freckles, putting her hand into mine. "Can I put the flowers on now?"

"Sure, Laurel," I handed her the bunch of cactus blossoms, their pink petals matching the shade of the sky. She stepped forward reverently, holding the flowers in both of her chubby hands. I smiled as she set them against the stone, engraved with these words:

Dedicated in loving memory of
ABRAHAM
1860-1904
Gone Too Soon

"Grampa," Laurel said, tugging at Pa's sleeve. "Hermit's eating Abraham's flowers!"

"Hey now, don't do that," Pa said, nudging the rabbit away with the toe of his boot. "Bad bunny! What, you think the West is some kinda lawless place or somethin'?"

"For him, it absolutely is," I shuddered, shaking my head at the rabbit.

Hermit the jackrabbit remains to this day one of Cactus Poke's most disturbing unsolved mysteries. Sadie and I were sure he'd been blown to kingdom come in the explosion that had collapsed the tunnel to Pa's hideout. But he'd come hopping nonchalantly into town a few days later, sneaking up behind me and nosing my pocket in search of a snack. I'd nearly jumped out of my skin, sure he was a ghost this time. Sadie and I couldn't figure out how he'd managed to survive—let alone get out of the tunnel—but he seemed supremely unconcerned by the whole ordeal, with nothing at all wrong with him except one slightly charred ear. And then…he just stayed. And stayed and stayed. And I'd thought Abraham had defied the laws of nature with her longevity. Each year that passed without Hermit dying of old age sparked yet another suspicious discussion of whether he really was a phantom rabbit or not. Eventually, Sadie and I simply agreed not to worry about it anymore. There are some things about this town we'd rather leave unexplained. Still though, I get spooked every time he sneaks up behind me.

"Look, Daddy!" Laurel said, pointing out beyond the ridge. "I can see our house!"

"Well what do you know about that? You sure can!"

I looked out over the sprawling town of Cactus Poke. Our house was on Old Main Street, sandwiched right between two new buildings: the office of *The Goldwater Gazette*, where I was editor-in-chief of the most widely-read newspaper in Arizona Territory, and the Starfire II, the Shakespeare company Sadie built from the ground up. A stunning production of *Hamlet* was set to open on Starfire's stage tomorrow night—with Sadie herself in the title role, of course.

The murmur of the town could just barely be heard from way up here—the laughter and chatter of busy streets, the hum of industry as the oil wells pumped life into the community, and the whistle of yet another arriving train chugging its merry way along the new railroad tracks, bringing with it more settlers and goods and stories and excitement.

Fifteen years ago, this broken-down ghost town had been nothing but one street and a handful of faded, empty buildings. Now, it was a thriving boom town, buzzing with life. And at its helm, strong and steady as Goldwater Ridge itself, stood Sheriff Lawrence Hodges.

The injuries he sustained from his showdown with Clint Pasadena set him back for a few years, and it was a long and uncertain road to recovery. But despite the blow his health took, the act of standing his ground and defending his town from notorious outlaws seemed to have a healing effect on his mind. Although some of his eccentricities never faded, he was, as Sadie said, his old self again. And as the town grew stronger, so did he. By the time news of the oil discovery was hitting the national newspapers, he was healed up enough to be reinstated as sheriff of his beloved town. A few years down the road, the citizens of Cactus Poke tried to elect him mayor, but he turned them down, saying that politics were a young man's game. Seeing his town thrive and grow and become a place for the people he loved to call home was reward enough for him.

After hauling the no-good Pasadena brothers back to St. Louis to face justice, the federal marshal returned to Arizona Territory to sort out the mess in Goldwater County. With a little convincing from Sadie, Pa, the sheriff, and me— and a whole lot of raised eyebrows and clarifying questions on the marshal's part—he eventually got the whole story. He decided to drop all charges and cancel all warrants against the so-called Outlaw Jack. Our family name was finally cleared.

Now that he wasn't a fugitive anymore, Pa started "OJ & Son Petroleum," the oil company that fuels the thriving economy in this part of the country. But he soon discovered life as an oil tycoon didn't suit him. His years of living in the mountains gave him a love for wild and rugged places. He'd much rather be the one out scouting the land than the one back in the office crunching the numbers. So, not long after the discovery, Pa wrote to Uncle Henry back home and offered him a job as the company's manager. He and Aunt Helen left Philadelphia to come live in Cactus Poke with us, which suited everyone just fine. Aunt Helen took over the Olde Towne Café, and although I never complained once about Sadie's cooking, I will say it sure is nice to have more angel food cake in my life.

And as for Sadie and me...well, maybe that's a story for another time. Suffice it to say for now that it ends happily ever after.

The sun slipped down beneath the western horizon, trailing the last tendrils of light behind it. As I looked at the stunning landscape before me, the buzzing town below me, and the dear friends around me, I smiled.

"Come on, ya bunch of beanheads," I said, hoisting Laurel onto my back and taking Sadie's hand in mine. "Let's go home."

THE END

ABOUT THE AUTHOR

Hannah Kaye is a lifelong daydreamer and lover of words. She wrote her first story when she was eight years old and has been practicing ever since. She enjoys a wide variety of books, but the *Chronicles of Narnia* will always have a very special place in her heart. When not writing, Hannah enjoys being outside, especially anywhere near water, where she's dabbled in kayaking, sailing, and SCUBA diving. Hannah loves travel and adventure and trying new things just about as much as she loves baking bread and sipping a cozy cup of tea in her own home. She lives in northeast Oklahoma with her husband John and her son Samuel. *Goldwater Ridge* is her first novel, and she never intends to stop writing.

You can connect with Hannah online at www.hannahkaye.blog or follow her on Instagram @hkayewrites.

Made in the USA
Coppell, TX
28 January 2022